WEALTH OF DECEPTION

DAN MORRIS

Wealth of Deception is a work of fiction and all names, characters, and places, are the products of the author's imagination or are intended to be used fictitiously. Any similarity to actual people, places, or events is purely coincidental.

Copyright © 2006 by Dan Morris

All rights reserved.

ISBN 978-1-84728-050-3

To my wife Eileen and my kids Alexa, Dillon, Sean, and Lindsay. You are the reason I'm following my dream and I'm lucky to have you.

ACKNOWLEDGEMENTS

Thank you to: my first editor and cheering section, Eileen Morris, for offering the encouragement to complete this project; my parents, Julie and Jack Morris for instilling in me at an early age a love of reading that has only grown stronger over the years; my sister and brothers, Roberta, Pete, Paul, and Dave for reading and editing; my Uncle Jim Shea for fitting my manuscript in among the vast amounts of material he reads; my father-in-law Roger Burns for being as excited as I am about this story and the possibilities; Barbara Schrager for taking the time to edit and offer valuable advice; my friends and readers/editors who each offered corrections and advice that made it into the final copy – Kurt Van de Castle, Timmy Dugan, Jim Anglin, Louis Ciccotto, Mark Trentmann, Dawn Franco, and Mike Burns.

WEALTH OF DECEPTION

CHAPTER ONE

Mike Brennan looked up at the digital clock on the wall. The noise on the floor of the New York Stock Exchange was deafening with only five minutes remaining before the bell would sound to open trading. As he pushed through the growing crowd gathering around his floor specialist, he recognized the guy from Goldman Sachs, his pad and pencil ready. Behind him was the girl from Bear Stearns, and next to her, with his nose in the air, was the young stud from Merrill Lynch. He knew they were here to pick up more shares of Dart Software. A stock that he was responsible for bringing to the public market. All the big firms had pre-ordered to get in at the opening price but also planned to increase their position before the price skyrocketed as was expected.

He made it to the small conference room just off the floor where the partners of his firm, BNL Securities, were gathered with the executive team from Dart. Instead of joining the celebration on the other side of the room, he turned to face the glass window to watch the activity after the bell. Two minutes to go. Over the next hundred and twenty seconds, he realized that no other feeling matched what he was experiencing at that moment. The world was watching. They expected big things and Mike planned to deliver.

Brennan had been with BNL for just under ten years, and his rise to Vice President of Equity Operations was considered by most to be meteoric. Several companies had been brought out through an Initial Public Offering under his watch but this one had special meaning to him. He got the tip that led BNL to Dart, a small company that was posting amazing numbers and whose client list was a virtual Who's Who of Wall Street. The fact that Brennan won the opportunity to lead the syndicate was an affirmation of not only his firm's standing in the pecking order on the Street, but his own. BNL was on the verge of making a boatload of money for their clients and for their own book.

Five seconds before the bell the floor fell silent. All eyes were on the clock. Four, three, two, one. The opening bell rang and the floor erupted with shouts from all angles. Mike couldn't see his guy in the middle of the frenzy, but he knew he was out there scratching orders on his pad.

The eldest partner of BNL, Melvin Barry, approached him. "It's an incredible sight, isn't it?"

Mike kept his eyes on the action. "Yes, sir. It is."

Barry smiled. "You done good, Kid." He carried his sixty-eight years well but Mike had noticed a bit of weariness from the old man over the past few months.

Mike had spent the last three years at BNL at the helm of the brokerage operations. He lost count of the IPOs he'd been involved with over the years but still reveled in the excitement when he knew they had a winner. "Do you ever get used to it?"

Barry stood with his hands behind his back, looking not at the frenzy out on the floor but at Brennan. "As with anything in life, Son, it becomes..." He searched for the right word "...commonplace."

Mike pulled himself from watching the growing crowd and took one last look at Dart's price. It was already up six dollars. He found it hard to control his excitement and wasn't expecting his boss to be sullen on such an exciting day for the firm.

He turned to face the old man. "I find that hard to believe."

The corners of Barry's mouth turned up into an expression resembling a smile but something was missing. The problem wasn't the lined forehead or the deep crevices coming from the sides of his nose and down both sides of his chin. Mike always said Barry looked like a ventriloquist's dummy. Mike squinted as he studied Barry's expression. *It was the old man's eyes*, he decided. *They've lost their gleam.*

"Do you remember the first client you closed?" Barry asked.

Mike went along with the game for the old guy's sake. Barry had taught him everything he knew about the market and he knew there'd be a lesson here as well.

"I'll never forget him. Dr. Overton is still a client."

"How much did you make? Five hundred bucks?"

"Six hundred and twenty four." He'd kept a copy of the trade ticket in the top drawer of his desk.

"Do you remember the tenth account you opened?"

Mike knew where Barry was going with his analogy. He thought hard, trying to remember the names of his clients and when he'd opened them. Since his promotion, most of his clients had been past off to other brokers. Careers chug along, and time passes quickly. He got the point but still considered picking a name out of the air and telling Barry he remembered each account. "I don't remember," he finally admitted.

Barry didn't respond but turned, hands clasped behind his back, and walked slowly toward the group on the other side of the room. Mike watched as he joined the managing partner of BNL, Philip Layden, along with the Dart people. Layden looked at Mike and lifted his champagne glass in the air. Mike smiled and nodded, feeling proud of his accomplishment. He turned to look at the activity on the floor one last time before joining the celebration.

On the thirty-eighth floor of the BNL building, a few blocks east on Water Street, the trading desk was alive with action. Brokers were pacing back and forth, fielding call after call, clients buying and selling Dart Software. Jack Darvish tapped a few keys on the keyboard and stood up. "You're all set."

The broker covered the mouthpiece of his headset. "Thanks, Buddy. You saved my life." Then he continued his pitch as if Jack were never there.

Darvish watched the rest of the brokers with amusement as he walked silently across the floor. They all called him when they had a problem with their computers but no one paid attention to him. Most didn't know his name. *And that's the way I like it*, he thought as he made a quick left at Mike Brennan's empty office and continued to his own cubicle down the hall. He was the main technology support for the trading desk. He had access to more information than the partners could ever imagine.

He sat at his desk and typed his password. A couple more clicks and within seconds he was on the Internet looking at the home page of the Banque Internationale de Zurich. He leaned back in his chair, hands behind his head, and smiled as he watched the computer code he'd written page through screen after screen, logging him on with his specially encrypted password until it finally ended up at his trading account.

It was certainly unusual for an employee at Darvish's level to have an offshore brokerage account. He was aware of that, but also knew he was not the usual employee. There were no stocks sitting in his brokerage account, just cash. He looked at the bottom of the screen for his balance. Twelve and a half million had never looked so good. The dollar sign on the left and all those commas and zeros were very exciting.

Feeling bad about what he was doing wasn't an issue. He was just tagging along for the ride on a victimless crime spree. He'd borrow shares from BNL's main trading account without actually laying out cash for them and then sell them to a fictional BNL client that he'd personally set up in the system. The cash came from the firm's technology budget, which had been pumped up to an unrealistic level by his boss on Darvish's own recommendation. Before anyone knew a transaction had gone off, he'd move the shares from his fictional account back to the firm's trading account. The partners and the high level employees were raking in the cash; they'd never miss a few million from the techie coiffeurs. Ripping off BNL without them knowing was a thrill he found hard to put into words, which he'd never done.

He watched in real time as the instructions he set up the previous evening were carried out.

"Like stealing candy from a baby," he whispered to the screen as he watched the exchange of two hundred thousand shares of Dart Software into his account at 9:31am.

"A big, fat, very wealthy baby." He smiled as his sell order quickly posted at 9:32am, leaving him with a pending cash balance of just over twenty two million. Jack marveled at his brilliance as he moved his mouse over a button and clicked. This time he leaned back in his chair and watched the screens automatically close, logging him out of his offshore account.

He flipped over to Fred Bigg's BNL account. He laughed as he thought about the name he'd made up. Mr. Bigg. He saw the buy of Dart Software followed quickly by the exchange back to BNL's trading account. The whole process took less than three minutes to execute.

One more click executed a script that erased the path of the three-way transaction that had just occurred. It would be virtually impossible to follow the origin of the cash or the shares. Mr. Bigg had done his job well and would recede into anonymity along with the thousands of other BNL account holders.

This was the third IPO where Darvish had worked his magic and it was by far the most lucrative. He planned on finalizing some travel details before cashing out and disappearing. He had no idea that he'd already overstayed his welcome at BNL.

CHAPTER TWO

Mike Brennan began to break a sweat after about two miles. All the work he'd put in on the Dart Software deal had begun to take a toll on his body. Two or three jogs a week were a far cry from his college and military days when he would be out at least five mornings a week by 5am.

Turning south on Lexington Avenue and into the final stretch was where it hurt the most. He could see the black, wrought iron gates of Gramercy Park two blocks ahead. Almost over, he thought. As he picked up speed, his breathing became labored and his legs heavy. He slowed his pace coming around the corner of Twenty-First Street and walked the last fifty yards to the door of his building. The entrance was directly in front of the one square block of meticulously maintained gardens of Gramercy Park.

As he approached the building, the doorman dragged himself out of his chair in the lobby to unlock the front door. He was coasting into the final couple hours of his night shift. "How was it today, Mr. Brennan?" he asked.

"I finally worked my way back to four miles. The only good thing I can say about it is that it hurts less than last week."

They stepped into the elevator with the doorman doubling as elevator man, working the controls of the eighty-year old lift. When they arrived at Mike's floor, the doorman slid the gate open. "Okay, Mr. Brennan. Have a good day."

Mike turned around to face his door, put his key in the lock as quietly as possible, and pushed it open. He placed the keys in their usual place on the table in the foyer and looked at the photos lining the wall. He noticed he'd looked a lot thinner when he was Lieutenant Brennan with his platoon on the deck of a carrier just before the invasion of Panama.

After graduating from Cornell University, he entered the Marine Corps as a Second Lieutenant. Four years of ROTC prepared him well for his short but extremely lively career as a commander of elite troops. He'd led one of the first groups of Marines into Panama in Operation Just Cause to capture General Manuel Noriega.

A Navy Seal team went in before the daylight hours to secure a landing zone on the beach and two Marine recon units followed just hours later to begin the drive inland toward the dictator's headquarters. Newly promoted First Lieutenant Michael Brennan achieved hero status, earning the Bronze Star and Purple Heart as he led his men into a heated battle with Panama's defense force. He was wounded early in the conflict leading a small advance patrol to recon the enemy's strong points. They came upon a machine gun battery which Mike destroyed by tossing a grenade from close range. The fire that followed set off some rounds, one of which caught him in the leg. The wound wasn't life threatening but caused him to sit out the rest of the short battle on a carrier and later at the US Naval Hospital in Maryland.

He took a step down the hall and looked at the next picture on the wall. He was in full battle gear jumping off a helicopter after being extracted from behind enemy lines during the first Gulf War. Just before this mission he'd been promoted to Captain and moved to a special infiltration force that worked hand in hand with the Seals. The team was created after the initial attack in Panama had worked so smoothly.

In late 1990, while the U.S. and Allied forces were preparing for battle, Mike's unit was inserted into Kuwait, behind the enemy, near the Iraqi border. When the order was given by President Bush to attack, the Seals and Mike's unit were already in position targeting Saddam Hussein's retreating troops for the bombers flying above. The Republican Guard didn't have a chance as they fled from the massive U.S. led onslaught from the south. The special Marine unit remained near the front lines for the entire invasion before being extracted to a rear base in Saudi Arabia. His unit in Kuwait unfortunately did not make it out without casualties. An errant bomb from an Air Force bomber landed on top of his communications tent killing the lone occupant and wounding his master sergeant. He had never gotten over the loss.

Captain Brennan was offered an early discharge after the Gulf War due to the government's downsizing of the military. He happily accepted early retirement at the ripe old age of twenty seven after having served six years.

He spent some time thinking about his future and decided it was time to head back to school. The fact that he wanted to do something with his life that was completely unrelated to his military career meant almost starting from scratch. His undergraduate degree at Cornell was in political science but since he graduated Suma Cum Laude, and had just completed a distinguished tour in the military, he had no trouble getting into Harvard's MBA program.

Michael Brennan did nothing half way. He graduated from Harvard near the top of his class which resulted in heavy recruitment. He eventually settled on BNL Securities because they offered him a healthy salary with guaranteed bonuses and perks that were hard to pass up. He saw that there was a lot of opportunity for advancement and concentrated all his effort on moving up the ladder. Mike was now heading up the brokerage operations of a world class firm and was reaping all the benefits of the high level executive that he had worked so hard to become.

The next picture on the wall was one he treasured more than any other. It was the first picture taken in his dress uniform immediately after receiving his Lieutenant's bars. His expression was stern and his eyes were an icy blue pool of determination. His six foot four frame held almost two hundred pounds of pure muscle that seemed ready to burst through the fabric.

He was brought back to the present by a voice coming from the kitchen. "Don't worry, you still look like that. Maybe with a little less hair."

Mike turned to see his girlfriend, Sam Brodworth, leaning on the doorframe.

"How was your run?"

"I tried not to wake you. I had a good run, felt pretty strong."

She had just rolled out of bed with no makeup. Her long, curly, light-brown hair was slightly amiss, which only made her more desirable. He walked to her and grabbed her around the waist, pulling her close. He kissed her as he slipped his hands inside her robe and felt her smooth, warm skin.

She kissed his neck and whispered, "Mmm, you taste salty. I love that." He held her tighter but she reluctantly pushed him away.

"I have to be at City Hall early today. You jump into the shower first."

"Only if you join me." She returned his comment with a look he knew too well. It said that if she joined him in the shower, neither of them would make it to work on time, if at all. She shoved him lightly toward the bathroom.

Mike asked, "Are you increasing your hours again? I was just getting used to you being here when I get home at night. You know I can't deal with sleeping alone. I'll call up Mayor Mad Dog and explain it to him if I have to."

"His name is Maddux and I had them put a clause in my contract that says I have to be home when my boyfriend gets home."

"He better treat you right because you're the best damn legal advisor on his staff." He tried to pull her close again.

"I'm very flattered." She pushed him away once again.

Mike gave up and walked to the fridge to grab a bottle of water. "Are your parents still coming in for the awards dinner tonight?"

"Just Dad. Mom is at some spa or other." Her tone suggested this was par for the course as far as her mother was concerned.

"That's a shame. You know I was looking forward to seeing them both and it's not that often I'll be winning the Man of the Year Award." Mike was only half joking.

"Don't worry, I'll be there. I'll clap and cheer so loud that I'll make up for anyone who doesn't show up."

"It's not like I'm Time Magazine's Man of the Year."

"Hey." She reached up to grab both his shoulders. "That youth center would be lost without you. Some of those kids look up to you as if you were their Dad."

"I know. I'm not knocking it but I would imagine your father could easily find something else to occupy his time."

"He's not a complete ogre. Let's stop talking about them. Daddy will be there but unfortunately for you you're not going to have Mom as a buffer. Dad can give you his full attention."

"I accept the challenge." Mike knew what she was getting at. The Brodworths came from incredible wealth in Connecticut and her father had a tough time with the fact that his little girl was shacking up with a former Marine who grew up in Queens. It didn't matter that Mike had done extremely well with BNL and lived in a multi-million dollar apartment in Gramercy Park.

It also didn't matter that Mike devoted a large chunk of his free time to a local youth center where he coached baseball. His team was made up of troubled teens from the Lower East Side of Manhattan. He'd been coaching them for almost six years and became involved in their lives and their family's lives. The boys, several of whom had no father at home, looked up to Mike because he offered them guidance and an ear to listen as often as he could.

He set up a scholarship fund through the center for anyone who made consistently good grades throughout high school and got accepted by any college. His first student, a girl named Josie Lopez, and sister of his third baseman, was just finishing up her freshman year at Cornell, his alma mater. The girl's mom was going to present him with his award.

"Are you going in the shower or am I?" Sam asked.

"Alright, alright." Mike walked around her and grudgingly went off to the shower alone.

CHAPTER THREE

"What the hell are you talking about, Charlie?" Philip Layden said calmly in the general direction of the speakerphone on his desk.

"I'm telling you that it happened yesterday, right after the bell. The firm's Dart balance took a two hundred thousand share hit. Two minutes later it was back to where we started," Charlie replied.

"Are you sure?"

"I'm not blind, Philip. I had the account up on my screen. When it dipped, I looked for a transaction to support it but there was nothing. While I was scrambling, the balance came back in line like it never happened."

"How many years have you been in charge of our trading desk?" Layden asked.

"I've been with BNL for twenty years. Eighteen as head trader," Charlie Walcott answered, slightly annoyed.

"We've been through five different computer systems since then. You know there are always bugs." Layden tried to ease his worries.

"This is highly unusual, Philip." Walcott stood his ground.

"How many cups of coffee had you downed by 9:35 yesterday?" Layden was trying to make light of a potentially serious situation.

Walcott huffed, realizing now that the head partner was screwing with him. "Just be warned that I told you about this Philip."

"Noted." Layden cut the line and immediately picked up the phone from its cradle. He pressed a speed dial button and listened to the beeps and chirps as the secure line on the other end picked up.

"Yes," the voice answered.

"Walcott saw the block move yesterday. Do we know who's fucking with our account yet?" Layden asked.

"Our tech people say it's coming from the inside."

Layden's head throbbed as his blood pressure climbed. "Inside BNL?"

"It will take a few hours to pinpoint but they say it can be done." Layden had nothing else to say as he waited for the instructions he knew would come.

"Philip?" the voice said.

"Yes, sir?"

"We don't know what else this person may have seen. After we identify him, he needs to be eliminated." The connection was cut before Layden could reply.

"Yes, sir," Layden said to the dial tone.

CHAPTER FOUR

The cab ride downtown took just a few minutes in the pre-rush hour traffic. Mike got out in front of the forty floor structure that housed BNL, its mirrored panels reflecting images of the Brooklyn Bridge and the South Street Seaport.

Up on the thirty-eighth floor, he made his way past the reception area and onto the trading floor. Brokers faced each other on several lines of trading desks, separated by multiple monitors displaying research, news, or anything that would help them make the sale. It wasn't yet eight o'clock and the room was already loud with brokers working the phones.

Mike's office was in the far corner of the floor. The inside walls were glass giving him a clear line of sight to the trading floor, the outside walls were windows from floor to ceiling, offering a magnificent view of downtown Manhattan.

He flipped the light on and before he made it to his desk, he heard footsteps behind him. He turned to see Jack Darvish.

"Good morning, Jack." Mike placed his briefcase on his desk and sat down.

"Mind if I sit?" Darvish was already sitting in Mike's guest chair.

"Your ass is already planted, Jack. Not much I can do about it now." Mike hit the power button on his computer and sat back, waiting for the screen to come to life.

Jack smiled. "You know I've been here for more than a year and I've never really thanked you for getting me this job. I appreciate it."

"Your brother saved my butt more times than I care to remember. The least I could have done for him was to hire his kid brother."

"He was a good soldier?"

"He wouldn't have been in my unit if he weren't the cream of the crop. It's hard for me to accept that he's not around anymore."

"Yeah, he thought they were going to be in and out of Baghdad. The insurgents had other plans."

"He died a hero."

"I know." Darvish changed the subject. "You free for dinner tonight?"

Mike shook his head. "Sorry, I've got that awards ceremony at the youth center up on Avenue D. How about tomorrow?"

Darvish stood abruptly. "Can't do tomorrow."

"Maybe next week?" Mike asked.

"Maybe." He turned to leave.

"Everything okay with you?"

Darvish continued to walk to the door and said, "No problems."

Mike got up from his desk and came around. "Hold on, Buddy. You know if you've got a problem, you can come to me. You don't have to take me out to dinner to get something off your chest."

"It's nothing. It's just…"

Before the thought was finished, the intercom sitting on the corner of the desk came to life. "Hey, Mike, you want to come up here, please?" It was the voice of Melvin Barry.

Mike pressed a button on the box. "I'll be right there, Melvin."

Mike put his arm on Jack's shoulder and walked him out the door. "We'll talk later. Okay?"

Jack nodded. "Sure. No problem." He turned and headed back to his cubicle down the hall.

Mike walked through the boardroom and looked up. The partners' offices were a floor above, but visible from one floor below. *Partners' Row*, they called it. It reminded him of a factory where the foreman could look out onto the assembly line. He went up the staircase and looked down at his brokers from the raised hallway and thought to himself how awesome the angle was when the guys in 'The Pit' were in a frenzy. Billions of dollars moved through those phone lines each year.

Barry's office was not as lavish a display as one might expect from a millionaire partner of a very successful firm like BNL. The inside walls, like Mike's, were glass. A few paintings and photos were scattered around a room just large enough to fit his big U-shaped desk and a small conference table that sat ten. Barry had views of the Brooklyn Bridge, the lower East River, and much of New York Harbor. The angle was breathtaking for the first-time viewer, but it seemed Melvin Barry never tired of it. He could often be seen standing at the window staring down at the boat traffic, the miniature cabs, and pedestrians.

Mike walked into his boss' office and found him in his usual position by the window, hands clasped behind his back. Philip Layden sat at the table tapping his fingers on the highly polished surface of the table.

As Mike entered the room, Barry turned around and pushed his small, round, silver-framed glasses up the bridge of his nose. "Good morning Mike. Take a seat."

"Good morning, gentlemen." Mike sat and Barry took the space next to him.

Mike looked at the partners' faces and knew immediately he wasn't going to hear good news.

"What's going on?" Mike asked.

As usual, Layden took the lead getting immediately to the point. "Dart lost one of their largest clients last night. Twenty-two percent of their expected revenue is gone."

At first Mike was speechless. As he got over the initial shock, anger quickly took over. "They never mentioned this as a possibility. We were with Billy Connors for most of the day yesterday." Mike referred to the CEO of Dart Software.

"Connors is claiming he was blind sided," Layden replied.

"God dammit." Mike slapped the table. "When will it be on the wire?"

"Reuters says 9am." Layden remained stone-faced.

Mike shook his head. "More than enough time for the market to generate a war party. We're going to lose big on this."

Barry interjected. "You've got to tell your guys to expect a flood of calls. We need people to hold their positions."

"We'll do our best." Mike stood to leave.

"Hold on Mike," Layden said. "This may not be our biggest worry."

Mike forced a smile. "It can get worse than this?" Dart was his responsibility from the beginning and the fallout from it failing could hurt his career.

"We've discovered that someone is borrowing shares of our IPOs from our trading account." Layden explained.

"Borrowing?"

"The shares disappear and end up back in the account within minutes with no record of any transaction."

"Someone hacked into the system?" Mike asked.

"No." Layden looked at Barry.

Barry moved a little closer to Mike as if someone may overhear him. "We think it's someone on the inside."

Mike's eyes narrowed as he understood what the partners were saying. "You think it's one of my guys?"

"Not necessarily," Barry said quickly.

Layden leaned forward in his chair. "We have to realize that your brokers have the easiest access to the trading and shareholder accounts."

Mike became defensive. "Can the transactions be traced to a specific shareholder account?" He knew the answer. If they knew, the perpetrator would be caught.

"Not yet, but I'm bringing someone in to look into it," Layden said.

Mike stood, hoping he could leave the room without any more comments from the partners. He struggled to keep his composure. "Please keep me posted."

He walked out the door thinking about how happy he felt barely thirty minutes earlier. If he had the ability to look into the future, he would be stunned at how bad things were about to get.

CHAPTER FIVE

Mike sat with his eyes closed, his head leaning on his hand, as he spoke in the general direction of the speakerphone.

"I'm going to be a few minutes late for the awards ceremony."

"The guest of honor can't be late." Sam was sitting in the back of a cab, heading north on Broadway.

"Please tell Maria to get started without me and I'll be there as soon as I can."

"Come on babe. Take some time for yourself," Sam pleaded.

"This has been the worst day of my professional career. I'll explain later."

"I'm sorry, everything was going so well. Can you give me a hint?"

"I'll see you in an hour or so. We'll talk more then." Mike broke the connection and turned his attention to his computer screen.

"Eight bucks," he said to himself and shook his head. Dart Software had lost almost everything it gained. Mike paged through the trading results for the day. His guys did their best to get customers to hold on to their shares. As expected, several investors dumped their position and closed their account with BNL. Even though he knew every IPO couldn't be a winner, his reputation at the firm was now tarnished. The partners were expecting this one to be big.

He flipped his screen over to the news service and re-read the story reporting Dart's loss of a big chunk of their future revenues. *It could have been a lot worse*, he thought. *It should have been worse.* He replayed the events of the day starting with the first couple hours. The price of the stock fell steadily throughout the morning. At noon, after losing a little more than eight dollars per share, it held steady. By the close, some support in the market kicked in to stop the bloodshed and the price crept up a few cents to end down exactly eight dollars.

"At least someone out there still thinks Dart's a good buy," he said to himself as he logged off the system and walked to the opposite side of his office. He looked at his reflection in a small mirror as he attempted for the third time to tie his bowtie. He could never get it quite right. Sam would fix it for him when he saw her in a few minutes. He took a deep breath and shut the light off, doing his best to put the day's events out of his mind.

He was one step out of his office when his phone rang. He turned back and leaned over his desk to look at the caller I.D. He recognized the number of one of his largest clients, Tony Davenport, from Atlanta.

"Shit. This is all I need." He picked up the receiver and leaned against the edge of his desk.

"Hello, Tony. How're you doing?"

The voice on the other end of the line was as angry as Mike expected. "Don't 'Hello Tony' me, you son of a bitch. Have you been watching the screen in front of you or do you have your nose stuck into someone's financials?" Davenport was shouting.

"Look, Tony, I told you this morning to hold onto your position but you said Dart's a dog. What more can I do? You said sell and I wasn't going to argue with you. Come on, you've been around the block, why are you coming down on me?" His voice was raised but calm. Tony Davenport was a client handed to Mike by Melvin Barry almost ten years earlier. They'd worked so many deals together since then that Mike knew how to stop him in his tracks.

He let Davenport continue his tirade, "Dart didn't lose anywhere near what the street expected after today's announcement. You must have known something was going on. BNL brought the goddamned company public!"

Mike didn't back down. "Come on, Tony, I know that weasel Wilson was the one who told you to get out when the news broke. Don't try to lay the blame on us when you know I supported this stock from the beginning." Mike knew that Davenport appreciated a little arrogance from the people who advised him, as was obvious in how he held his second-in-command, Louis Wilson, in such high regard. Wilson was a shrewd financial mind who had connections Davenport used for his own profit. Mike didn't get along with him from the beginning and didn't attempt to hide his feelings.

After a pause, Davenport spoke calmly. "Okay, Mike, I probably would have sold anyway even if you had called, but I would appreciate being kept in the loop."

"No problem, Tony. Next time I tell you I feel good about a stock, I hope you remember this." Mike hung up the phone still not knowing what had stopped Dart's skid.

He left his office again and walked by the trading desk toward the elevators. He realized how angry he was not only at the Dart executives for keeping information to themselves, but also the fact that one of his brokers was possibly doing something illegal with the firm's trading account.

Was Layden right? Who was it? He scanned the young faces as he continued through the room, the brokers saying goodnight to him, commenting on his tux. He grunted replies, not really hearing their words. These people were making money as long as the firm did well and they were having a record year. Why would they take the risk of going to jail for a few more bucks? He hired each one of these people himself and he thought he knew them. Something didn't fit but he knew with BNL's resources, they would find out soon enough what was going on.

As he continued toward the reception area, he looked up to Partners' Row and saw Layden inside Barry's office. They were in a heated discussion. Even from this distance, he could see Barry's face was red with anger.

"This is really getting old, Melvin," Layden said calmly. "For the same reasons I couldn't tell you twenty five years ago, I can't tell you now. It's something you need to accept."

"How do you know they're not the ones screwing with our trading account?" Barry yelled.

"They want to find who it is as badly as you do."

Barry rubbed his chin as he thought. After a moment he said, "Can I offer to buy them out?"

"These are not people you offer to buy out," Layden chuckled. "Do you really not understand what's going on here or are you playing games?" He walked closer to the older man and continued. "When you made that agreement it was for life. Not just until you thought it no longer benefited you."

"Dart should have lost thirty percent of its value but it only lost eight dollars. Don't you think that's going to raise some flags?"

"We got some support in the market!" Layden raised his voice.

"That support is on your payroll," Barry said through clenched teeth. "Maybe you can make the regulators go away as you've accomplished for more than two decades. I'll give you that. What do you plan on doing when this phantom BNL employee starts screwing with other customer accounts? Once the public becomes involved, we're going to have trouble."

"Have you thought about taking some time off to relax?" Layden asked, knowing the answer.

Barry ignored the question. "We've had many close calls with the regulators over the years but we're not going to twist out of this one."

"We will twist out of it. That's just the point," Layden said confidently.

"I'm getting too old for this shit!" Barry was talking more to himself than to Layden.

"Then why don't you retire like we've asked several times?"

This time Barry stepped closer to the younger Layden. "Because this place is my life. I'm the 'B' in BNL and that means something to me."

"You don't want to end up like Nellington, do you? The 'N' from BNL isn't faring so well these days." Layden referred to their late partner, Pierce Nellington, who disappeared with his sailboat off the coast of Rhode Island. Neither the boat nor the body was ever found.

"Go fuck yourself, Philip." Barry turned to the door.

Mike watched from the trading floor as Barry walked to the door and thrust it open with enough force to produce a loud bang as it met the wall. The old man came down the stairs and walked by Mike without looking at him.

Mike caught up to him. "What the hell was that all about?"

"Nothing Kid, don't worry about it. That guy can be a jackass sometimes," Barry complained.

They stepped onto the elevator and Barry turned to Mike, changing the subject. "How about Dart today? Looks like we may have been worried about nothing. All we needed was a little support, and it came through today."

Mike looked down at the shorter man. "It was certainly better than expected but that wasn't just a little support. There must have been some heavy hitters out there to carry the kind of trading we saw today."

"All you need is to place a call to the right people at the right time," Barry responded grimly.

Mike looked at the old man but before he had a chance to ask what he meant, the elevator doors opened and several people got on laughing and being generally loud, preventing further conversation. When the doors opened on the ground floor, Barry got out first and made his way quickly through the small lobby to the revolving doors. After being delayed by the crowd, Mike got outside only to find that Barry was in a cab pulling away. He stepped to the curb and looked after the moving cab still wondering about Barry's last comment. He shrugged it off and grabbed his own cab up to the youth center on Avenue D near 10th Street.

CHAPTER SIX

Mike was a few minutes late. The noise of the crowd could be heard as soon as he opened the main doors to the youth center. The small gymnasium was just ahead beyond the small lobby. He pushed open the swinging door and was immediately hit by the smells of his youth. Hardwood mixed with sweat and dust.

"Mr. Brennan is here!" one of the kids called out.

The crowd turned. Members of his team got up from their tables and approached him.

"You ready for the big night?" Juan, his left fielder, asked.

"I'm ready kid," Mike answered confidently, slapping the teen on the back.

Jorge, the first baseman, said as he pointed to his left, "Check out Ricky."

Mike looked at Ricky Lopez who was wearing a suit and tie. Mike had never seen him in anything but the baseball uniform he'd donated to the team. Ricky wore it to all the practices and games.

Mike approached him and shook his hand. "Looking sharp Ricky."

"I got an A in biology, Mr. Brennan. An A." He grinned.

Mike shook his hand tighter. "You keep that up and you'll follow your sister to Cornell."

Ricky replied with a bigger smile.

Mike broke away from the kids and approached the dais, a line of folding tables under the far basketball hoop. On his way, he waved to several parents and grandparents of the kids on his team. Sam was sitting near the podium talking to the center's director, Maria Villanueva.

"Good evening, Ladies. You both look beautiful tonight." Mike leaned down and kissed Sam. "Maria, I'm honored you got all dressed up for me."

"Keep dreaming, man. I'd be wearing sweats if it weren't for them." She pointed over her shoulder.

As Sam reached up and began retying Mike's bow tie, he followed Maria's thumb to a group of men and woman standing near the side of the gym. "Press?"

"You're going to be big news."

"Great. You know how I love the spotlight."

"You'd better love it. You'll be at that podium in ten minutes in front of a hundred and fifty people and photographers from every New York paper." Maria seemed to enjoy making him uncomfortable. She and Mike had a good relationship but she wouldn't be caught admitting that she liked him.

"Sorry if I held you up but I couldn't get out any earlier," Mike said.

Maria smiled. "Luckily, the sound system was messed up. They just got it working. Are you ready?"

Mike looked from the tables filled with kids and their families to the photographers. "As ready as I'll ever be."

Maria stood. "You're not so tough for a former marine."

"Bullets and bombs don't scare me. Kids and cameras are another story."

"Let's get this over with then." She said and walked up to the microphone.

CHAPTER SEVEN

Sitting at his desk on Partners' Row, Layden reached inside his jacket pocket to retrieve his vibrating satellite phone. He pressed the green button and listened briefly to the beeps and clicks as the voice scrambler kicked in.

"Yes."

"He's online right now. Our guys still don't have him identified but they traced the transactions back to a computer footprint unique to BNL's connection. This man is very adept at staying hidden."

Layden stood from his desk and looked through his glass wall, down to the trading desk one floor below. From his vantage point, he could only see a few empty seats.

"How the hell am I going to identify him?"

"It's late and there are only three people logged on to the system. You can walk around and flush him out."

"I'll call you back." Layden opened his office door.

"Hold on, Philip. This guy may be dangerous. I've sent two of my men over to the building to assist you. They're on the way up in the elevator."

Philip became angry. "We can't make a scene here, sir."

"We have no choice," the voice said and paused. "We can't take a chance that this guy hasn't done more damage than borrowing shares of an IPO. If he saw anything else, we could be finished."

Layden knew he was right. "I'll meet them at reception."

He walked down the stairs and started across the trading floor. On his right was Mike Brennan's darkened office. Straight ahead, almost in the middle of the floor, was a young man tapping away on his keyboard. The kid's back was to Layden as he walked quietly toward him.

Layden stopped as he arrived behind him. "Working late?"

The young man turned his head quickly toward him, startled. "I didn't hear you come up, Mr. Layden."

"What are you working on?" Layden leaned down and looked at the screen.

"I'm working up a call list for tomorrow," the broker said.

Layden nodded. "How'd you do today?"

"I lost a couple of clients over the Dart news but I got most to hang in there," he answered proudly.

"Good job, son. Why don't you head home now? Get some rest."

"I've only got a few more minutes…"

Layden cut him off. "It's not often a partner tells you to go home. That's a direct order, kid. Go home."

"Yes sir." He cut the power to his computer and stood. "See you tomorrow." He went to the elevator bank and pressed the down button. Layden walked casually in the same direction and heard the bell as the car arrived.

The young man stepped aside as two very large men in suits stepped into the reception area. The doors slid closed and he was alone with the new arrivals.

"Good evening Mr. Layden," the larger of the two said as they approached Layden.

"Thompson." Layden nodded, but made no move to shake his hand. Thompson's short dark hair and ramrod straight posture had him easily marked as former military.

Layden looked at the second man. He was smaller and more refined. A leader among a very well trained, well paid, and well armed security staff. Mark Hailey had been in his position for almost seven years, a record for Layden's wealthy associate who employed them.

"Have you been briefed, Hailey?" Layden asked.

"Yes, sir." He tried to make it clear that he was involved and on top of the situation. "A member of my team is tracking your thief."

Layden looked back over the empty trading floor. "Looks like there's only two people left. They must be in the offices and cubicles behind us." He pointed to a large entryway opening on a sea of six foot cubicles.

"Let's head back this way and make a full circle to end up back here." Layden started to walk in the opposite direction from the trading floor.

Hailey put his hand out. "Let us take the lead, sir."

"No. The surprise of seeing me will make it very hard for them to keep their composure. Let's go." He led them down the left aisle. The two security men stayed about ten paces behind, their hands under their jackets.

Jack Darvish knew he was taking a risk staying online for an extended period but he needed to confirm that his money had arrived safely.

He decided to transfer his cash out of the Banque Internationale de Zurich and into another offshore account for another layer of protection.

"I don't see the incoming wire, sir," the man on the other end of the phone line said in heavily accented English.

"What the hell are you talking about?" Darvish struggled to keep his voice low. "The money left my bank an hour ago."

"I'm still checking, sir. Is there a number I can reach you at to keep you abreast of the situation?"

Darvish clamped his teeth together. "There's no way I'm hanging up. Please just find my twenty two million dollars."

"Oui, monsieur." The man slipped into his native language.

Jack flipped his screen to his Banque Internationale de Zurich account and looked at the zero balance. His money should have arrived in his new account at the Banque de Rue St. Gabrielle over an hour ago. He rechecked the wire instructions to make sure he hadn't made a mistake. *They look fine*, he thought as he racked his mind for a step he may have missed. With a click of his mouse he was looking at the BNL account that he used to borrow the shares. There was a zero balance as expected. A couple more key strokes and he had all of BNL's cash accounts on his screen.

He brought up the firm's main trading account and looked at the recent activity. His fingers were frozen over the keys as an entry half way down the page caught his eye.

"This can't be happening."

"Excuse me, sir?" The banker was still on the phone looking for Darvish's lost wire.

"I'm talking to myself. Can you call me back in half an hour?" He gave the man his cell phone number and hung up.

He ran his fingers down his screen from the top to make sure he read it correctly. Right there in the center of the page was a wire for twenty two million at exactly the time his wire should have arrived at a three floor brick structure on Rue de St. Gabrielle in beautiful Geneva, Switzerland. He clicked on the wire instructions and read the source of the funds. Mr. Frederick Bigg, Banque Internationale de Zurich, Oranjestad, Aruba.

"Shit!" he said too loudly. He stood and looked over the walls of his cube and down the short hallway to Mike Brennan's office. No one was in sight. He sat back down, his hands shaking slightly as he continued typing.

"There's no way I screwed this up." He studied the other entries to the account. "What's this?"

He scanned the firm's main account coming to rest on the total. He did a double take when he realized the cash balance was in the billions, not millions. He also noticed the balance changing constantly with no corresponding transactions.

"These dogs," he whispered as he realized what was happening. "I'm trying to beat them at their own game. They're hiding these transactions from the regulators." He stood again and looked around to make sure he was alone. Jack knew he was in trouble if they were on top of things enough to intercept his wire. They found out that the transactions were initiated from inside the company. He knew it was possible that they could trace the activity back to BNL but he was still confident that they couldn't isolate his unique computer ID. He still had a few minutes to try to get his cash back.

"This is one bold son of a bitch, sir," the tech specialist said.

The older man looked over his shoulder at the gibberish on the screen. It may as well have been in Russian.

"What are you talking about?"

"He took the bait. He's in the firm's main cash account right now."

"He knows we took back the stolen cash?"

"You can bet on it. He's pissed off and he came looking for it."

"Who the hell is he?"

The young techie was typing non-stop as he spoke. "He's good, sir. I still can't trace his desktop." He paused, stopped typing, and banged the keyboard.

"What's wrong?"

"He froze me out!" He started to type again, but it was no use.

"What does that mean?"

"It means I can no longer access BNL's system."

The older man grabbed his satellite phone and dialed a number.

"Fuck you too!" Darvish said as he looked at the screen and smiled. "I know you're out there, but you don't know me, do you?"

He started to print off pages of strange transactions along with the wire instructions identifying the sending banks.

"I may as well cover my ass while I'm in here." He looked over at the small laser printer on his desk as it began spitting out the confidential information.

While he waited for the printer to finish he initiated another transaction. This time he went directly to BNL's trading account and set up a wire back to his BIZ account. He quickly accessed that account and watched as the money arrived.

"I would have been happy with twenty two million, you fools." He set up his final transaction. "This is twenty four hour internet banking at its best."

Layden continued his slow walk around the thirty-eighth floor. As he was about to turn down another row of cubes, he heard the tapping sound of a keyboard. He inched closer to the last desk in the row and saw the long blond hair of a woman, working intently at her computer.

The thought hadn't crossed his mind that a woman could be hacking their system. He pointed in her direction to let the two security men know someone was there. They stopped walking, allowing Layden to continue.

"Good evening," he said as he entered the small space.

No response.

He leaned in closer and saw the thin headphone wires hanging from her ears. She couldn't hear a thing. He could see on her screen that she was on the internet getting some shopping done while listening to music. She just completed a purchase when Layden knocked loudly on the cabinet hanging above her head.

She looked toward the noise, then at Layden and let out a loud scream. She pushed her chair to the opposite side of the cube, which was only about two feet.

Layden said, "I'm sorry I startled you."

She yanked the headphones out of her ears and said breathlessly, "I'm sorry I screamed, Mr. Layden. I didn't think anyone else was here."

"It's okay. Why don't you take off for the night?"

"I was just about to leave anyway." She stood and grabbed her pocketbook, nodded to the two security men and started to walk down the hall toward Mike Brennan's office.

Hailey stuck out his arm, pointing in the direction they just searched. "Can you please go that way, Miss?"

"Sure." She shrugged and quickly walked away.

As soon as she was out of earshot Layden said, "He's got to be down this hallway." He started to walk down the hall but stopped as his phone vibrated again.

"Yes." Layden had the phone to his ear, looking down the hallway.

"You've got to pick up the pace. He's just frozen us out of the system."

"There's only one hallway of cubes left. He's got to be there."

"Go! Now!" the voice yelled.

Layden put the phone back into his pocket and said to the security men, "Let's move it!" He turned and ran down the hall with the two cronies following closely behind.

Jack had just shut the power off on his computer when he heard the loud scream. He stood and peered over his cubicle, down the hallway toward the noise. Empty.

He grabbed the papers off the printer and walked quickly to the trading floor. He turned right at Mike Brennan's office and looked up at Partners' Row. Layden's light was on but he couldn't see inside from his angle. He was barely halfway across the floor when he heard the voice behind him.

"Hey!" It was Layden.

Darvish turned to see the head partner standing in front of Brennan's glass walled office flanked by two very large men he'd never seen before. He decided immediately that he wasn't going to stick around and see what they wanted. He turned quickly and ran. He'd never heard a gunshot before in his life but knew that the deafening noise, followed by a searing pain in his right shoulder, was his first. He groaned loudly but continued running.

The second shot hit the exit sign just above his head as he entered the reception area. The glass covering on the sign shattered and hit him in the back of his head and neck. The elevator doors were just shutting as Darvish dove for the opening and landed on the floor of the car. The doors slid shut behind him as he heard another shot hit the metal doors. He grabbed the railing, struggled to a semi standing position, and looked into the terrified face of the woman whose scream he heard moments ago.

"Late night, huh?" Darvish joked as he grabbed his shoulder and winced in pain.

The woman was too scared to speak. She was pressed up against the wall, trying to stay as far away from him as possible.

Jack looked down at his white shirt, quickly turning red from his wound.

"Don't worry. I think it just nicked me." He pushed back his shirt revealing the source of most the blood, a two inch gash on the top of his shoulder.

He looked over at her. "I'll give you a little advice. Resign tomorrow and never put this place on your resume."

The bell rang as they reached the lobby. Darvish ran quickly out of the elevator, leaving the woman alone, on the verge of a breakdown. He past the sleeping guard and pushed through the revolving doors to the street. Across Water Street, near the Seaport, he got into the backseat of a waiting cab.

CHAPTER EIGHT

After the awards ceremony, Mike and Sam stood in front of the youth center saying goodbye to the kids. After the last one left, they walked to the corner to hail a cab.

"Your dad never showed," Mike said.

She put her arm through his and leaned into him. "I'm sorry about that. He probably got caught up at the office."

"I can use this against him now when he digs into me. What do you think?"

Sam laughed. "Good luck."

"He just didn't want to be caught in a photo with me that may get published."

"Oh, please Mike. You know he likes you."

"My blood isn't blue enough for him and you know it."

"Are you calling me a blue blood?"

He stopped walking and put his arms around her waist. "You're blood is very blue but I love every ounce of it."

She tried to ignore him and continued walking. "Can we talk more about what happened at the office today?"

"Let's wait until we get home," Mike said as they reached the corner. Before they could cross the street a taxi skidded to a stop in front of them.

"Now that's service," Mike said. "I didn't even put my hand up yet. Maybe this is your dad."

Sam shook her head. "In a yellow taxi? I don't think so."

The rear door opened and Jack Darvish got out. Blood was covering most of the right side of his shirt.

"What the hell happened, Jack? We have to get you an ambulance." Mike pulled his cell phone off his belt and was about to dial.

"Hold on." Darvish put his hand out and continued. "It looks a lot worse than it is."

Mike reached over and pulled back Darvish's shirt, looking at the wound. "That's a bullet wound, Buddy. And you've got fifty little cuts on the back of your neck. What the hell is going on?"

"I'll explain on the way." Darvish said turning back to the waiting cab.

"Hold on," Mike said as he grabbed Jack's good shoulder. "Explain now."

"Alright." Darvish stood as tall as he could, looking up at Mike. "I stole twenty two million dollars from BNL using shares of your IPOs."

"It was you?"

"Hold on. Let me finish."

Mike pushed him and bent him backwards over the trunk of the cab, holding his chest to keep him down.

"Ow! Just let me finish, man." Mike wouldn't let him go as Darvish struggled to speak, his pain growing.

"What else could you possibly tell me to make me not call the cops?"

"BNL is processing transactions in some kind of shadow system." He tried to hold up the papers with his good arm.

"What?" Mike let him up but still held his shirt.

Darvish breathed easier as he continued. "The firm's cash account was receiving millions in wires but there were no transactions posted to the ledger. They were virtually invisible."

Mike shook his head. "Then how did you see them?"

"Because they took back my twenty two million and when I went to look for it I found these!" He held up the papers.

"What's that?"

"Account numbers from banks all around the world. Someone's running money through BNL and probably right back out. I didn't see the other side but I'll be willing to bet there's no trace of these transactions except for these." He shook the papers.

Mike was still angry and not convinced. "Let's go to the office right now and call in Barry and Layden."

"That's not a good idea, Mike."

"Why?"

"Because Layden was at the office with two men. One of them almost blew my head off, but luckily they just tore a hole in my shoulder. The next shot shattered the exit sign, spraying glass into the back of my neck."

Mike stared at him, but didn't speak.

"There's also a good size hole in the wall and one of the elevator doors." Jack tried to smile. "And one frightened girl from accounting who probably won't show up for work tomorrow. I advised her against it."

Sam reached over and pulled Mike's hand off Darvish's shirt. "Let's go back to Gramercy Park and clean him up. We'll sort things out," she said in a calm tone.

Mike looked at her and nodded. He took off his tuxedo coat and handed it to Darvish saying, "Put this on. I think we've drawn enough attention to ourselves already." They looked around at the small group of people watching them. They got into the taxi, leaving a very confused crowd of strangers.

CHAPTER NINE

The beautiful building on Park Avenue sat just south of Eightieth Street. Layden approached with the two security men, Hailey and Thompson, in tow. He entered the code from memory into the digital keypad, the only modern intrusion in the beautifully carved nineteenth century wooden doors. He listened for the bolts to roll back into the doorframe. The door swung open automatically and he walked through alone. The two security men went back to their vehicle to wait for their next orders.

Inside the front hall, Layden looked around but wasn't impressed with the opulence. He had grown up in a similar building on Fifth Avenue overlooking Central Park. He climbed to the top of the marble staircase on the second floor and followed a long hallway lined with a collection of millions of dollars worth of original Van Goghs, Monets, and Gauguins that led toward the back. He entered a large sitting room with a full bar set up against the wall. The stools were dark wood with deep red upholstery covering the seat and back. Layden took a seat off to the side in a high-backed soft leather chair and put his feet up on an ottoman.

The owner of the building was a corporation. The taxes were always paid on time and it was maintained exquisitely. No unnecessary attention was drawn toward the property or the owners. That's the way they wanted it and the way they needed it.

Layden had been in the dwelling several times since taking over as head of BNL and never before had he been so uncomfortable. He knew that much more was at stake now than just his job.

"Good evening, Philip," the voice of his host boomed from the doorway. "Please follow me."

Layden turned to see a man whose advanced age and seemingly frail body did nothing to diminish the authority he projected. His wealth went back several generations and his attitude showed it.

He turned and Layden quietly followed him down the hallway to a large conference room. Inside the dimly lit room, they sat near the head of the long table. A flat screen television on the wall came to life and an image appeared of a downtown Manhattan office building well known to each of them, and probably to every New Yorker. The photo of the BNL building, taken from the air, included the South Street Seaport and part of the Brooklyn Bridge.

The man spoke in a monotone without a hint of emotion. This was business. "Since taking over after your father's tragic death almost twenty-five years ago, you've done an extraordinary job. But now I think you'll agree that it's time to make some changes before we lose BNL."

Layden was thankful the room was dim as he felt the blood drain from his face. He knew his fate was out of his own hands since his father was killed in a suspicious small plane crash while on company business for one of the old man's subsidiaries. He could only pray that he would be kept on at the firm because there was only one way out of this arrangement. In a box.

Layden and Dowd, Inc., a small investment company, earned millions during the late sixties and seventies. A few months before the crash that killed his dad, the younger Layden was brought into the company and learned the function they performed for an organization that had been around for more than half a century.

When the dust settled, the general consensus was that it would be a good idea to put the Layden name in the background, making it less prominent. That's when Philip took on two partners. Melvin Barry, a finance specialist in the New York City government, had local contacts that were considered invaluable. Pierce Nellington came from an old money family and was a brilliant financial mind. BNL was born.

The man continued, "When Nellington got out of hand ten years ago, his sailboat was lost at sea off the coast of Rhode Island. The Coast Guard finally called off the search after five days." He paused and looked at Layden sitting in the shadows, letting the younger man digest his thoughts. "Before we concentrate our efforts on the thief inside BNL, we need to decide the fate of Mr. Barry. He's not the same man we brought into the firm years ago. We can't have someone in his position not willing to go along with the game."

Layden turned toward his host. "Are you suggesting a forced retirement?"

"I had something a bit more permanent in mind."

Layden shoulders sagged not out of sadness for the death sentence just imposed on Melvin Barry, his partner of more than two decades, but out of relief that someone else was about to take the fall.

His mouth was dry but he forced a reply. "I agree."

"Fine. Please take care of the details." He pressed a button on the remote and focused his attention on the next image, the subject of Melvin Barry's fate forgotten.

This was nothing new for Layden but he was still amazed at the ease with which an order was given to snuff out someone's existence. It could have just as easily been an order for lunch or new stationary.

Layden looked at the screen which showed a BNL ID card with a picture of a young man in the corner. Layden recognized the picture immediately. "That's the bastard who ran out of the office tonight. Your guys got a few shots off and I think they hit him."

"They did, as you'll see in a minute. Jack Darvish is a techie who's been with BNL just over a year. The unusual transactions involving the last three IPOs, as well as an offshore account with the Banque Internationale de Zurich containing twenty-two million dollars, have been traced to him." The man shifted his gaze to Layden.

He continued. "Do you know how this man was hired, Philip?"

The guy's a techie for god sakes, Layden thought. *I've never even heard his name before tonight.*

"I don't know."

"He was brought in by one of your high level people. A personal favor to a dead friend."

Layden raised his eyebrows, thinking of who it could be.

His silent question was answered as the projector flipped to the next photo. An image flashed on the screen showing Jack Darvish standing next to a cab, its door still open, his white shirt drenched in blood. Mike Brennan was taking off his tuxedo jacket.

"Brennan?" Layden was shocked.

"We had a man outside who followed Darvish as he got into a cab in front of the Seaport. He stopped on Avenue D and met with Brennan and Brennan's girlfriend."

The screen changed again, showing them inside the cab, pulling away from the curb. "After a heated discussion, Mr. Brennan and the girl got into the cab with Darvish."

"Where did they go?" Layden asked.

The screen changed one last time to show a well kept building with a doorman standing just inside the glass doors.

"Brennan's Gramercy Park apartment."

The old man was watching the screen intently. He finally broke his silence, his eyes remaining on the screen, "Brennan was in the Marine Corps with Darvish's older brother. Joseph Darvish was killed two years ago in Baghdad. Do you think Brennan could be in on it with Jack Darvish?"

Layden thought for a moment before answering. "I can't imagine Brennan would take this risk for twenty two million. Even if he did feel some kind of loyalty because of the guy's brother, his salary and bonus were five million last year alone."

The Old Man shook his head. "Twenty two million was the original amount."

"What?" Layden said.

"After we intercepted the wire, Darvish came looking for his cash and posted another transaction. We're short five hundred million."

Layden's face drained of blood all over again. He hoped his heart would continue beating under the pressure. "Five hundred?"

The question was ignored as the image switched back to the three people standing outside the cab. He zoomed in on Brennan and Darvish's faces.

"I think we have the perfect goats in these young men. Before we find out too late that Brennan's involved, you need to make sure the authorities know he's involved. Brennan's the brains behind the transactions and the tech guy is the worker bee. Once they're convicted and sent to prison, I'll take care of him on the inside."

The overhead lights turned on and the two men stood and walked toward the door. The man reached out and grabbed Layden's arm.

"The Attorney General is on a witch hunt and his focus is now on the stock market." He gripped Layden's arm tighter. "This has to be taken care of immediately."

"I'll handle it."

"My associates will not accept weakness, Philip. BNL is a major link in the chain and they won't risk losing it."

"I understand, sir."

"I hope you do."

Layden took one last look at the image on the screen. Brennan, the clean cut All-American boy was a threat to topple an organization that had been in place for nearly three quarters of a century. It was now his responsibility to stop him.

CHAPTER TEN

Another image of Michael Brennan was projected on the bare wall of an office building in downtown Manhattan. The small projector sat on a card table in a darkened room. Two men on folding chairs were drinking stale coffee from the twenty-four hour deli across the street. Their ties were loosened hours ago and suit coats had been tossed haphazardly on the lone empty chair.

David Reynolds and Pete Battaglia looked like they could have been lawyers, accountants, or investment bankers. In fact they held jobs like that in the not too distant past. Special Agent Reynolds of the FBI had a successful career in finance before joining the Bureau. Assistant District Attorney Battaglia had been with the US Attorney's office for most of his professional life and would probably return there when the task force he was helping to run completed its task.

"What do you think?" Battaglia asked.

Reynolds looked at the screen and shook his head. "What I think obviously doesn't matter because we haven't got shit on this guy. He's clean."

"I know all that." Battaglia slapped his hand on the flimsy table. "A year of my life has been flushed down the toilet while we've been trying to find something on these people. There's just nothing we can prove."

"That's where you're wrong. The Attorney General hand picked us for this task force for a reason. He expects results and we're going to give him results."

"Are we going to fabricate evidence?" Battaglia asked.

Reynolds smiled. "You've been an ADA for way too long. You're mind has been irreparably damaged"

Battaglia ignored the insult. "Okay Mr. FBI. You worked on Wall Street for how long before becoming Super Agent Reynolds?"

"Ten years."

"You tell me how we're going to pin something on BNL and their poster child here, Michael Brennan." He pointed to the photo on the wall showing Brennan walking on Water Street, about to enter the BNL building. He looked sharp in his thousand dollar suit, square jaw, and close cropped hair. "They're presenting him with the Man of the Year at that god damned youth center as we speak. I heard this morning he helped a little old lady cross Second Avenue."

Reynolds lost his smile as he tried to re-focus. "Are you finished?"

"Please go on. I can't wait to hear your plan."

"Some of the companies brought public through BNL don't have the track record to maintain their price levels." Reynolds held up a sheet of paper that listed all the IPOs that BNL brought public since the company's inception. "Dart should be trading at half of where it ended up today." He was excited now, the ideas falling off his tongue. "We charge them with market manipulation, citing a few instances of heavy trading, and get a subpoena to tear through their books."

"That'll fly with a judge?" Battaglia asked. "It's going to be hard to argue supply and demand. These guys can sell ice to Eskimos for Christ's sake."

"You leave that to me. Write up the charges and I'll bring it to Judge Price and convince him. How long will it take you to get me something?"

Battaglia thought for a moment before responding. "I wrote the damn thing six months ago. I'll tweak it a bit to include market manipulation and I'll change the date. Give me half an hour."

"Perfect. I'll be back in twenty minutes." Reynolds stood to leave.

"I'll do it but we're going to need some time to prepare to go into their offices. You get Price to sign it tonight and I'll worry about setting up the forensic team."

"I'll tell you something right now my little Italian friend. We're going to get them and I'm not kissing another year goodbye. I feel it. Something is going to break soon."

"You feel it? Who the fuck are you, Columbo?" Battaglia shook his head and grinned. "You watch too much television."

Reynolds disregarded the comment. "We're about to break this wide open."

"Get outta here and let me finish. I miss my wife." Battaglia walked over to his desk.

Reynolds took a hard look at the picture on the wall before shutting off the projector. He grabbed his jacket and walked to the door.

"Come to think of it, I miss your wife too." Reynolds smiled.

"Do I need this shit from you?" Battaglia shook his head as the door slammed shut.

CHAPTER ELEVEN

"That hurts, man!" Darvish winced in pain.

"Don't expect sympathy from me." Brennan expertly dressed the wounds as his patient sat on a stool at his kitchen counter. He removed the last piece of glass from Darvish's neck and taped a large bandage in place.

Darvish stood up when he was done and put on one of Mike's shirts. His thin frame barely filled out the shoulders and he had to roll the sleeves so he didn't look like a little kid wearing his dad's shirt. He walked to the refrigerator, grabbed three beers and handed one each to Mike and Sam. He continued into the living room where he fell into the leather couch. He moaned as he slowly put his feet up on the coffee table.

Mike followed him in. "By all means, make yourself comfortable."

Darvish took a long pull of his beer. "I understand that you're pissed off. I tried to tell you today but I couldn't bring myself to do it."

"And how would that have helped?" Mike sat on the other couch, opposite Darvish, the coffee table separating them.

After another sip he responded. "I'm not saying it would have helped. I guess I wanted to apologize more than anything."

"I've got to be honest with you. Right now, I couldn't give a shit about your predicament. You stole the firm's money and you'll pay the price."

"Thanks."

"What I'm worried about is this." Mike held up the pile of papers Jack brought with him, some of them stained with blood. "And the fact that someone with Layden took a shot at you."

"Three shots," Darvish corrected. He turned to Sam and pointed to her unopened beer sitting on the table. "You going to drink that?"

She laughed and pushed it across to him. "Are you always so pushy? Maybe you can come over to work at City Hall."

Mike interrupted. "After he gets out of jail, you can set up an interview."

"Jail?" Darvish sat up a little straighter.

"You think you're going to get away with this?" Mike's anger had not subsided. "If they don't kill you first, there's no way to avoid going to prison."

Darvish again looked to Sam. "You're an attorney. Do I have a chance here?"

Sam shrugged and replied, "These white collar crimes are easy to plead out if you've got something to offer the other side."

"I've got these." He reached over and grabbed the pile of papers in front of Mike and waved them in the air.

Sam directed the next comment to Mike. "On the other hand, it will be a lot harder for someone in a senior position at the firm to deny knowledge of these transactions."

Mike snatched the papers back from Jack's hands. "I don't even know what these transactions are. I had no idea about this and I can prove it!"

"How?" Sam asked.

Mike glared at her. "Whose side are you on?"

Sam moved closer to him on the couch and put her arm around his shoulder. "Yours. I'll do anything to help you. I hope you know that."

"Can we get back to the situation?" Darvish asked.

"You're really getting on my nerves, Jack." Mike took a sip from his bottle.

"I have that effect on people after a while. That's why my plan to take this money and disappear from society was so good but I never thought for a second you'd turn me in. After I saw those transactions I thought I owed it to you to let know."

"Thanks for being such a good citizen and warning me but even if I don't turn you in, twenty two million won't last forever. Certainly not if your living on some Caribbean island."

"Well, I haven't exactly been honest with you."

Mike's anger welled up again. He leaned forward with his elbows on his knees. "Tell me everything you know. Now."

Jack opened his mouth to reply just as his cell phone rang. He pulled it off his belt and flipped it open. "Hello." He put a finger up to Mike, telling him to hold on.

He listened for a few seconds before saying, "Thank you… nothing else today. I'll be in touch."

"Who the hell was that?" Mike demanded.

"That was my banker in Switzerland."

"Switzerland?"

"Yeah. He just confirmed my wire for me."

"The twenty two?"

Jack looked down before answering. "When they took the cash back I got angry. My plans were snuffed out before my eyes. Instead of taking back my original amount I thought I'd teach them a lesson. I didn't feel bad about it after seeing those wires."

"How much, Jack?" Mike seemed ready to pounce on him like a hungry lion.

Darvish looked him in the eye. "Five hundred million."

Mike stood suddenly, causing Darvish to sink lower in the couch. Mike pointed at him as he past him. "You're a dead man, Jack. No wonder they took a shot at you. I'd probably kill you myself if it were my money."

Mike walked into the bedroom. Sam followed and found him putting clothes in an overnight bag.

She sat on the bed. "What the hell are you doing?"

"We've got to get out of here, Sam. It's guilt by association. Jack screwed us by showing up tonight because I'm sure they're following him. He should have just walked away." He went to her closet and grabbed a bag, tossing it on the bed next to her.

"Who are you running from?"

"We're not running. If there's one thing I learned in the Marine Corps it was this. Always strike first. I only play offense, babe. No defense."

She nodded, understanding his thought process. "What's the plan?"

"I need to talk to Melvin Barry. He acted strangely when we were talking on the way out of the office tonight. He just got out of a shouting match with Layden before I met up with him. I'm wondering if he was trying to tell me something."

"What did he say?"

"We were talking about how lucky it was that the bottom didn't drop out of Dart. He said, 'All you need to do is place a call to the right person at the right time.'"

"That's true isn't it?" Sam started throwing clothes in her own bag.

"It's just the way he said it with an odd look on his face. We got separated in the elevator and he hopped in a cab before I got the chance to talk with him in the lobby. I need to confront him."

"Do you think he's dangerous?"

Mike shook his head. "I know he's not."

CHAPTER TWELVE

Over the years, Philip Layden had forged relationships with people of varied backgrounds. He had contacts in law enforcement, government, and of course the business world. The contacts he valued more than any others were the ones that no one else knew about. For the right price, they would handle just about any job and meet short deadlines. He placed a call as soon as he left the mansion on Park Avenue to a man who fell into this last category.

The sun had set long ago over Rockaway Beach in Queens, on the southwestern edge of Long Island. It was approaching midnight and the boardwalk was nearly empty on a beautiful moonlit night. The boardwalk ran the length of the beach starting way down in Far Rockaway and making its way through all different types of neighborhoods starting with Hispanic, moving into African-American, then Irish, then Jewish. Layden walked quickly past One Hundred and Twenty-Eighth Street, looking for a familiar face.

He pressed the spot under his suit coat to feel the small Baretta he never left home without. Layden knew the man he would be meeting would be carrying at least one weapon in his belt, probably one stashed in an ankle holster, and another at the small of his back. Sean Sullivan didn't take any chances. Although Layden didn't expect any trouble he knew there would be others close by to back Sullivan up if something went wrong.

There were just some jobs that Layden had to go to the outside to bring in the right people. He'd done business with Sullivan several times over the years and each time was pleased with the results.

Layden stopped walking and leaned on a railing. He watched the waves crash on the beach forty yards out. The dark blue curls turning to foamy white as they approached the shore. He heard a slight noise behind him and turned quickly to see a man in a wet suit holding a surfboard. From a distance Sean Sullivan could have been mistaken for a twenty year old. His shoulder-length blond hair was bleached by the sun and his skin was nicely tanned. The black suit hugged a very trim body that the forty-three year old kept in top shape by surfing and swimming on a daily basis.

"Hello Sean. Still the stealthy one I see." Layden pushed himself up to sit atop the railing.

"You have to be in my line of work. It's a necessary skill if you like to stay alive." Sullivan moved forward with his hand extended.

"It's nice to see you, Sean. You surf at night?" Layden shook his hand and slapped him on the shoulder.

"The amateurs leave at sundown."

Layden smiled. "How've you been?"

"I'm doing just fine." Sullivan didn't look Layden in the eyes for more than a couple of seconds at a time. Always wary, he was scanning the boardwalk and the beach.

Layden got to the point of the meeting. "I need some work done."

"How soon?"

"Before sunrise." Layden tried to gauge Sullivan's reaction. There was none.

Sullivan looked out to the ocean. "You've always been a great client but I've got some bad news. My rates have doubled."

Layden started to speak but Sullivan held up his hand. "I have to live, don't I? You'll receive the same impeccable service you've come to expect."

"Fine." Layden knew he didn't have much of a choice.

"Call the same number and leave the details." Sullivan vaulted himself over the railing onto the sand and grabbed his board again.

They shook hands and Sullivan trotted off toward the ocean. Only then did Layden notice two other figures, dressed in dark wetsuits, waiting near the water. *God dammed spooks*, Philip thought as he watched the three surfers enter the water and paddle beyond the breakers.

CHAPTER THIRTEEN

Agent Reynolds exited the basement garage on West Street. He drove his BMW to work every day but made sure he parked a few blocks away from Federal Plaza. There were other agents at the office driving nice cars, but they flaunted them. They wanted everyone to see the expensive hunk of metal and rubber as they made their way to one of the lowest paying jobs in the nation.

Reynolds came from humble beginnings. His father was an agent at the Bureau. His mother a school teacher. After finishing his degree at Yale, David was torn between a career at the FBI and Wall Street. As far back as he could remember in his childhood, he wanted to be a lawman like his dad. When he played cops and robbers, he had to be the cop and he had to win.

It was that winning attitude that helped convince him to take a job with a large brokerage house. It was a hard decision but when the money started rolling in, he was able to make his parents and the rest of his family very comfortable. It was very satisfying. With ten years under his belt in the market, after he moved from broker to running his own small hedge fund, his sense of satisfaction was gone. He was seeing things going on in the business world that he knew his father wouldn't be happy knowing. Things that were so far outside the law, the perpetrators should have gone to jail for a very long time.

He eventually got to the point where he could no longer turn his head and ignore the facts. He sold his piece of the business to his partner and walked away. He knew he didn't belong in the white collar world. He was blue collar no matter how you sliced him.

He'd normally drive up to East Seventy-Sixth Street and park the car under his building but tonight he needed to conduct some business. Twenty blocks south of his building, he turned east on Fifty-Sixth Street toward the river and Sutton Place. The building he was looking for sat on the east side of the street. He pulled up to the empty spot in front of the entrance and a doorman immediately approached the car as Reynolds got out.

"Good evening, sir. Can I help you?"

Reynolds opened his badge case and held it up for the man to see. The protective doorman looked at it closely.

"I'm here to see the Judge."

"Yes sir. Is he expecting you?"

"Yes," Reynolds said as he followed the doorman to the house phone. No one got upstairs without a call to the resident.

"Judge Price? Special Agent Reynolds is here to see you." He listened for a moment and hung up the phone. "Go right in, sir. George will take you upstairs."

The elevator operator let Reynolds out on the top floor where he found the only door on the hallway and rang the doorbell. The door opened and he was led by the housekeeper through the apartment to a room in the back. She opened the door and motioned for him to step inside.

"Have a seat Reynolds. Can I get you a drink?" The Judge was already behind the bar with two glasses. It was hard to refuse.

Reynolds scanned the row of bottles on the shelf behind the bar until he found what he was looking for. "Makers Mark on the rocks."

"Excellent choice." The judge poured two glasses and came around the bar. The judge was a tall man with a full head of white hair. He looked like a tough guy and was. They sat in soft leather chairs facing each other, an antique coffee table between them. Although the Judge was an intimidating figure, Reynolds was comfortable with him. They were on the same side.

"You didn't come to shoot the shit at midnight, Reynolds. What can I do for you?" Price didn't mince words.

Reynolds smiled. "I want to take BNL down."

Price pretended to choke on his drink. "Why stop there? Why not take out Merrill Lynch and Goldman Sachs while you're at it?"

Reynolds reached into his pocket for a sheet of paper. He was prepared. "These are some of companies that BNL brought public in the last twenty years. The first half shows stocks that for all intents and purposes should be trading below a dollar." He handed the paper to the Judge. "The bottom half are going for a thirty percent premium."

"That's supply and demand, son."

"I'd like to believe that Judge Price, but I have the analysis to back up my conclusions."

"I own some of these stocks." He dropped the paper on the table.

"So does the rest of the country. That's why we need to stop them now." Reynolds reached into his pocket again and returned with the subpoena Battaglia drew up earlier in the evening.

The Judge took it, scanned the words quickly, and looked up. "You're effectively declaring war on the securities industry." He dropped it on the table between them. "Are you prepared for the fallout?"

Reynolds moved forward to the edge of his chair. "I've been preparing for this battle since before I got to the Bureau."

"How does Attorney General Jacobs feel about it?"

"He's already taken on the mutual fund industry and won. These are the same players trying to skim profits at the public's expense. He's looking forward to the fight. That's why he set up the task force with the FBI and the US Attorney's Office."

The Judge locked eyes with his visitor momentarily. "The Bureau's recruiter must have been drooling when you dropped your resume on his desk."

Reynolds didn't handle compliments well. "I'm just a hard working agent, Judge."

"Bullshit. How many new agents do you know that owned their own firm before signing up?"

Reynolds shifted uncomfortably in his seat. "None."

"My point exactly." The Judge took a pen from his shirt pocket, leaned over the coffee table and signed the bottom of the subpoena. When he was done he stood up.

"I trust that you know what you're doing. Just be careful, Agent Reynolds. Old brokerage people aren't cut from the same cloth as the guys running mutual funds."

"That's where we disagree, Judge. I think all thieves are the same."

The judge handed him the signed subpoena. "Prove it."

"I plan to."

CHAPTER FOURTEEN

"Do you think Jack will be safe at the Plaza?" Sam sat in the passenger seat of Mike's black Range Rover.

"I was able to pay cash and sign him in under a false name. As long as he stays in the hotel and doesn't go online to check his bank accounts, he'll be fine."

"What if we're being followed?"

"I don't think we were followed out of Gramercy Park. Nobody knows about that tunnel to the next block except for the doormen."

"How do you know about it?"

He smiled. "Don't ask. Let's just say that it doesn't hurt to supply the guys with a few sandwiches and coffees every once in a while. I've got to tell you, it's a lot better than walking all the way around the block in sub-zero weather to get to the market."

"Thanks for telling me about it."

"They swore me to secrecy."

"You're very honorable." Sam punched him in the shoulder.

Mike was heading north on Central Park West, about to turn into the park to cut through to the east side.

Sam became serious again. "What are the chances of Jack not going on the Internet?"

"He's a computer geek. I'd say the chances are slim but I plan to work quickly." Mike jerked the wheel left to avoid a cab that stopped short in front of him then rolled to a stop at the red light.

Sam reached over and put her hand on top of Mike's. "Are you going to be safe?"

The light turned green and he kept his eyes on the road, following the line of traffic into the park. "I'll be fine. I can take care of myself."

"How can you say that when you have no idea what you're dealing with yet?"

He was tailgating a bus, following the curves of Seventy-Ninth Street as it wound its way past the carousel and softball fields.

"I'm confident that after I talk to Melvin, I'll have the answers I need."

Sam remained silent. Mike looked over at her and took her hand in his. "Don't worry, babe. I'll call in to the office and leave a message that I need a few days off. We'll head out to the house in Southampton. I haven't even told anyone at work about it yet and it's in my mom's name. We'll be safe there."

She looked out the window at the trees rolling by. "We've got a lot of commitments coming up. The mayor's fundraiser at the Plaza is tomorrow night and Maddux would flip his lid if we don't show up."

"We'll take the helicopter service back here tomorrow night."

"Isn't Albert Claire's barbeque out in Amagansett in a couple days?"

"Southampton is just a few minutes from Claire's place so don't worry."

"I'm not worried about the events themselves. I'm worried about someone coming after you while we're there." She tried to maintain her strong attitude but it was becoming harder as the night wore on.

Mike looked over at her. "I'm sorry I dragged you into this but you're going to have to trust me."

He pressed a speed dial number on his cell phone and put it to his ear as he exited the park and turned south on Fifth Avenue. Mike pulled over in front of Barry's building, just across from the park and waited for the other end to pick up. He looked out the driver's side window and up toward the penthouse, as if he'd be able to see Barry on his terrace.

"Hello Maria, this is Mike Brennan. Can I please speak with Mr. Barry?"

He listened for a moment. "When?" He cut the connection and turned to Sam. "Apparently Senor and Senora Barry left for their house in Cove Neck. We'll stop there on the way out east."

"It's almost midnight!" Sam was looking at her watch.

"There's no way I'm sitting on this until the morning." He pulled out into traffic.

"This doesn't feel right, Mike."

Mike lifted the armrest between them and removed one of his most prized possessions. A Sig Sauer P226 9mm he got from some friends when he left the Marine Corps.

Sam slid away from the weapon, closer to the door. "I hate that thing."

Mike shrugged. "I said I can take care of myself but I never said I was going to do it alone." He lifted his shirt and stuck the weapon in his waistband.

Fifty minutes later Mike pulled off the Long Island Expressway and took the local roads heading toward the north shore of the island and the hills of the beautiful Gold Coast. He'd been to the Barry's house several times and he was still in awe of the splendor of the house and surrounding property. The Barry's winding driveway was lined with hundred year old great oaks and the house was an incredible sight with the moon hanging low behind it over Oyster Bay Cove in the distance. They past the smaller guesthouse, its pond filled with water lilies, and came to a stop in front of the main house, the gravel crunching loudly under the tires.

They hopped down from the SUV and breathed in the fresh air, heavy with the moisture of the bay. The massive trees surrounding the house formed a canopy keeping the area cool and dark. They walked up the wooden steps to the outdoor porch that wrapped itself around three sides of the house. It was almost one in the morning but there were lights on in several rooms. Someone was up. Mike rang the bell and the door opened within seconds of pushing the chime. Barbara Barry was visibly upset, her eyes red and puffy. She didn't seem surprised to see them.

Mike stepped in, kissed her on the cheek, and held her at arm's length.

"Is everything okay, Barbara?" Mike was looking behind her to see if Melvin was in view.

"I don't know, Mike. He won't tell me what's wrong. He's sitting in the den staring into the fire and he keeps telling me that everything is going to be okay. You've got to talk to him. Please find out what's going on with him." Barbara was holding back tears.

Sam stepped in to hug her and Barbara held her tightly. "Hi, honey. I'm so glad you're here. What made you drop by so late?"

"Mike said he needed to talk to Melvin about work. I'm not really clear on the details." It was obvious Barry hadn't told his wife anything about the stolen shares from BNL's accounts and the shooting at the office earlier in the night.

Mike was already half way down the long hallway leading to the back of the house. He opened the door to the den and looked to the far side where the fireplace was located. Two large leather armchairs sat in front of the fireplace, facing away from the door. He could see Barry's arms on the chair to the right, holding a martini in his hand. The walls were lined with bookshelves. A rolling ladder allowed access to the top shelves. He stepped quietly around the chair on the left and stopped directly in front of the old man.

Without looking up Melvin said, "Sit down. You wanna drink?" His eyes were fixed on the crackling fire. The room was extremely warm with the windows closed and the fire roaring.

"I think a dip in the pool would be better than a drink after sitting in this sauna." Mike forced a smile.

"I'm glad you came out here, Son."

"Why do you think I came out here?" He was interested in what Barry thought his reasons were.

Melvin looked at Mike for the first time. "I'm done. Finished," he said with the weariness of a sixty-eight year old man who felt his age.

"What are you talking about? Done? We're having one of the best years in the company's history. How could you quit now?" Mike wasn't expecting this. He knew something strange was going on but he never expected this.

"I don't think you understand, Mike. I don't have a choice in this matter. They want me out and my hands are tied."

"Who the hell is they? You can't be forced out because someone is screwing with our trading account. You've got way too much support and influence for that!"

Melvin stood and walked toward the fireplace.

"Listen to me, Mike. Just listen. I thought after today you'd understand but you don't get it. Just forget it. Maybe I overestimated how smart you are. Just get out and leave me alone here. I've got some thinking to do!"

"Take it easy." Mike felt they were talking about two different things. "Do you know what happened after hours at the office?"

Barry turned from the fire and looked at Mike with a blank expression. He didn't know.

Mike was confused. "Have you spoken with Philip tonight?"

"No. Why?"

"Layden somehow found out that the guy stealing shares of our IPOs was Jack Darvish."

"The computer kid that you brought in?"

"Yes. Two men with Layden opened fire on him on the trading floor."

Barry put his hand to his mouth and shook his head. "That idiot. Was anyone hurt?"

"A bullet grazed Jack's shoulder but he'll be okay." Mike took a step closer. "Why the hell wouldn't Layden just call the cops?"

Barry didn't reply.

"Is something going on at the firm that I should know about?"

Barry remained silent.

"Dart should have bottomed out today and it didn't. How did you phrase it? 'All you need is to call the right people at the right time'. Darvish uncovered millions of dollars coming into our cash account. Is that what this is all about?"

Melvin sat back in his chair and continued to stare into the fire. "I'm surprised you didn't find out years ago."

"Find what out?" Mike raised his voice, his anger now apparent

Barry continued speaking as if he were alone. "The real problem is that I should have told you years ago." He took a sip of his martini. "Or never hired you in the first place. My problem was that I liked you and I wanted you to taste the high life. After a while I realized that if I liked you so damned much, I shouldn't have gotten you involved in all this shit!"

Mike was still puzzled. He had grown steadily nervous as Barry continued babbling to himself. Mike had done nothing illegal in all his years in the business but his name and reputation would be ruined if the partners of the firm were involved in illegal proceedings. No one would believe that he didn't have a hand in it.

There was a long uncomfortable silence after Barry's last outburst. Mike finally broke the tension. "Melvin, let's talk about it and we'll try to clear it up. What can't we handle now that we haven't handled before?"

Melvin turned to face Mike. He seemed to be aging by the minute. His back hunched over, his shirt wrinkled.

"It's too late to clean this one up, son. It started way before you joined the firm. We've been manipulating the market for years now."

Mike felt like he was hit in the head with a baseball bat. His ears were ringing, his vision blurred. Now he understood how so much could go right for him over the past few years. They were breaking the law. His firm had been manipulating prices for their own benefit as well as for their clients. Mike doubted his business smarts if he didn't see this coming.

He should have been able to recognize the pattern. He was trying to narrow down the many deals they had done over the years. *Which ones had been pumped up?* He could think of a few that had done unexpectedly well, but his last thought was of Dart. The price held even after the bad news was released.

Mike came out of his daze and looked at Melvin. "Tell me this is just a joke, Melvin."

Mike walked to the window and looked into the yard and saw Sam and Barbara sitting at a small table by the pool.

"Does Barbara know about this?"

The old man shook his head sadly. "She suspects way more than she actually knows because I've tried to keep it from her much the same way I tried to handle it with you. I didn't want to hurt you but we just got in too deep. There was no turning back after the first time."

"Who else is involved?" Mike was still thinking to himself that there was a way out because he refused to believe his career was over. He was also trying to keep Sam out of his mind because he dreaded the moment when he had to explain this to her. She'd be crushed. Not just emotionally crushed, her career as a political legal advisor would also be cut short.

Barry answered, "I have no way of knowing but I'd guess half the street is involved. It's ballooned to such a point that I can't believe the authorities haven't caught on yet. At least the officials who haven't been paid off."

Mike began to think about the investigations that were sure to begin when the news broke. He would be arrested and publicly humiliated. Even if he were exonerated, which he knew deep down, he wouldn't be, he could never get a job in the business again. He'd be lucky to get something in the back office of a non-profit.

"I thought we were a legitimate firm when we started out. Philip brought me in and we did pretty well. Turns out he wasn't happy with the huge gains we were taking when the market was exploding. I'm just as guilty for going along with him but I didn't want to dissolve our partnership and have to start over somewhere else. I was already past my prime and the sound of all that cash flow didn't sound that bad. I convinced myself that no

WEALTH OF DECEPTION 71

one was really getting hurt." Melvin sighed and resumed his gaze into the fire. His face was gaunt with dark circles under his bloodshot eyes.

"Who's sending all those wires through BNL's accounts?" Mike asked, wondering where it all began.

"There are several silent partners but I don't know them. We've been dealing with shell companies of shell companies. I never actually met with anyone face to face, but I know Philip has." He put his head in his hands for a second and then sat straight in his chair, grabbing Mike's arm. "Layden's men took a shot at the kid tonight because he feared what may have been uncovered. Not because of some stolen money."

"It wasn't just some money, Melvin. It was five hundred million."

Barry let go of Mike's arm but didn't seem phased. "I'll bet Layden didn't even know how much was stolen. His number one fear would be someone finding out what we've been doing all these years." He paused. "Now they think you're involved because you brought this kid into the firm."

"I've already realized that."

"You've got to protect yourself, Mike." Barry leaned forward in his chair. "I hope you realize that if you turn him in he'll kill you. I'm sure he's already planned how to get rid of you. He knew you'd eventually find out and that you wouldn't go along with him. You've got to keep this to yourself for your own safety, as well as for Sam's."

Mike again looked out the window at his girlfriend sitting on a lounge chair with her feet up, sipping a drink. She had finally gotten Barbara into a better mood. It wouldn't be long before they both found out about the trouble the firm was in, and neither would take it well.

"You've got to tell me who's involved, Melvin."

"It's bigger than you can imagine, son. I don't even think I know the full extent of what we've been enabling for years. I certainly know of a few others involved, but I've always believed that we were one of many firms out there being controlled by a central entity. Philip is the point man."

Mike slammed his hand on the mantle. "I can't believe what I'm hearing. You're saying there are firms out there operating the same way you've been. It could be the whole fucking market for all I know!" He pulled the other chair around in front of the old man and sat down. "You've got to give me more details so I can somehow prepare myself for the crush."

Barry looked at Mike for a long time before he spoke. "Mike, I'm exhausted right now. I feel so tired I can barely speak." He closed his eyes and rubbed them. When he opened them again, they were redder than a moment earlier, more sunken into his skull. "I'm tired from the years of keeping secrets and wondering when I'd be caught. Come back in the morning and I'll lay it out for you. We can figure out a plan so you can leave the firm without Layden getting suspicious. Just do me a favor, don't let Barbara know anything. I'll tell her when I'm ready."

Mike looked at the older man with a mixture of emotions, anger leading the list. He couldn't force the old guy to talk. "I'll be back here first thing in the morning. Get some sleep Melvin, because we've got a lot to talk about."

Mike pushed himself out of the leather armchair. Barry had no intention of getting up with him. "Don't worry, I'll let myself out."

Mike called out the back door to Sam. They said goodbye to Barbara, went back through the house, and out the front door to the Range Rover. Mike opened the passenger door for Sam and walked around to his side. Before he opened the door, he stopped and looked into the darkness surrounding the house. The foliage was dense and the trees thick.

He took a couple steps toward a group of tall pine bushes and stared into the deep green needles. He knew he heard a sound but it could have been a raccoon or a cat. He put his hand to his waistband, feeling for his

9mm. After a few seconds, satisfied he was alone, he turned back to his vehicle wondering if he was just being paranoid.

The SUV pulled away leaving the front of the house quiet. There wasn't a sound in the still air except for the same rustling in the bushes that Mike thought he imagined moments earlier.

CHAPTER FIFTEEN

Mike rose early the next morning after a fitful night, thinking about the disturbing conversation with his boss. When Sam awoke, they took a walk along the beach. Afterwards, they sat on the sand a few feet from the crashing waves talking about the possibilities.

Sam's attorney's mind was working overtime. "There's a back door out of just about every legal battle. You could cut a deal and give the authorities everything you know."

"If I cut a deal, I'd be admitting some level of guilt."

"There may be no other choice." She stated the obvious.

"I have to find another option because I did nothing wrong!" He got up and started back to the house.

"Mike!" Sam called after him.

He turned and waited for her.

"I'll do anything I can to help you. You understand that, don't you?"

He put both his hands on her cheeks. "I know it. I'll just never accept the fact that I have to lie and say that I was involved in this shit just to walk away." They walked back to the house silently, hand in hand.

He left Sam in the house, got into the Range Rover, opened all the windows and blasted *The Doors* as he sped back west toward the Barry estate. *Break on Through* was reaching its peak as he pulled off the highway to follow the same route through the hills he drove not eight hours earlier. He pulled onto the gravel driveway and approached the main house where he spotted an ambulance and a police car parked in front. Mike's heart leapt to his throat as he skidded to a halt behind the empty ambulance. He took the stairs three at a time and ran through the open front door of the house.

Looking down the long hall into the back of the house, he could see the EMTs near the pool. He sped through the kitchen and out to the yard where they already had a body on the stretcher covered with a sheet.

"What happened?" Mike yelled to the men wheeling the stretcher toward an opening in the fence.

A policeman walked quickly from the other side of the pool. "May I help you, sir?

"I'm a friend of the Barry's. What the hell happened?" He was trying desperately to keep calm.

Beyond the cop, he could see Barbara sitting at one of the tables, her head in her hands, sobbing uncontrollably. Mike slipped past the officer and knelt beside her.

"Barbara, I'm so sorry. What happened?"

She raised her head and looked at him through bloodshot eyes soaked with tears. "I woke up and found him in the pool." Her voice was just above a whisper. "He was still in his clothes." She paused, her lip quivering. "He must have fallen in."

Mike stayed with her until her sister arrived. The cops told him that Melvin had way too much to drink, decided to go for a walk, got too close to the pool and fell in. With all those martinis in him he didn't have a chance.

After Barbara settled down and her sister showed up, Mike set out for his house on the South Fork, thoughts flying around his head at a hundred miles an hour. His thoughts were first of Barbara, the poor old widow, all alone now. Then as if flipping the pages of a photo album, images of BNL and Layden appeared in his mind. He never got the whole story from Barry but how could he possibly show up at work as if nothing had happened?

He set his vehicle on autopilot and somehow ended up at his destination. He shook himself out of the daze as he turned down his small street and pulled into his driveway to find a police car blocking his path. Barry's words from the previous evening sprang to life. *You've got to keep this to yourself for your own safety, as well as for Sam's.* He ran through the front door to find an empty house.

"Sam!" he yelled with no response. He ran to the kitchen pushed through the screen door. It swung open and hit the house with a bang. He stopped in his tracks when he saw Sam sitting on the deck with a policeman.

The officer looked up from his beer. "Do you always run like a madman through your own house to greet your girlfriend?"

"You scared the hell out of me, you son of a bitch!" Mike's heart was pounding, sweat dripping down his back.

The cop looked at Sam and shrugged, then looked back to Mike. "Why don't you come over here and give your big brother a hug. You don't call to let me know you're coming out?"

Mike skipped the hug and fell into the chair next to him. "You're still a son of a bitch, but I'm glad to see you, Tim. I've had a rough morning."

Mike told them what happened to Barry. Sam was upset and wanted to go back immediately to see if Barbara was okay. Mike convinced her to stay, in light of everything they'd just found out about the company.

Tim, a lieutenant with the Suffolk County Police Department, had close to fifteen years on the job. He, unlike his younger brother, wasn't very fond of the city. He'd been trying to get Mike to move out East for years and was glad when he decided to get a summer place nearby.

Sam disappeared into the house to let the brothers talk alone. They sat facing the ocean with their feet on the railing, breathing the ocean air.

Mike inhaled deeply, let it out slowly as he turned to his brother. "I've got something I need to get off my chest but you've got to keep it to yourself until I've decided just how I'm going to handle it. I'm going to need your help." Mike proceeded to tell Tim the whole story about Jack Darvish, the strange wires, the shooting, and Barry's story about a possible central entity controlling BNL. Tim listened intently to every word and didn't interrupt.

When Mike finished, Tim was brutally honest. "This doesn't look good for you. How the hell are you going to prove that you didn't know about any laws being broken when you held such a high position in the firm?"

Mike knew the reality of his problem but still refused to accept blame. "I've got a little time to figure it out. I can probably take a few days off because of the funeral and I'm hoping Layden doesn't know I visited Barry last night." He paused, collecting his thoughts. "Think you could take a few days off to give me a hand figuring this one out?"

"You didn't even have to ask. I'll do anything to get you out of this mess. I just hope there's a way out."

"Do you know a place on the North Shore where you can launch your boat?"

"I've got a friend who runs a marina up in East Setauket. What do you have in mind?"

"While Layden is in the city today, I want to cross the Sound and search his house in Connecticut."

Tim smiled. "That's breaking and entering."

"Thanks for the lesson in criminal justice but I don't have many choices. These bastards are into something and I need to take drastic measures to come out clean."

"And alive."

"That's also important. So are you still in?"

"I told you I'd help you, little brother. What's lined up after that?"

"Tonight, Sam and I are heading into Manhattan for a fundraiser at the Plaza Hotel hosted by Mayor Maddux. Tomorrow night is a party at Albert Claire's over in Amagansett."

"That's the Claire Cosmetics guy?"

"That's him. He's been a client at BNL for twenty years and I've been handling his personal account since I was brought into the firm. We've got a pretty good relationship. I'll talk to him. Maybe he's got some ideas."

"You've got to be careful now, Mike. How do you know they won't come after you at the Plaza?" Tim was concerned.

"I think security will be pretty tight at the fundraiser. All the Democratic Party hacks will be there. I heard Vice President Browning will be making an appearance. That means Secret Service."

"Okay. What about out here or at Claire's?"

"The house is in Mom's name and I've told no one about it. I think we'll be okay here. At Claire's I'll be on my own but I can take care of myself."

"Sorry. I forgot you were a big tough Marine. Do you still remember your hand to hand combat skills or do you need a refresher course?" Tim teased.

Mike ignored the jab. "Can you pick me up in an hour?"

"I'll be here."

CHAPTER SIXTEEN

"This is some place, huh?" Agent Reynolds said as he pulled to a stop behind a Cove Neck patrol car in the Barry's gravel driveway.

"Not bad," Battaglia answered sarcastically.

They got out of their government issued Chevrolet and walked up the steps to ring the bell. After flashing their badges to the uniformed policeman who answered the door, they were shown to the same den that Mike had been in with Barry the previous evening.

"We're here to keep the press away," the cop explained as he led them through the house. "Mr. Barry's death hasn't been made public yet but you guys know how fast word gets around."

"You should probably post a car at the end of the drive and I.D. anyone trying to enter the property," Reynolds suggested.

"Good idea, I'll have dispatch send over another car." He left the room.

When the door was closed Battaglia said, "We're a fucking stone's throw from Manhattan but it still feels like we're in some backwards small town. How does that happen?"

"It's one of life's mysteries. No one knows…" He was cut off by the door opening and a well dressed man coming into the den. He stood straight as an arrow, walking confidently up to the two lawmen.

"Can I help you fellas?" the man asked.

Reynolds stepped forward and answered, "I'm Special Agent David Reynolds with the F.B.I. and this is Special Investigator Pete Battaglia with the US Attorney's Office." Reynolds was holding up his badge and I.D. "We'd like to ask Mrs. Barry a few questions if we could."

The man didn't hesitate. "Oh, I don't think that would be possible gentlemen. She's understandably very upset and has been sedated by her doctor."

"Do you mind if I ask who you are?" Battaglia asked.

"Of course not. I'm Philip Layden, Mr. Barry's partner at BNL. I came over to help Mrs. Barry with the arrangements."

The two men knew very well who Mr. Layden was and weren't surprised to see him handling inquiries.

"We were under the impression that Mr. Barry's death was already found to be an accident. Why would the F.B.I. and District Attorney's office need to be involved?"

"As I'm sure you're painfully aware, Mr. Layden, there's been an ongoing industry-wide investigation of securities related violations that includes your firm. It's standard procedure for our task force to follow up on the death of any person involved in an investigation. No matter how remote their involvement might be." Reynolds was being purposely vague. He felt that BNL was the center of his case, but he had yet to prove it. Hopefully, the piece of paper in his breast pocket, with Judge Price's signature would help change that.

"That's understandable." Layden said coolly, turning toward the door. "If there's nothing else I can help you with, I have some urgent business to attend to."

"Actually Mr. Layden, there is something you can do for us." Reynolds reached into his coat pocket. "Please take my business card and call me if you think of anything that we should know about."

Layden took the card. "I'll be sure to do that."

"Thanks." Reynolds enjoyed watching the man take the card and smile, as if he really intended to keep it.

In the car on the way back to their office Battaglia asked, "Did that guy give you the creeps?"

"I feel like I need a shower. I don't think he liked us very much." Reynolds was at the wheel, speeding toward the city on the westbound LIE. "He was scared."

"Scared of us?" Battaglia asked.

Reynolds shook his head. "Not us. I'm not sure of what or who, but he's certainly not scared of us."

"Maybe he'll come running when he's ready to cave in."

"I doubt it." Reynolds was watching the road in front of him without actually seeing it.

"Me too."

"We'll be seeing Mr. Layden soon enough. As soon as Attorney General Jacobs finishes reviewing the subpoena the judge signed for us, we'll be tearing apart BNL Securities."

Battaglia nodded happily. "I can't wait to see his face when we arrive on his doorstep with fifty investigators and agents. He's going to have a heart attack."

CHAPTER SEVENTEEN

"Are you staying out of trouble, Jack?" Mike stepped off his back deck, cell phone to his ear, his bare feet feeling the heat of the sand.

"I could get used to this."

"That's what I was afraid of." Mike stopped a few feet from the shore. "We've got to make this conversation quick because they could be trying to track our positions. This whole thing just got a bit more serious. Barry's dead."

There was silence on the other end of the line.

"Jack?" Mike listened for his breathing to make sure the connection wasn't broken.

"I'm here. Did they kill him?"

"They ruled it an accident but I can't say I have confidence in that."

"Why would they kill him?"

Mike looked out over the ocean and thought for a moment before answering. "Something to do with the wires you saw. I stopped at his house last night on the way out here. He told me Layden wanted him out of the firm."

"They must have really wanted him out."

"He told me a bit more which is why I'm going to ask you to do something that could put you in danger."

Again silence. Mike realized that there was nothing to keep Jack in the room where he was sitting right now at the Plaza Hotel, at Central Park's southern edge. He needed to pull something out that he knew would work.

"Your brother always told me that you were the guy in the family with the guts. Not him."

"He said that?"

"He had a great deal of respect for you, Jack. You have the chance to make this right and I need you to help prove I had nothing to do with any of it. Whatever it is they're doing."

This time there was no hesitation. "What can I do?"

"I knew you'd come around, buddy." Mike laid out the plan for him as quickly as he could, conscious of the fact that someone could be trying to locate them using their cell phone signals.

CHAPTER EIGHTEEN

"I'm in," Sean Sullivan said into his headset from the hallway outside Mike Brennan's Gramercy Park apartment. "Have you got the street covered?"

"Roger that," the voice came back.

Sullivan's support team was waiting on the street in a dry cleaner's delivery truck. He had entered the building moments earlier through the unmanned service entrance and arrived at his destination using the rear stairway. The doorman, who was snoozing in the lobby, had no idea there was an uninvited guest in the building.

The intruder easily picked the lock and entered the quiet apartment. Sullivan used a system when searching a target's house. Starting in the back bedroom and working his way forward, every paper he found was looked at quickly and expertly for any of the information he'd been instructed to retrieve. He felt a pang of guilt as he scanned the wall where Brennan had hung his Marine Corps memories. With the country at war, Sullivan's sense of patriotism was at an all time high but he quickly shook off his feelings and focused on his immediate task.

He found several different reports about the companies on the list Layden provided, but nothing to do with earning large sums of money on specific days or separate bank accounts. He searched through Mike's computer and some disks that were lying on the desk. Sullivan thought to himself that if this guy were stealing from the company he was smart enough not to keep any clues in his home.

He took a small package from his back pack. Inside were several tiny devices the size of shirt buttons. He placed each of the high tech listening devices throughout the apartment, behind picture frames, under lamps, and even in the medicine cabinet in the bathroom. The last piece of equipment he needed to install was a somewhat low tech wire tap on the phone. He spliced the phone line near where it came out of the wall, connected a transmitter, and pushed the wire back into the wall. This method was virtually undetectable, unless Brennan had pros sweeping the place for this specific device.

In the bedroom, Sullivan looked at the open closet doors and the unmade bed.

"This guy's not coming back," he said out loud.

He took a large envelope from the pack and opened a closet door, flipping on his flashlight to look around. He took a roll of duct tape from the pack, ripped off a two foot section and laid it across the envelope. He reached up above the door frame on the inside and secured the envelope to the wall. One more length of tape was attached to make sure the envelope stayed put and he was satisfied that the job was complete. The package was now exactly where Layden had told him to place it.

He didn't know what the envelope contained but he was following the instructions of a client. A very wealthy client. Sullivan was never one to frame a man for a crime but he needed to keep his return customers happy. Now he would sit back and wait for a phone call on his monitoring equipment or for the slim possibility that Brennan and his girlfriend would return to the apartment.

CHAPTER NINETEEN

Philip Layden tried to relax in the back of his limousine on the way into Manhattan from the Barry estate on Long Island. His day was already planned out. They needed to find Mike Brennan and Jack Darvish. He'd been informed that Brennan had called the office taking a personal day. He hoped Sullivan would get results quickly because failure was not an option.

The ring of his cell phone interrupted his thoughts. He'd normally ignore it but when he looked at the incoming number, he knew he needed to answer it.

"Layden."

"Our problems our growing, Philip. I need you to make a stop on your way to the office." The man spoke cryptically.

"Is it who I think it is?" Layden asked.

"The same. Another block went off today after the bell. A hundred thousand shares."

Layden sighed. "I'll talk to him."

"He's a trouble maker and we can't have unrest in the ranks. Especially now. Do you have the envelope?"

Layden patted the briefcase sitting on the seat next to him. "I was hoping not to use that but it seems we have no choice."

"Check in with me when you're done." The line went dead.

He called up to his driver, "Hey Mick, we need to stop off at Seventh and Fortieth."

"Yes sir." Mick slowly made his way to the right lane and turned west on Thirty-Fourth Street. Within a few minutes he pulled to the curb in front of their destination.

The offices high above Seventh Avenue had magnificent views to the north and east. Albert Claire, the man whose company leased the space in the building, had an unexpected and very unwelcome visitor. Years ago, Claire very much appreciated Layden's attention but now he couldn't stand the thought of him, much less the sight of him.

Layden moved forward in his seat. "You do understand the predicament we're in, don't you Albert?"

"You keep saying 'we' Philip, I could get out any time I feel the need."

"That's where we obviously disagree, my friend." Layden rubbed his trademarked flat top haircut. "You're in this up to your neck." Philip Layden was an imposing figure at six feet three inches. At fifty-eight years old, he was in better shape than most thirty years olds. He watched the beads of sweat form on Albert's brow.

Albert Claire was the Chief Executive Officer of Claire Cosmetics, one of the largest and most successful manufacturers of women's products in the country. He had grown cocky over the years and Layden often paid him a visit to bring him back to reality.

Layden stood up, jarring Albert Claire from his thoughts.

"The only reason I came here personally today, Albert, is that I like you." He walked slowly around to the other side of the massive hand carved oak desk, moved Albert's glass of twelve year old scotch to the side and set his massive frame in its place. "I don't want to see you get hurt."

Albert rubbed his short gray hair and smoothed his perfectly trimmed goatee. He looked up from his comfortable leather chair and locked onto the eyes of his guest. "Are you threatening me Philip?"

"Of course not." Layden's grin was barely noticeable. It showed more in his eyes than his mouth. "At least not physically." He hated to admit it to himself but he really loved this part of his job.

"Are you insinuating that you'll bring my business down? I've built it from nothing before so don't think I couldn't do it again!" Albert pushed his chair away from Layden.

"I wouldn't dream of doing that. I hold too much of your stock to want that to happen. And besides, your whole notion of building this empire by yourself is a fairytale for the media and the Street. I think you're actually starting to believe it. That's sad, really sad."

"Screw you, Philip."

Layden picked up his drink and moved to the large windows behind the desk. The view of Bryant Park to the east behind the New York Public Library and Times Square to the north was quite beautiful.

"You've come a long way Albert, but you have to admit you owe my firm a little bit of that. Wouldn't you agree?" Albert Claire knew nothing of Layden's associates. He only knew about Philip Layden and his father before him who offered him the financing that got his company off the ground and started him on the road to success. Layden didn't turn around to see if there would be an answer to his question. He knew that admission would never be made.

Albert, looking very tired, leaned back in his chair, rubbed his eyes and said, "You weren't even around when I made the financing agreement with your father."

Layden laughed out loud. "Is that what you call it? A financing agreement?"

Claire answered with an icy stare.

Layden moved back to the desk. "Once we offered trading support to keep your stock price at high levels, the 'financing agreement' as you like to think of it, ended." He leaned in close to Claire's ear and whispered, "That's when the collusion and market manipulation started."

Claire struggled to maintain his composure. "Anything I agreed to with Layden and Dowd all those years ago should have been voided when your father was murdered."

Layden's face was very serious. "My father died in a plane crash. He wasn't murdered."

"You believe what you want," Claire replied.

"Are you threatening *me* now, Albert?" Layden smiled, knowing Claire was backed into a corner, grasping for straws. He couldn't deny the fact that the crash was suspicious but it didn't serve a purpose to worry about the past. His father was dead and he was called upon to head the new firm. His ability to feel any emotion about the incident was stunted long before his father died. He, like so many of the men he worked with and socialized, was raised in boarding schools by strangers and his family was mainly there to pay the bills and bail him out of trouble to keep the name intact.

Albert finally answered. "You're not in any danger from me. I just like to point out that people who operate the way you and your company do seem to get what's coming to them in the end."

Layden allowed the man to go on long enough. He needed to return to the offensive. "Maybe you're right Albert, but I now control the arrangement you made all those years ago when you were a struggling start up shop." Layden's brow furrowed with mock concern. "As I told you before, I wish there was a way out for you but let me refresh your memory about the reality of your situation. If it weren't for my father you'd still be in that tiny office selling second rate lipstick."

He let his statement sink in for a moment and then continued, "And one more thing, the next time you want to sell a block of Claire Cosmetics stock the size you put through today, you call me first!"

Claire put his face in his hands. "I want out. I can't be a party to this any longer. I'll buy out your shares at whatever price you want." Desperation crept into his voice.

"You should know that there's no amount of money that could pay for what we did for you." Layden could see that the man was on the edge. Claire wanted out and he didn't seem to care about the cost, which made it the perfect time to give him a dose of reality and put him back in his place in the pecking order. "Just keep it in a straight line and we'll be fine." Philip said as he returned to the desk from the window. "But I guess the word *straight* may have a different significance for you."

Albert stood. "What's that supposed to mean?"

"I know about your weekend getaways to your estate in Amagansett and who your guests have been."

Claire knew where he was going but tried to keep his strong appearance. "I have hundreds of guests to my house, Philip. In fact, there will be a couple hundred people at my house tomorrow night for a party."

Layden smiled. "I guess my invitation got lost in the mail?"

Claire clenched his teeth. "I believe our meeting is over, please leave now." He pressed a button on his desk. "Lori, please see Mr. Layden out."

The door to the office opened within seconds and Philip walked toward it. "I think we'll need another minute." He closed the door in Lori's face before she had the chance to say a word.

He turned back to his host. "I don't think your wife would be happy to know about your special relationship with Rick Jeffries, do you?"

Claire didn't flinch. "We've been married for twenty years. I think by now she knows about my lifestyle."

Layden expected this response. He put his head down slightly as if he were defeated and took a step closer to Albert. "Do your daughters know?"

Layden knew that would be like a knife in his heart. Albert Claire's daughters were his life. They were sixteen and eighteen going on thirty and led the ultimate socialite existence. Private schools, world travel, the absolute best of everything.

"You have no proof of anything." Albert sat down again and looked at the empty surface of his desk, trying to put Rick and his daughters out of his mind.

"You're still so naïve after all these years. How the hell did you ever make it this far?" He paused. "Oh yeah, I remember now. Because we wanted you to make it, you arrogant bastard!" He pulled an envelope from his inside coat pocket and threw it on the desk.

Albert stared at it briefly before picking it up and dumping the contents. Spilling out were very graphic photos of himself with Rick Jeffries, male supermodel, and the face of the Claire Cosmetics product line for men. He recognized the bedroom of his Amagansett home and the unmistakable naked bodies in the throws of passion.

"How did you take these?" The fury was building inside him.

"It's easier than you think." Layden's imperceptible smile almost appeared again. "Maybe instead of showing these to your daughters, we'll send them straight to the board of trustees of the foundation that runs their precious little school. Or even better, directly to their friends." Layden moved back to the door. "Now, I believe our meeting is over. Have a pleasant day, Albert."

He opened the door, stepped through and closed it quickly behind him. Lori, the secretary, tried to walk around him but he purposely blocked her path.

"Give him a minute alone, okay?"

He only had to wait about three seconds for the sound of the glass shattering against the inside of the door. Albert Claire was too predictable, as usual.

"He's all yours." He waived his hand in dramatic fashion and made his exit.

CHAPTER TWENTY

With the quiet north shore town of East Setauket almost out of sight, Mike stood on the deck of his brother's thirty foot Boston Whaler, holding a guideline as they cruised across the smooth Sound toward Connecticut.

Tim had one hand on the wheel and the other on the throttle. He raised his voice to be heard above the roar of the engines. "How do we know Layden won't be home?"

Mike kept his eyes on the Connecticut coast in the distance. "He hasn't missed a day of work in twenty-five years."

"Don't you think the death of a partner is something that may change his schedule?"

Mike shrugged. "My guess is that he went out to see Barbara Barry for few minutes and he's been back in his office for hours."

"Sounds like a nice guy."

"A real sweetheart. There's a way to make sure he's not home."

"How's that?"

"If his limo is gone, he's gone. He doesn't drive."

Tim shrugged. "Not exactly scientific but it'll have to do."

They tied down the boat in an empty slip at a marina in Norwalk and walked along the main road to within a few hundred yards of Layden's house. It was a large Victorian built in the eighteen hundreds on the water with its own private beach and dock. They left the road and entered the rocky beach to be in position to access the property from the water side. The beach was desolate as the two brothers strolled along the water.

They scanned the nearby houses carefully and when they were sure they saw no movement in the area, they made their move. A path led through the high grass at the top of the beach to the back of the house. At the edge of the grass, Mike held his hand out to stop Tim before he left the cover of vegetation. The next property was barely visible in the distance but Mike took one last scan of the perimeter before stepping onto the paved area next to the garage. The doors were swung wide open, showing an empty space that normally housed Layden's limousine. He wasn't home.

They moved quickly to the rear of the house and stepped up on the large deck. Mike turned around at the back door as Tim began working on the lock of the metal box attached to the wall next to the door.

"It's a typical security system. Nothing too complicated." Tim opened the tiny door and looked at the circuit board. "All we need to do is bypass this wire and we can open the door."

Mike put his hand on his brother's shoulder. "Are you sure you want to do this? Once your inside, there's no turning back and it could cost you your job."

Tim replied without hesitating. "I told you I'm in for the long haul. There's nothing stronger than blood."

"Thanks." Mike turned away from the door. The marina where they left the boat was visible down the shoreline in the distance. As his brother continued to work on the alarm, Mike looked out over the water and tried to focus in the direction of Cove Neck and the Barry house. The haze was a little too thick for him to see all the way across.

"Got it," Tim whispered as he pushed open the door.

They entered the house, closing the door softly behind them. They knew Layden was probably in Manhattan but they couldn't be sure that the house was completely empty. He'd divorced years ago and had no children but cleaning staff might be present and they had to be sure they were alone before beginning the search. Stepping silently through the kitchen into a large dining area, Mike took two ski masks from a pouch tied around his waist and threw one to Tim. He pulled the mask down over his face and took his nine millimeter pistol from a holster at the small of his back. If anyone happened to be in the house, they would appear to be common thieves, not a stockbroker and a police lieutenant.

They swept the first floor, finding it clear. Mike stayed in Layden's home office while Tim slowly crept up the stairs to the second floor to confirm that they were alone.

Mike felt strange as he sat in Layden's chair. It was a violation of someone's privacy but he was left with no other choice. He knew the only way to prove his innocence was to have proof in his hands that showed what BNL had been perpetrating for years.

He turned on the monitor and found that there wasn't a password preventing access to the system. He scanned the drives to find which contained Layden's personal files and found many concerning the deals that BNL had been involved in over the past few years. There were letters to chief executives thanking them for their business as well as letters to other brokerage firms detailing plans for future business. Nothing unusual.

Mike took a pack of blank discs from his pack and placed one in the empty drive. He couldn't take the time right now to go through every file but he was convinced that something would be there that could help him. He had just finished burning the files when the door to the office opened.

Mike turned quickly to see Tim entering the room. "You scared the shit out of me!"

"I'm glad you put your gun away. A little jumpy, huh?"

"I don't often break into houses and search through people's belongings. It also doesn't help that this guy would rather see me dead than alive." Mike removed the last disc and stood.

"This guy's got a decent spread here. Maybe I'll buy it at auction after we throw him in jail!"

"Let's concentrate on keeping me out of jail before we think about shopping sprees."

Tim was casing the room, picking up different items, opening cabinet doors.

"Who the hell is this?" He had a small gold statue in his hands. The figure of a man was laying sideways, almost in flight.

Mike pushed the chair away from the desk and walked toward his brother. "Someone from Greek mythology, isn't it?"

"I've seen it somewhere before, but I can't place it." Tim put the statue back in its place and picked up another figure. A muscle bound man holding the world on his shoulders.

"That's Atlas." Mike took the small piece in his hands, feeling its weight. "Layden's got a thing for Greek mythology."

Tim looked around the office, making sure nothing looked out of place. "Let's get out of here. We're pushing our luck."

They took a quick walk around the first floor making sure they had left everything as they found it. At the back door, they checked for neighbors in the distance. When all was clear, they stepped onto the back deck where Tim quickly removed the wires he attached to trip the system.

He closed the metal box and they quickly disappeared into the tall grass. This time they walked on the beach most of the way back to the marina until they reached the fence of the parking lot.

They arrived at the boat without encountering anyone. Mike untied the ropes, threw them on the deck and jumped aboard as Tim started the engines. The boat maneuvered its way slowly through the marina and then made its way across the Sound. Mike was standing on the aft deck holding a side guideline, feeling the sea spray wash across his face. He felt as if he were sinking into a deep pit with no way out. He had high hopes of discovering some information at Layden's house, but there was nothing obvious in any of the files that showed anything illegal going on at BNL.

They rode east along the coastline of Long Island to the marina where they had put the boat in the water that morning. The drive from there to Mike's house in Southampton was relatively short on the back roads traveling from the North Shore to the South Shore. The traffic during the summer months could get very heavy on the narrow roads, which crisscrossed the small beach towns. During the week, late in the day, the roads were filled with workman traveling in the opposite direction, out of the high priced towns. Tim soon turned off the street onto the gravel driveway next to the house.

"I'm going to take a quick shower." Tim grabbed a bag from the back seat of the car.

Mike stepped up on the wooden front porch and pushed open the unlocked door. "I've got a call to make. I'll be out on the deck."

The windows of the house were open and a light breeze was gently moving the curtains. A note on the kitchen counter from Sam said she had gone into town to do some shopping. She'd be back in time to get ready for the fundraiser in Manhattan. Mike took a beer out of the refrigerator, grabbed the phone off the counter and went out the back door.

CHAPTER TWENTY-ONE

The three elevators opened at the same time on the thirty-eighth floor of the BNL building. Thirty FBI agents poured out, led by David Reynolds and Pete Battaglia. As they past the shocked receptionist, Reynolds held up his badge in one hand and the search warrant in the other.

"Where's Mr. Layden's office?"

She paused and looked up toward Partners' Row. "I...I'll call him down for you, sir."

He followed her gaze to see the offices above. "Don't go to any trouble, we'll find him."

An agent walked around the high desk and disconnected her phone before the group of agents fanned out through the trading floor. Reynolds went directly to the stairs and took them two at a time. Before he made it to the top, Layden, hearing the commotion from the brokers, came out of his office to look into The Pit.

"Good afternoon, Mr. Layden. Nice to see you again." Reynolds handed him a copy of the warrant and continued past him into the partner's office with two agents in tow.

Layden still hadn't said a word. After scanning the warrant, he looked over the edge to the far end of the trading floor. A man was just shutting the door to Brennan's office. Layden caught his eye and nodded. The man nodded back and slipped into the crowd of agents and brokers on the floor. Layden smiled and followed Reynolds into his office.

CHAPTER TWENTY-TWO

"What have you got, Jack?" Mike walked along the hard, wet sand at the water's edge.

"Plenty. This is easier than I thought."

"Are you being careful not to reveal your identity or location?"

Darvish laughed. "If anyone's watching, which I doubt, I'm Gertrude Steinman from Miami. I've been online all day and I think I'm alone."

"Great. Now tell me some good news, man."

"I can't say I've got good news but we certainly know more than we did this morning. Did you know that before BNL was formed, Philip Layden's father was a partner in a firm called Layden and Dowd?"

"No. What did they do?"

"Venture capital."

"Okay, anything else?" Mike asked.

"Wait a minute. You haven't asked me who Layden's dad provided financing to almost thirty years ago."

"Who?"

"A young go-getter by the name of Albert Claire received ten million dollars to launch a woman's product line that became marginally successful over the years."

"I wouldn't exactly call Claire marginally successful."

"That was a joke, Mike. He's in every department store in the country and there are at least five billboards in Times Square alone with his advertising on them."

"I'm not sure if I care that Albert Claire was financed by Layden's father. I think the real question is who financed Layden and Dowd."

"I've already thought of that and I've got something. There are a couple of shell companies that held a majority stake and I've got a copy of one of the corporate resolutions."

"I'm not even going to ask you how you're getting this information."

"Good. Don't."

"What are the names of the shells?" Mike asked.

"Prometheus Holdings and Atlas Consultants."

Mike was silent as he remembered the small statues at Layden's house in Connecticut. The Greek mythology class he took at Cornell was coming back to him. Prometheus made his father, Zeus, angry by giving the gift of fire to mortals. And Atlas had the burden of carrying the earth on his shoulders for eternity.

"You there Mike?"

"Yeah, I'm here. What does it say on the corporate resolution?"

"The Prometheus paper is signed by someone from D&A Inc. Of course it's illegible so I can't read it."

"Did you look up..."

Jack cut him off. "I'm well ahead of you Mike. D&A Inc. is a company based in Atlanta but that's where the trail ends. I can't find an address or anything but I'll keep trying."

"Anything on the wires?" Mike turned away from the water and walked back toward the house.

"I've only drilled down as far as cities. I've got a bunch in Atlanta and a few in Oranjestad, Aruba. That just happens to be where I used to do my banking."

"You mean where you hid your stolen money?"

Jack ignored the comment and continued. "Until I wired it to a lovely little bank in Switzerland."

"You're unbelievable. You've got to find me something more concrete. E-mail me a copy of the corporate resolution and I'll e-mail you back some files I got from Layden's PC in his house. I'm hoping that by the time I get to the Plaza for the fundraiser, you'll have something for me. Just give me a call and I'll come up to your room. I don't want you to risk coming out. Okay."

"Yes, Dad."

"I shouldn't give a shit if you get killed but I do, alright?"

"Alright."

"See you in a few hours."

CHAPTER TWENTY-THREE

Sullivan slammed down his twelfth raw clam at a bar called Live Bait on Twenty Third Street, near the southern edge of Madison Square Park. After leaving Brennan's apartment, he walked a couple blocks north to the NYU hangout as much for the fresh clams as for the college girls. He was about to approach a couple of young ladies whose fake IDs probably added a few years to their ages when his cell phone rang. He looked at the screen and smiled.

"The fruits of my labor," he said to himself.

He listened as the bug he planted picked up Mike Brennan's voice saying he wasn't there to take the call and waited for the caller to leave a message. "Hey Sam, missed you at the office today. The mayor just wanted to confirm that you guys are showing up at the Plaza tonight. Give me a call back."

Sullivan smiled as he walked by the young girls and pushed the door open to the street. He dialed a number and put his phone to his ear.

"It seems our young millionaire will be heading to the Plaza tonight for the Mayor's fundraiser. I'll be there waiting for him"

CHAPTER TWENTY-FOUR

Layden sat alone in his quiet office after the agents had gone for the day. His computer was gone, with the promise given by the FBI of a replacement. He put the satellite phone on his desk, set it to speakerphone mode, and dialed a number.

When the connection was made, the voice on the other end resonated through the office. "What did they find out, Philip?"

"Exactly what we wanted them to find out."

"It pays to be prepared. Should we be concerned about this Reynolds fellow from the FBI? He spent ten years on Wall Street before going over to the Bureau."

"He's very smart but I still believe we can lead him in the right direction." Layden was confident.

"Is there any way for him to dig through the records and come up with anything substantial?"

"We've led him by the nose away from the source and toward a believable stooge." Layden believed they could steer the investigation any way he pleased. "Have you seen the papers today?"

"I have. Brennan's Man of the Year pictures made almost every one."

Layden couldn't help smiling. "After they get a hold of information that our boy isn't so virtuous, they'll have a field day. The networks will pick it up and he'll be guilty before he hits the courts."

"I'll be at the fundraiser tonight so I hope our man will be discreet when dealing with Brennan. The place will be packed with security and Secret Service," the old man warned.

"I'm sure the whole thing will be transparent. We've used this man and his team on several occasions and they're very good at what they do. That's why I chose him for this assignment."

"I look forward to it. Is Davenport on the line yet?"

"I'll loop him in." The sound of beeps and clicks filled the room as the scrambler was activated.

"Hello."

"Glad you can join us," the old man huffed.

"It's always a pleasure, sir." Davenport's drawn out southern accent was immediately grating.

"How's old Atlanta?" Layden attempted to separate his two associates. Davenport did not get along well with the old man.

"Hot."

"Do you have anything to add, Anthony?" Layden wanted the conversation over as soon as possible.

"I lambasted Brennan yesterday about letting me out of that stock. If he knows anything, he's one cool cucumber."

Layden leaned forward in his chair. "It doesn't really matter what he actually knows. By now the authorities have their main suspect in Barry's death and in the market manipulation."

"So we're clear?" Davenport asked.

The old man answered, "It's a bit early to say that. I'm calling a conference of the members at my Cooperstown estate. We need to reassure our associates that we've got these issues under control."

Davenport pressed. "Are they under control? We've got to catch the marine and your little techie before you say that."

Layden answered immediately, confidently. "I'm taking care of that. We'll have Brennan tonight and I'm sure he'll lead us to Darvish." His job and probably his life depended on containing Brennan and Darvish.

"I hope you're right." Davenport pushed harder. "Maybe during the meeting we can also talk about how the associates up North are fairing better than the ones on this side of the Mason Dixon line."

The old man didn't back down. "Are you ever going to give up on your Southern bullshit, Davenport? You've got to get over the fact that the North won the war."

"Are you referring to the War of Northern Aggression?"

Layden knew his two colleagues could go on for hours so he quickly brought them back to the topic at hand. "Gentlemen, can we please focus here?"

After a few moments of silence the old man said, "We'll follow up tomorrow. Keep me posted." He cut the connection as soon as he finished speaking.

CHAPTER TWENTY-FIVE

Mike checked his bowtie in the mirror before walking outside to see Tim off.

"Are you sure about going in there tonight?" Tim was rechecking the straps holding his boat on the trailer.

"Don't worry. I'll be fine." Mike opened the driver's side door. "Get some rest because I have a feeling this thing has only just begun."

Tim got in and started the engine. "You know I've got a friend, Paul Schmidt, who went through the academy with me who's now at the FBI in Atlanta. I'm sure he'd help you out if I asked."

Mike thought about it for a second. "It would be good to have some high powered help but I have no idea who this guy Schmidt is. He could have been a great guy when you knew him but maybe now he'd do anything to advance his career."

Tim shrugged. "You've got a point but I don't think he's like that. He's always been a good friend."

"It's good to know we can fall back on that, but I'd rather keep the number of people involved to a minimum. Let's see what Jack can do from his room at the Plaza. Can you meet me here tomorrow morning so we can sort out the next step?"

"I'll be here bright and early."

Mike returned to the house. He entered the living room to see Sam leaning over slightly, fixing her makeup in a wall mirror.

"You look incredible!" Mike said

She turned toward him in her full-length black gown, nothing covering her shoulders except her long curly hair pulled away from her face in a clip.

"You don't look half bad yourself." Sam admired Mike in full black tie regalia.

"We've got twenty minutes to make the flight, are you ready to go?"

"Let's go."

He kissed her on the cheek to avoid smudging her lipstick.

They drove five minutes to the heliport where a small hangar housed two helicopters. The attached shack had the dual purpose of waiting room and headquarters of Bricker's Helicopter Service. The owner, Ross Bricker was one of the active pilots.

Ross was a local guy who began a tour in Vietnam late in the war. His stay was cut short when President Johnson decided to withdraw the troops. His experience as a chopper pilot may not have been long, but it consisted of some extremely intense flying under heavy enemy fire as they pulled the troops out of the jungles. He had no choice but to become a highly aggressive flier who could handle himself under the worst conditions. Ross' last mission included the evacuation of the U.S. Embassy on the last day. He landed on the deck of a ship of the seventh Fleet waiting out at sea. Ross watched as flight after flight of South Vietnamese helicopters landed on the U.S. Navy ships, only to be pushed into the ocean to make room for the next incoming chopper. Pilots packed their entire families onto the crafts in an effort to escape the North Vietnamese. Those last hours changed him forever in ways that he would only be able to talk about years later.

Mike had gotten to know Ross well at the end of the previous summer when he was making frequent house hunting trips to the Hamptons. When there was no one else on the flight, which was common for a weekday morning when the majority of commuters were heading toward the city, Ross would let Mike sit in the co-pilot's seat, headset on. Since both were veterans there was an immense amount of mutual respect. Ross opened up to Mike and found a friend who understood the ugliness of combat.

After a couple of months of regular flights, Ross talked about his career after the war. He wouldn't go into detail, but he told Mike he flew for a government agency for many years in the late seventies and early eighties. When he finally decided to return to civilian life, his love for flying was still strong enough for him to want to make a living at it. Unfortunately for him, in the beginning, his flying style was a little too aggressive for many of the passengers and it was hard for him to get return business. It appeared that people didn't appreciate the way he swooped low over the water and made ninety degree turns before setting his chopper down on a landing pad.

His habits were hard to break, but he calmed down enough to build a steady business of regular commuters and vacationers. But when he and Mike were alone, he easily slipped back into his old military methods, which brought back memories for Mike.

Mike parked the SUV and they walked to the waiting helicopter with its rotors already turning. Ross was circling the chopper making his final pre-flight check of the equipment. The couple instinctively lowered their heads as they came close to the spinning blades. Ross waved to them as they stepped up into the body of the craft and followed them into the cabin. It was considerably quieter inside with the door shut but they still had to raise their voices to hear each other.

"How're you two doing? I haven't seen you in a while." Ross put on his headgear and microphone.

The cabin held nine passengers comfortably in three rows of three. Mike and Sam had taken the first row because they knew Ross liked to talk.

Mike leaned forward. "We're doing okay. Just came out to work on the house a little. How's business?"

"It's always better in the summer. We're back up to full schedule and I've been thinking of trying to get my hands on some financing for a third chopper to expand the flight schedule after last year's rush. I hate to turn business away if I can avoid it."

"That's great to hear, Ross. I hope it works out."

"And how're you doing pretty lady? You headed for a big party tonight?"

"That's right," Sam said. "There's a fundraiser tonight at the Plaza."

After lifting off the ground, Bricker turned the French-made Eurocopter Dauphin AS365 a hundred and eighty degrees to a westerly heading. He had told Mike that the helicopter was originally owned by the U.S. Coast Guard and sold at auction. Ross knew that the engines were kept in impeccable operating condition and had thought the price for the used bird was a steal. He had to refit it for hauling passengers instead of running sea rescue missions but it was still worth the life savings he poured into it.

After leveling off at cruising altitude, a mile off the shore of Southampton he turned half-way in the pilot's seat. "Now I remember. You work for Mayor Mad Dog, right?"

"One and the same," Sam replied.

"And Mike, was that your company that I've been seeing on the news today?"

"Probably." Mike was hesitant to speak openly about BNL.

Ross was persistent. "One of the partners bought the farm, huh? Did you know him well?"

"Very well. Melvin Barry hired me and I worked with him almost every day. He was a good man."

Mike hadn't taken much time out to think about the loss of Barry. He'd been concerned mainly with saving his freedom and livelihood, and had ignored the fact that he'd lost a friend. Even though he thought of Barry as a good man, he now had to question everything he knew about him. There was no way for him to know what else the old man kept from him.

"Sorry to hear that, Buddy. Does this mean a promotion for you?"

No, Mike thought. *One of the biggest investment banking firms in the country is going to go down fast and hard.*

"I think it'll be business as usual." Mike looked out the window at a string of lights in the Great South Bay. Probably a group of fishing boats bringing in snappers or fluke this time of year.

Mike considered telling Ross that he was in trouble but decided against it. Ross was a good friend and if he needed some kind of help in the future, he knew the pilot would be willing.

"Are you going to be around for the return trip later tonight?" Mike asked.

"I'll be here. Just page me and I'll start her up so she'll be warm when you get here."

"Thanks." Mike looked toward the land and saw the number of houses increasing as they past the more densely populated towns closer to the city. They'd arrive at their destination on the west side of Manhattan within a few minutes. He thought about how he'd had no contact with Layden other than leaving him a voice mail telling him he was taking the day off. Layden never called him to tell him about Darvish so he had to assume they believed he was in on it and were attempting to find him. He hoped he made the right decision to come back to the city.

CHAPTER TWENTY-SIX

David Reynolds and Pete Battaglia sat in a conference room at 26 Federal Plaza. Ten senior agents, along with New York State Attorney General Doug Jacobs, who rolled up his sleeves and dug into the investigation, sat around the large table. They were surrounded by boxes of documents from BNL. In front of Reynolds was Mike Brennan's computer that they had taken from his office.

"This Brennan guy was smart enough to pull off these trades for all these years but not bright enough to keep the trail of evidence off his PC at work?" Reynolds asked.

Attorney General Jacobs looked up from the document he was scanning. "You shouldn't be surprised by the arrogance of these people, David."

Battaglia chimed in. "You were one of them once."

Reynolds looked over the top of the screen. "I wouldn't be stupid enough to leave all this information in full view. It's not even password protected."

One of Reynolds' team, Agent John McCoy, came through the door and stopped at the head of the table. "You're not going to believe the shit we just pulled out of Brennan's apartment." He looked down the table and saw the Attorney General. "Oh. Excuse me sir."

Jacobs smiled. "Don't worry. I have actually heard bad language before."

McCoy handed a large envelope to Reynolds who proceeded to dump the contents on the table in front of him.

"What the hell is all this?" Reynolds picked up the first sheet and started reading. "A bank account with B.I.Z., Banque Internationale de Zurich, in Aruba. There's almost seventy five million in there." He slid the paper toward Jacobs and picked up another sheet from the package.

Battaglia had moved his chair closer to look over Reynolds' shoulder. "Those are trade confirms, right?"

Reynolds took a sheet of paper from his pocket containing the same list of stocks he had shown Judge Price. He leafed through the pile of confirms and looked down his list. "Now we know why these stocks still have any value. These trades were timed to keep the market thinking there was still demand out there."

The Attorney General grabbed one of the sheets. "What accounts were used to set the trades off?"

Reynolds spread the papers out in front of him. "My guess is that they were trust accounts where the executor didn't pay attention to the activity or the names on the accounts are just made up. Brennan would have had access to the system to create any accounts he wanted."

Reynolds looked up at Agent McCoy. "Call the NYPD and get an APB on Brennan. We've got to bring this guy in."

CHAPTER TWENTY-SEVEN

The lobby of the Plaza Hotel was buzzing with heavy hitting Democrats and their entourages. Sean Sullivan looked around at the couples coming in wearing tuxedos and gowns but none looked familiar yet. He couldn't get too close to the action because security was tight and anyone entering the ballroom needed a pass.

As he walked around the end of a leather couch in the waiting area he saw a man looking through the window of the gift shop. The young man, dressed in jeans and a button down shirt, had something familiar about him but he couldn't place the face. Sullivan walked slowly forward to get a closer look.

The lobby was crowded. Sullivan had to walk around several people to get to the gift shop. As he approached the young man, he brushed against him.

"Excuse me." Sullivan looked into his eyes.

"That's okay."

The hair was shorter and much lighter, Sullivan thought as he remembered the photo that Layden e-mailed him. It was Jack Darvish, techno wizard extraordinaire. Layden explained that this was the kid who was messing with BNL's accounts along with Brennan. Darvish was next on Sullivan's list after Brennan so he figured the order in which he took care of Layden's problems didn't matter.

Sullivan continued into the gift shop, keeping Darvish in his sight. After a moment, Darvish turned and slowly made his way through the lobby to the elevator bank. Sullivan followed and slipped onto the crowded elevator along with him. When the doors opened on the third floor, several people got off including Darvish. Sullivan kept his distance, making a note of the room his mark entered.

After showing ID and picking up their passes, Mike and Sam entered the grand ballroom at the Plaza and immediately ran into some of the Mayor's staffers.

"We thought you weren't going to make it," someone said.

"We wouldn't miss this for the world." Sam didn't stop to chat. After some quick small talk, she led Mike to one of the bars set up along the wall.

The bartender served them champagne as they leaned against the bar to survey the crowd. Sam knew about half the attendees. She saw the governor, Ted Gately, speaking with the Vice President, Joseph Browning, surrounded by at least six Secret Service agents. Across the room talking to another Democratic Party bigwig was Mayor Maddux. He was an imposing figure at six foot five and two hundred and twenty pounds. He played football at Penn State and probably would have made it to the pros if it weren't for a career ending injury in his senior year. He didn't let that ruin his life. After law school, and some time in the D.A.'s office, he started a successful law practice in Manhattan where Sam Brodworth was given her first chance fresh out of school.

Mike took a sip of champagne and made a face. "Too early for me to order a beer?"

"At least wait until I walk away before you start carrying around a bottle of Miller."

"Come on, babe, this is a special occasion. I'd probably order something fancy like a Budweiser."

She continued to scan the room. "I think we need to be careful here, Mike."

"You mean we can't have our picture taken with me drinking a Bud?"

"You know what I mean. We shouldn't underestimate the danger we're in. Don't you agree?"

"Absolutely." He looked at the gaggle of Secret Service agents surrounding Vice President Browning and then over to the undercover NYPD lurking around the mayor. "But I think we're safe here tonight."

Mike barely finished the last remark when the Mayor walked up to the bar.

Sam pointed to Mike. "Mr. Mayor, you remember..."

"Of course I do." He cut her off and reached out and grasped Mike's hand in a bone crushing grip. "The Man of the Year and I have played golf together on more than one occasion. Nice to see you again, Mike."

"I guess you saw the coverage in the papers?" Mike was embarrassed.

"Damn right I did. That's very admirable work you do over there."

"Thank you." Mike wanted to change the subject. "Can I order a drink for you, your honor?"

"A martini, thanks. Very dry."

"Looks like a great turnout, doesn't it sir?" Sam commented.

"The Democrats should be happy as hell with the numbers they're dragging in tonight." Mike handed him the martini. "So, Mike, I see your firm has come onto some sad times."

"That's true." Mike glanced at Sam who was trying to duck out of the conversation nicely. Mike picked up on it, nodded his head, and continued his conversation with the mayor.

"Excuse me, gentlemen, while I get to work." Sam turned away into the crowd. Although she had no intention of straying far away from Mike's side, she needed to give the mayor the impression that she intended to network a little bit.

"The death of a partner must have shocked you and the rest of your company. I've known Melvin Barry for years. He was a good man." The mayor took a big sip of his drink.

"We're going to miss him." Mike tried to stay positive about the future of the company, which wasn't easy since he was sure it wouldn't last another two weeks. The conversation drifted from the condition of BNL to the market place in general. Maddux was well versed and from the conversation, Mike guessed that the mayor was worth well into the millions.

After a few minutes, Vice President Browning came over, skillfully interrupted them without acknowledging Mike's presence and steered the mayor toward a group of gentlemen standing nearby. Mike recognized one of the men as Ernest Browning III, the Vice President's brother and chairman of Browning Aerospace. The company was a leading manufacturer of fighter jets, bombers, and had recently gotten into ship building with the acquisition of another industry giant. During the presidential campaign, the issue was brought up by the opposition that Vice Presidential Candidate Browning was seeking office to help his brother land government contracts. As the election wore on, other issues took center stage and the relationship was rarely mentioned in the media.

Mike had never met Ernest Browning but he was a well known business figure in New York and a large political contributor. Mike was surprised his talk with the mayor lasted as long as it had when the room was filled with so many big money people. Sam always claimed that the mayor was never a true political animal and Mike saw the first signs of that tonight.

He looked around the room and finally located Sam talking to Governor and Mrs. Gately. He thought it a good time to slip out and pay Jack a visit upstairs to find out if he progressed on his research.

Mike got off the elevator on the third floor and walked the empty hallway to Jack's room. Mike paid cash for a week in advance which helped in the night manager not asking Jack for any ID.

He stopped at room three twenty and knocked softly. No answer. He listened through the door for a shower running but heard nothing. He pushed on the door and found it wasn't closed all the way. Immediately inside the main door, on the left side of the foyer, was the bathroom. The light was on and the door was wide open.

Mike approached slowly and called out. "Jack?"

He inched forward and peered into the bathroom around the door jamb. It was empty. He pushed back the shower curtain to find an empty tub. Stepping back into the foyer, he looked into the darkened room and wished he had his Sig Sauer 9mm. He'd have never gotten through the metal detectors at the ballroom downstairs. The bad feeling in the pit of his stomach was growing.

"Jack?" he called again.

He reached around the corner and felt for a light switch, finding it after a few seconds of groping. The room lit up instantly from three table lamps arranged around the room. The only problem was that they were all on the floor. The room was wrecked. The empty dresser drawers were upside down on the floor. The bed was off its frame and the stuffing shredded all over the place.

"Holy shit!" Mike lifted a corner of the mattress to make sure Jack wasn't lying under it.

"Where the hell are you, Jack?" Mike realized he couldn't stick around to find him. He'd get Sam out of the fundraiser downstairs and get back to the Hamptons house as quickly as possible. Maybe Jack decided to go for a walk and someone came in while he was out. Mike knew the more likely scenario but tried to keep it out of his mind.

He turned toward the main door and stopped before touching the handle. He heard a key being dipped into the electronic lock on the hallway side. Mike quickly backed up to the main room and flipped off the light. He just got his body behind the wall and stood silently in the darkness as someone entered the room.

Mike tried to control his breathing as he felt the sweat dripping from his forehead down his face. Whoever entered the room was moving slowly. If it were Jack, he'd probably have walked right in and turned on the lights. The figure was getting closer to the darkened main room. Mike held his breath as he moved silently away from the light switch. He saw a hand reach around the wall to flip on the light.

Mike made a decision on the spot that he was getting out of the room alive. He grabbed the hand and pulled the unsuspecting man off balance. Mike flipped him around quickly, wrenched the arm up toward the shoulder, and pushed him hard into the wall. The man quickly spun out of the hold and caught Mike in the jaw with a punch followed quickly by a kick to the stomach. As Mike doubled over in pain he grabbed the leg, reached out with his foot, and swept the standing leg out from under him. He hit the ground hard and was dazed enough for Mike to jump on top of him.

Mike still couldn't make out any features in the darkness and only saw the man's silhouette against the light from the bathroom. It certainly wasn't Jack. Mike could tell the man had long hair and Jack would have cried like a baby after the first thrust into the wall. Mike sat on the man's chest and cocked his arm but before he was able to uncoil the man bucked his body and pushed Mike over his head into the wall headfirst. *He's strong as hell*, Mike thought as he tried to push himself to a standing position.

He heard movement behind him and knew his own body was moving too slowly to fend off another attack. His hand made contact with something on the floor. It was one of the lamps that had been knocked over. Mike heard the footsteps running toward him and he quickly spun around, half standing with the lamp in hand, and swung it as hard as he could and connected solidly with the man's head. Mike moved to the side and the intruder continued his forward motion into the wall. The drywall broke with the force and the man stopped moving.

Mike dropped the lamp and backed away into the dimly lit foyer. He turned, ran to door and pulled it open. The bright light in the hallway stung his eyes as he sprinted beyond the elevators to the exit sign on the opposite side of the floor. As he pushed the door open he looked back to the room and saw his attacker coming out. He had long blond hair and was holding his head.

His feet barely touched the stairs as he made it down three flights in seconds. The sound of the man rushing through the door on the third floor hit Mike's ears just as he entered the lobby at full speed. He realized immediately that he needed to slow down. He couldn't sprint through the lobby toward the ballroom when the Vice President of the United States was inside. Secret Service would have him on the floor and cuffed within seconds.

He walked as quickly as he thought he could toward the ballroom and didn't realize what he looked like until several people in the lobby gasped. He pulled out a handkerchief and wiped is face. His nose was bleeding and he could feel his eye swelling up. He showed the guard his pass and waited for the approval.

The guard looked from the picture to Mike. "Are you okay, sir?"

Mike nodded. "I went out for a smoke and slipped down the stairs. I'm fine, thanks."

"Get some ice for that eye."

"Will do." Mike smiled at the guard and noticed for the first time that his mouth hurt. He moved his tongue around his mouth to make sure there were no teeth missing. All accounted for. Before he walked through the metal detector, he turned back to see the man from the room walking toward the ballroom. He was well dressed in a dark blue sport coat and collared shirt. He was much more composed than Mike felt. Mike thought for a second that the man could also be a guest at the fundraiser but realized if he were, he'd be wearing a tux. He spotted Mike and stopped halfway through the lobby. Mike turned his back and entered the ballroom through the metal detector and immediately put his head down to avoid attention. He scanned the room for Sam and caught a glimpse of her with the mayor and his security team.

The mayor saw him and waived him over.

One of the police bodyguards immediately grabbed one of Mike's arms. "Is this the guy, sir?"

Sam looked at his face and tried to put her hands on his cheeks but he pulled away. "What happened to you?"

"I'll explain later. Can you tell me why this nice police officer is holding my arm?"

The mayor spoke up. "Let's move to the side room, out of the way." He pointed to a door a few feet away.

Several undercover officers entered the room first followed by the mayor, Sam, and Mike who was still being held tightly by the cop. The room was empty except for a few folded up tables and chairs leaning against the wall.

Mike knew they couldn't have heard about what just happened in Jack's room. He estimated it to be no more than three minutes since he barreled down the stairs and entered the lobby.

The mayor looked at the man holding onto Mike. "You can leave us alone Lieutenant. I'll handle it from here."

The man didn't let go. "Sir, with all due respect. The FBI says there are serious charges against this guy."

Mike looked at Sam who gave nothing away from her expression. He knew she had left girlfriend mode and entered attorney mode. He was very confused.

"You'll have to trust me on this, Bob." The mayor was going to get his way.

"Yes sir." The cop turned and left them in the room alone.

When the door was closed, the mayor got down to business. "My men got notified of an APB for a Michael Brennan of Gramercy Park. Wanted for murder one and embezzlement."

Mike was stunned. The thought had crossed his mind that Layden would try to pin Jack's scam on him but murder?

"Who the hell did I murder?"

"Melvin Barry."

Mike looked at Sam again. "Did you tell him we were there together?"

The mayor answered for her. "She did. She also told me about this Jack Darvish and the wires. That's why you're here talking to me instead of in the back of a squad car heading to the Midtown North precinct. There aren't many people in this godforsaken world I trust as much as this lady right here. She told me everything."

Mike reached over and took her hand in his and turned to the mayor. "What did they say about me?"

"On top of your offshore accounts totaling almost one hundred million dollars and the trail of market timing trades, you drowned Melvin Barry in his pool."

Mike shook his head but didn't reply.

"The Nassau County ME changed his original finding from accidental death to murder just a few hours ago. Someone held Barry under the water until he was dead."

"Those bastards."

"Did you run into someone from BNL outside the ballroom?" The mayor was sizing up Mike's swollen eye.

"I didn't recognize the guy. I went up to see Jack and found his room ransacked. This guy came in while I was in there." Mike touched his eye and winced.

"Did you get the better of him?"

"I don't know about that but I got away from him."

"We'll get his description out to NYPD. Do you know where Darvish is?"

"I can only imagine."

"We'll have PD look out for him as well. Now, what do you propose we do about these charges against you?"

Mike looked the mayor in the eye. "I need more time to prove I had nothing to do with any of this and I can't do that from a jail cell."

"That's what I told him you'd say." Sam tried to smile.

"Because of Sam's word, I'm going to put my neck on the block here, Mike. I'll give you forty eight hours. After that, I'll trust that you'll turn yourself in."

"That's all I need, sir. I can't thank you enough."

"Don't thank me." He pointed at Sam. "Thank her."

Maddux stood, walked to the door, and opened it a crack. After whispering with the head of his security detail, he returned. "Two of the officers will escort you out a side door and take you where you need to go. Where are you headed?"

"To the heliport on the West Side."

"Good luck." He reached out, shook Mike's hand, and disappeared into the crowd.

One of the two cops who were left approached Mike. "Follow us."

They walked along the back wall and into an empty hallway along the massive kitchen. The cop lifted a small handheld radio and spoke into it. After a few seconds, they pushed through a door onto an alley behind the hotel. An unmarked car was waiting with the back door open. Mike, Sam, and one of the cops slipped into the back and the other got into the front with the driver.

The driver turned around. "Where to?"

"West Side heliport," Mike replied.

"You got it." The tires squealed as the car lurched forward onto Central Park South, crossed traffic and headed west.

Mike dialed a number on his cell phone. "Ross, we're heading back a bit early. Can you be ready in ten minutes?" He listened for the reply. "Thanks."

The cop next to them in the back seat looked over Sam at Mike. "Can you give me a description of the guy who roughed you up?"

"Shoulder length blond hair, blue blazer, strong as a goddamned bull."

The man relayed the information into his radio, hoping to catch the perpetrator before he left the hotel. Mike knew that wasn't going to happen and he also knew he had probably not seen the last of the guy.

They rode the rest of the short trip in silence. Mike couldn't get the image of Jack's room out of his head. He knew Jack would have been defenseless against the man he encountered. His only hope was that Jack had left the room to get some dinner.

Back at the plaza later in the night, the mayor stepped up to the podium. "Ladies and Gentlemen, can I please have your attention."

He waited briefly for the noise to die down before he continued. "We'd like to thank each of you for your support tonight. As you know, we're coming up to an election year and it will be an important and exciting time for our nation. Someone would like to come up here and say a few words. Please welcome The Vice President of the United States, Joseph Browning!"

The mayor stepped off the small stage and Vice President Browning bounded onto the platform to raucous applause from the crowd.

After the noise died down, the Vice President began. "On behalf of the President and the Democratic Party, I would also like to thank you all for your support tonight. It's been my distinct honor to have the opportunity to spend time with you this evening and I'm confident we can count on your continued support as we carry on our journey…"

Off in a quiet side room, where the mayor and Mike Brennan had a conversation not two hours earlier, the Vice President's brother, Ernest Browning III was on his secure satellite phone.

"What do you mean you can't pinpoint his location? I saw him here with his girlfriend a short time ago. I would have grabbed him myself if I knew I couldn't count on you!"

He listened briefly as he paced back and forth in the empty room.

"I told you before Philip. Our associates are worried about the current state of affairs. There's no room for failure."

He paused again as he opened the door and looked at his brother on the podium. "Yes, I know you've neutralized the techie kid but we need Brennan to make our story stick. Don't call me again until you have positive news."

He stepped through the doorway and caught the Vice President's eye. Ernest Browning nodded to his brother as he continued his speech. The associates had to know that the situation was under control.

CHAPTER TWENTY-EIGHT

Albert Claire's house in Amagansett could hardly be called a house. It sat on a hill overlooking the ocean and upon initial observation gave the impression of a farmhouse. It was certainly in the farmhouse style but in its most modern, extravagant form. There were two large wings that came off each side of the main part of the house that formed a courtyard in the front. From the road, nothing was visible except a long lane bordered on both sides by thirty-foot high manicured bushes. When Mike emerged from the tunnel of hedges he was greeted by a team of valets ready to park his Range Rover in a meadow to the side of the house.

The barbeque was on the ocean side on the multi-tiered deck and already quite lively by the time he arrived. Considering the events of the previous evening at the Plaza and the fact the media picked up on the Man of the Year gone bad, he needed to keep out of the public eye. After checking in with the man at the door, who checked his name off a list of attendees, he pulled his baseball cap lower and began searching for the host.

Mike made it to the back of the house without encountering anyone he knew. He looked beyond the deck to the beach and saw people crowded around a large hole in the sand where two chefs were pulling out steaming lobsters, clams, shrimp, and corn and placing them on the hungry guests' plates.

He saw Albert Clare coming up the stairs to the deck, several reporters in tow. Albert's parties weren't a success without reporters from all the popular rags present. He needed to see his reveling in print with a few scattered photos to validate a major bash. Mike needed to get him alone to see if he could supply him with any useful information. Luckily the reporters allowed him to go to the bathroom alone.

Claire continued into the house and staggered down a hallway off the kitchen. Mike noticed he already had too much to drink and the party barely started. Mike followed him down the hall to a bathroom and just before the door swung shut, he pushed the door in. He slipped inside and shut it quickly behind him.

"What the hell are you doing?" Claire didn't recognize Mike with his hat pulled low. He moved toward the door.

"Hold on Albert." Mike moved in front of him and took off his hat.

Claire forced a smile. "Michael Brennan." His words were slightly slurred. "I have to admit I didn't expect you to show up tonight."

"I didn't do it Albert."

Claire closed the lid of the toilet and sat down. He was obviously scared, knowing that Mike was all over the papers and news programs as a murderer.

Mike tried again. "You've known me for a long time Albert. I'm not capable of what they say I did to Melvin."

Claire was skeptical. "Then why are you the main suspect?"

"Because someone that I hired saw something he shouldn't have seen. When he brought it to me, I guess they assumed I knew more than I actually did. They set me up."

"I didn't want to believe it, Mike. We've been friends a long time, but the stories are very convincing."

"That's why I'm here. I need your help to get to the bottom of what we uncovered. Once I'm arrested, I'll be useless."

"Why do you think I can help?"

"Because I know that you were financed by Philip Layden's father when he ran an outfit called Layden and Dowd. You've been in a business relationship with the Layden's for a long time."

"That doesn't mean I know about the inner workings of BNL."

"No. But I thought you could shed some light on how Philip Layden operates."

There was a knock at the door and Mike put his hand against it to make sure nobody came in.

"I'll be out in a minute." Claire called out. He stood and turned on the water in the sink. He reached down and scooped some cool water in his hands and splashed it on his face. "I recently got a visit from Philip at my office."

"Does he do that regularly?"

"Every few months." He splashed another handful of water and wiped his face on a hand towel. He looked at Mike in the mirror, standing behind him. "Listen Mike. I'm not really at liberty to discuss our business relationship."

"But it may be helpful to me in understanding why we saw hundreds of millions in wires flying through BNL's accounts. And also why I'm being railroaded for something I didn't do."

Claire turned around and looked Mike in the eyes, trying desperately to focus. He took a deep breath and let it out slowly. "You know what? This may be the vodka talking but fuck him. I really don't care anymore. BNL has been supporting Claire Cosmetic's stock price in the market since day one. Once I agreed to that they had me by the balls and I've been screwed!"

Mike put his hand on the older man's shoulder. "Thank you for telling me. Do you have any proof?"

Claire smiled. "I've been taping his conversations with me in my office for the past five years. He's been threatening me with blackmail. I spent more money on the recording equipment than I did on the swimming pool out there."

"What were you planning on doing with the tapes?"

"I've been saving them for the right time. I guess this is it, huh?"

"Where are they?"

"In my office in Manhattan. I'll have copies made and I'll call you in a couple days."

"I'm not sure I have a couple days, Albert."

"That's the best I can do for you. I want to keep copies for myself and it will take some time."

"Okay. Please call me on my cell when you've got them. You won't regret it."

As Mike turned to open the door, Albert sat back down on the toilet.

"I already regret it."

Mike put his hat back on and left Claire in the bathroom. He gave the valet the ticket and a five dollar bill and he was on his way back to Southampton within a few minutes.

He pressed a speed dial on his cell phone and waited for the connection.

"Hey, brother."

"Are you ready to go Tim?"

"Yes, sir."

"I'll be there in a few minutes. Did you talk to Ross Bricker?"

"It's all been arranged. Tomorrow morning, he'll fly Sam to the East Side Heliport and Mr. Brodworth's bodyguards will meet her and take her to one of his apartments."

"Perfect. I need her to be somewhere safe."

"She'll be fine there."

"I've got some bad news for you, man."

"What is it?" Mike asked.

"I just got word from my contact at the NYPD that Jack Darvish's body was found in the laundry room of the Plaza Hotel. I'm thinking the guy you met up with inside the room was probably disposing of the body when you went to the room and returned to continue his search when he ran into you."

"How did he die?"

"There wasn't a mark on his body. The ME said his neck had been broken cleanly and professionally. Instant death."

Mike didn't allow himself to grieve for Jack. He felt slightly guilty that it was his idea to set him up at the Plaza Hotel but he'd still be happily chugging along at BNL if it weren't for Jack and his scheme to defraud the company. He'd have time to feel sorry later, after he found whatever it was he was looking for and he was proven innocent. Until then, he had to focus on his current task.

CHAPTER TWENTY-NINE

It's amazing what you can do when you use cash, Mike thought as he sat alone in the rear of a six seat chartered business jet, taxiing down the runway at Republic Airport in Farmingdale. He didn't show ID and the name he gave, John Simon, was a ninety-two year old neighbor on the street where he grew up in Queens. It was the first name that popped into his head when the clerk asked him. He'd have to look into the reason why he chose that name on the spot when he had a little more time for self psychoanalysis.

After dropping his car at Tim's house, they picked up a rental from a local guy, again using cash and fake name on the paperwork. From this point on, Mike wanted everyone in his life to avoid leaving a paper trail. The FBI and Philip Layden would be all over anyone connected to him and he needed to make it as hard as possible to track them down. His parents were already sitting on a beach in Puerto Rico. As soon as the news broke that he was involved in Melvin Barry's death, he called and told them the truth and arranged for them to leave the country to avoid the media storm that was sure to hit. Sam would stay with Tim and his wife for a night before Ross Bricker flew her into Manhattan to stay at her Dad's.

As the small plane lifted into the air over suburban Long Island, Mike's thoughts turned to his own survival. Claire's taped conversations would give him a little bit of ammunition but he needed more. That was why he was headed to Atlanta to pay a visit to Tony Davenport. Another client handed to him by Melvin Barry in the early years, they had built a rapport that Mike felt he could use to help him get information. Since Davenport had been with BNL for so many years, maybe he had a feeling for what was happening.

Another piece of information that Mike wanted to explore further was the two shell companies that Jack discovered behind Layden and Dowd, the precursor to BNL. He felt that if he found out who owned Prometheus Holdings and Atlas Consultants, he would have an important part of the puzzle. He knew there was a connection between Prometheus and Atlas outside of his current situation, but he couldn't place it.

The wires coming through BNL out of Aruba and Atlanta had to be monitored from somewhere and he was determined to figure it out. Now that Jack was gone, his ability to conduct clandestine research was hindered and he was now forced to take a more aggressive approach. He was counting on Davenport to point him in the right direction.

Mike leaned back in his comfortable leather seat and watched New York slowly disappear as the jet gained altitude. The lone stewardess approached and took his drink order. With the week he'd been having he felt a few drinks would help him relax. He only ordered one because after the first few sips, he fell into a deep sleep and a recurring dream that he'd had a hundred times over the years. It was when he was deployed in his first major operation as a marine during the invasion of Panama. The dream usually followed actual events and was so realistic, Mike always woke up sweating, his heart beating out of his chest. After taking out the machine gunners and taking a bullet that was set off in the resulting fire, he was carried out of the jungle on a stretcher. A helicopter landed on the beach and his men loaded him in. The only difference between his usual dreams and this one was that this time around, instead of being carried out on a stretcher, he was in a body bag.

CHAPTER THIRTY

The catering team packed the last van and drove down Albert Claire's long drive to the street. The few remaining guests that held out until 3am fell into their cars and would somehow make it home without wrapping themselves around trees. Rick Jeffries walked around the first floor locking doors and shutting off lights before walking up the grand staircase that led to the master bedroom and several guest suites.

The first door on the right was opened just a crack. He pushed it all the way open and walked through. In the dim light he could make out a figure on the bed. He took a few steps closer to see Albert Claire, still fully dressed, face down and snoring loudly. Rick had helped him into bed a couple of hours earlier when the older man's words had become so badly slurred that his guests could no longer understand him.

That's what their relationship was about. Claire had made Rick his number one model which had helped make his face known around the world. In return, the ruggedly handsome young man tried to keep the alcoholic cosmetics magnate from embarrassing himself. And also on occasion, when Albert wasn't drunk, they shared a bed.

Rick turned him over, lifted his head onto a pillow, and folded a comforter over him.

"You stupid old drunk," he whispered. "One of these days you're going to drink yourself into the grave."

Although they both knew their friendship was based mostly on material gain, Rick had to admit he had a certain amount of affection for the old man.

He left the room and closed the door gently behind him. He didn't know why he was trying to be quiet because Albert wouldn't wake up now if the house fell down around him. Maybe he felt he had to sneak around because of the person he knew was waiting for him in the next room. Rick and Albert certainly didn't have an exclusive relationship but sleeping with someone in Claire's own house while he was there made him somewhat uneasy.

He opened the door at the far end of the hallway and stepped into the darkened room. He walked toward the open French doors leading to a balcony facing the beach. The curtains were flowing lightly in the wind. As he got closer, the fresh smell of the ocean mixed with sweet perfume.

The outline of her body was backlit by the moon hanging low over the ocean. She turned to face him and smiled with anticipation when he stepped onto the balcony. Cynthia Highsmith had been waiting for this moment all night. The ironic part about what would inevitably happen in the next few moments was that she was personally invited to the party by Albert Claire. She wasn't really a friend of the millionaire, but one of many in the media with whom he liked to surround himself.

Her career was moving along with incredible speed mainly because she'd go the extra mile for a story. If that meant she had to suffer through sleeping with a supermodel, she'd do it. Her role as an on-air reporter in the New York market had recently been expanded to a nationally syndicated prime time news show that was quickly moving up in the ratings. Not long ago, she had done a special on the plight of the male super model, with Rick Jeffries as the headliner. He owed her.

She reached out and put her arms around his neck. "What have you got for me?"

He put his hands around her waist and pulled her body tightly against his. "I've got something for you."

She kissed his neck, ran her hand slowly down his ripped abs and opened the zipper of his jeans. She reached in and squeezed gently and put her lips close to his ear.

"I've missed you too Rick, but you know why I'm here. This will have to wait a few minutes."

She pushed him lightly away and picked up a pad and pen from the table.

Rick shook his head. "You're positively cold blooded."

"I think *driven* is the correct term."

"Whatever." Rick sat in one of the wicker chairs.

"You know the deal baby. You give me all your pillow talk with Mr. Claire and I give you face time on my show along with a little pillow talk of our own."

Cynthia's next prime time special focused on corporate corruption and she knew from the tidbits that Rick had been feeding her that Albert Claire was quite possibly involved with something illegal. She couldn't get a grasp on the whole picture but she knew Claire was unhappy with certain business arrangements that he made years ago. The next really big coup for her would be to get a personal interview on the subject with Claire. Rick promised to work on him in return for a follow up show giving himself more prime time exposure.

After taking several pages of notes she closed her notebook, got up from the table and went back toward the bedroom. She turned around at the doorway. "Are you coming?"

Jeffries got up quickly. "Hell yes."

CHAPTER THIRTY-ONE

The bar was filled with smoke despite the city's ban on smoking. Of the fifty or so people that packed into the small tavern on One Hundred and Eighth Street in Rockaway Beach, roughly half were NYPD but they weren't there to enforce the ban. They were there to enjoy themselves and unwind after a day of dealing with the scum of the city. In the dimly lit corner booth sat two men drinking beer, their heads leaning in so they could hear each other over the boisterous crowd.

One of the men, affectionately known as "The Surfer" among the younger locals, was doing most of the talking. Sean Sullivan was trying to explain how Brennan slipped through his hands at the Plaza hotel. Philip Layden was listening patiently as Sullivan pleaded his case. The fact that the NYPD and the Secret Service were all over the hotel provided little solace to Layden.

"I'll get him Philip. You've relied on me before and I don't plan on letting you down this time."

Layden slapped the table hard. Sullivan's beer bottle tipped over and he caught it just before it fell on the floor. "This isn't like any of the other times!" Layden looked around at the crowd. A few nearby patrons turned to look at him. He ignored them and continued in a lower voice. "This is the most important job of your life, Sean. Of my life too."

"I took out Darvish and you have his laptop. Your tech guys can find out what he's been up to."

"That's great but with Brennan still out there we're at risk. My associates do not like being at risk."

Sullivan smiled confidently. "I know how to get him to walk into my hands."

"How?"

"I'll hit him where it hurts. Tug on his heart strings."

Layden took another sip of his beer and stood. He leaned in close to Sullivan's ear. "I don't care how you do it. Just get it done." He pushed his way through the crowd to the exit.

CHAPTER THIRTY-TWO

"Sir?"

Mike could hear a voice in the distance but couldn't make out the words.

"We're landing in a few minutes, sir."

Mike opened his eyes and looked around the small cabin. After a few moments, he remembered where he was. His face was wet with sweat and he felt out of breath.

The stewardess stood above him and spoke softly, a look of concern on her face. "We're on approach to Dekalb Peachtree. You have to fasten your seatbelt."

Mike looked out the window as he put on his seatbelt and saw the lights of a large city in the distance. It was about an hour until sunrise and Atlanta was just beginning the process of waking up. As the ground got closer he could make out the houses, strip malls, and factories. The pilot touched down smoothly on the runway at the small airport on the outskirts of the city.

As the plane slowed and turned toward the small terminal, Mike could see several groups of hangars that housed charter services. Dekalb-Peachtree was a tiny airport with short runways that couldn't be used by commercial airliners. Most of the traffic was chartered business jets or small props.

The stewardess opened the door and lowered the small set of stairs. As Mike grabbed his small carry-on bag, the pilot turned to him.

"Do you want to book a return flight Mr. Simon?"

"No thanks, Captain. I'm not exactly sure when I'll be returning."

"Okay sir. Just remember we're just a few hours away."

"Thanks for the smooth flight."

"You're welcome."

The pilot turned back to his control panel and Mike went to the door and stepped into the heavy Atlanta heat. It was the kind of heat that caused an immediate sweat. The sun was just on the horizon and the temperature was already near ninety.

On a normal business trip he'd have a car waiting to pick him up but this wasn't a regular client visit and he couldn't afford to leave any traces. He walked through the empty hangar that served as a terminal and went to a pay phone to call the local taxi service. While he waited he thought about what he and his brother had spoken about before he left. Tim reminded Mike that he had a lot of experience dealing with enemies in jungles and deserts but navigating through urban settings with possible enemies present was brand new to him. And that wasn't even the biggest twist. This time around he wasn't the hunter. He was the prey. He had to avoid desolate areas and make sure that the only way out of a place wasn't through the people who may be following him. He took his brother's warnings seriously but he wasn't afraid. He had a mission to complete. An ill defined mission but it happened to be the most important one of his life.

Mike paid the driver and stepped out onto a downtown Atlanta sidewalk in front of an office building not unlike the BNL building in New York. The structure was shorter but had similar reflecting panels. He caught an image of himself in the lobby windows and noticed he looked tired and worn out. This ordeal was taking its toll on him physically as well as mentally. The last couple nights were spent tossing and turning thinking about spending years in prison. He tried not to think about the other alternative that could leave him in the same condition as Melvin Barry and Jack Darvish. Dead.

He straightened his tie and buttoned his sport coat as he continued beyond his destination and entered a coffee shop in the building next door. He had an hour to kill before Davenport would be in his office and he needed to think about how to approach him.

CHAPTER THIRTY-THREE

Cynthia Highsmith sat behind her big desk at the station's headquarters in Rockefeller Center. Aside from technical personnel who were around twenty four hours a day, and the early show personalities, she was one of the first to arrive at six in the morning. She ate, slept, and breathed her work and thought nothing of eighteen to twenty hour workdays. She came directly from the party at Albert Claire's house in Amagansett and showered in her private bathroom.

The executive producer of her new show pushed for her to get the vacant office that was more like a small apartment overlooking Rockefeller Plaza. Not that she didn't appreciate it, but now she needed to think about decorating the damn thing and she would rather focus on her work. If she pleaded hard enough, she knew the same producer would get the company to pay for a decorator.

There was never any doubt in her mind that she deserved everything that was currently going right in her life. Straight out of school she got her first gig as a traffic reporter in Cincinnati. Her dedication paid off a year later when she got hired by one of the major networks in Los Angeles. Knowing that getting to New York was really the big time, she worked hard at her job as well as on her contacts. She wasn't always proud of the methods she employed for advancement but she was the one with the nationally broadcast weekly show, not them. If some men were stupid enough to let certain parts of their body make their decisions for them, they deserved what they got.

She opened the file for her next series of shows on corporate corruption. The tidbits she got from Rick Jeffries were great but she needed something more substantial put on the air. She wanted him to name names but the hard truth of it was that Rick just didn't know the details. Albert Claire was a very private man until he had a few too many drinks and then the window of opportunity to gather information was usually too short from the time he began to babble to the time he ended up face down on his bed.

She had been trying for months to convince Rick to get Albert to agree to a face to face interview and it was finally going to happen. The CEO of Claire Cosmetics granted an off the record meeting to explore the possibility of an exchange of information. The problem was that every high profile executive knows that there really is no such thing as "off the record". She knew that with her determination, he'd eventually do something on camera. The problem was pushing him fast enough with just the right amount of finesse to get him on board before her series aired on the scum of the business world.

Albert did reveal enough information to get Cynthia interested in the first place. He told Rick about a business relationship that he agreed to years ago that was putting a strain on not only his ability to conduct business but also on his bottom line. This arrangement was costing him too much money and he was ready to end it but that's where he was having problems.

All he would tell Rick was that there were complications that he wasn't willing to talk about.

She knew that the Claire Cosmetics piece could put her series over the top and she didn't want to have to leave it out. Her meeting with the head of Claire Cosmetics was extremely important because she couldn't reveal small details she learned from Rick without knowing the whole story. That could put Mr. Claire in danger and possibly alienate Rick. He was too good a contact and too good in bed to lose.

The big news this week was the scandal at BNL securities and the executive who was charged with embezzlement and the murder of a partner. She could fill a whole show with people who knew Mike Brennan and experts who would speculate why he did it and where he was hiding. She could wait for the Claire story to unfold but she was never one to wait for something to fall in her lap.

CHAPTER THIRTY-FOUR

Special Agent David Reynolds was also in the office early. After having trouble sleeping, he came in to 26 Federal Plaza early and sat quietly in his bare office. In front of him, laid out on his small desk was a chart measuring about three feet square. His personal method of charting a case included nothing scientific but he believed every crime was a puzzle. If the pieces were shuffled enough, the answers would fall into place. On the chart were removable tags that represented all the companies and people that had any level of involvement in his investigation. Every tag was color-coded. Red tags represented those believed to be heavily involved in illegal activity. A green tag had an unknown level of guilt.

He had two tags in his hands. Philip Layden, the lone living partner at BNL in his left hand and Mike Brennan in the right. He placed the red Layden tag back on the chart under the heading of BNL. Although he had no proof, the partner's guilt was pretty much sealed in Reynolds' eyes after meeting him out in Long Island. Brennan's tag was green. Reynolds wanted to talk to him but bringing him in was proving difficult. Although he believed that there was no way Brennan could be innocent, he'd give him the benefit of the doubt for now.

He was drawn out of concentration when Pete Battaglia walked in without knocking.

"Do I get any privacy around here, Pete?" Reynolds was only half joking.

"You sound like my daughter." Battaglia sat on the folding chair next to the desk. "The face recognition techies in the basement are working on the tapes from LaGuardia and Kennedy as well as the smaller Long Island airports."

He leaned forward and pointed to the colored tags, knowing his partner's system. "You think that Layden character is guilty too, huh?"

"There's no doubt in my mind."

"Who's that?" He gestured toward the green tag.

Reynolds looked down. "Michael Brennan."

Battaglia smiled. "Is he your new obsession?"

Reynolds ignored the insinuation. "I wouldn't go so far as to say obsession, but he's certainly an anomaly."

"Are you telling me that a fellow Ivy League puke couldn't possibly be a criminal?"

"You're too ignorant for words, man. You know damn well what I mean."

"Please explain." Battaglia put his hands behind his head and his feet on Reynolds' desk.

"Fine. This Brennan guy grows up in a lower middle class family in Queens. He gets into Cornell based on his smarts and goes on to join the ROTC and gets a commission in the Marine Corps. This is no ordinary guy, he's dedicated. Love's his family and his country. He fought in Panama and the Gulf War."

Battaglia played devil's advocate. "Maybe he was sick of making a military salary, hated the fact that he was borderline poor growing up, and would do anything to make money and live the high life."

Reynolds held up the newspaper with Mike's picture at the youth center. "He donates a percentage of his salary to his high school and local church. He just won Man of the Year from the Lower East Side Youth Center."

The two lawmen played off each other. That's what made them so good at what they did.

Battaglia shook his head. "He's not going back to Queens no matter what. He's dating a woman from one of the richest families on the East Coast. He stole seventy-five million dollars, hid it in an offshore account, and murdered his boss." He took the chart off the desk and pinned it to the wall. He took a blank red tag, wrote 'Brennan' on it and slapped it in the middle of the BNL section. "He's guilty."

Reynolds walked to the chart and pinned his green tag next his partner's red tag. "Let's leave them both up, I'm still not convinced." He took a step back to take in the whole puzzle. "We've got work to do, my friend."

"You got that right." Battaglia admitted.

CHAPTER THIRTY-FIVE

The elevators opened into the reception area of Davenport and Associates and Mike stepped forward onto the marble floor. On the wall behind the receptionist was the name and corporate logo in large gold letters. The girl at the desk looked up and smiled as she spoke into her headset. She pressed the hold button and said, "How can I help you?" Her accent was the same as the girl in the coffee shop downstairs.

"I'm here to see Tony Davenport. I'm sorry I don't have an appointment but please let him know that Mike Brennan is here." Mike turned and walked slowly to the couch and sat down. The woman who regularly answered the phones must have been out. She would have recognized his name.

The receptionist spoke into her headset in a hushed tone, preventing Mike from hearing her. She then swiveled in her chair toward Mike. "I'm sorry to keep you waiting sir, Mr. Davenport will…" Her sentence was cut off as Anthony Davenport opened the door next to her desk and entered the room.

He was not a large man but he commanded a presence that made him appear larger. Without knowing him, someone could feel the authority seeping from his pores. His impeccably tailored lightweight tan suit didn't have a wrinkle in it, as if he put it on only five minutes before. His grey hair was coifed perfectly without a strand out of place.

"Mike! What the hell are you doing here? Your face is all over the news." He approached Mike with his hand extended and stopped very close to him. He looked at Mike's bruised face and winced. "What the hell happened to you?"

Mike was suddenly nervous. It was much easier to talk on the phone than in person but he couldn't risk anyone hearing what he needed to tell Davenport. "I had nothing to do with Melvin's murder." He let go of Davenport's hand. His palm was beginning to sweat. "Can we go to your office and talk?"

"We've known each other a long time but I'd be taking a tremendous risk here."

Mike expected this response. "I've never lied to you before Tony. We've done a lot of deals together and I've always been up front with you. Give me just a few minutes of your time."

Davenport nodded sternly and turned to his receptionist. "Hold my calls, Darling."

He motioned for Mike to follow him through the door he entered moments ago. He led Mike down a wide hallway leading to the rear of the floor. Most of the offices lining the hall were closed with the exception of the door next to Davenport's corner office.

A man stuck his head out of the doorway. "Brennan? What the hell are you doing here?" It was Louis Wilson whom Mike had met on a number of occasions. He thought the financial wizard's mind wasn't worth the abrasive personality that came along with it. From what Mike could tell Davenport trusted Wilson with a lot of the company's financial decisions.

"Hello Louis." Mike extended his hand. Wilson was the last person that Mike wanted to deal with at the moment. "I need a few moments of Tony's time. When I'm done, Tony can fill you in. Please excuse us." Mike closed Davenport's door almost hitting Wilson's nose.

Davenport smiled, enjoying the interaction. "You don't like him much do you?"

"Honestly Tony, I don't like his attitude and if I don't have to deal with him, I won't. Can I trust that he won't call the police while I'm in here?"

"Wilson doesn't order lunch without running it by me first. You're safe for now."

Mike was feeling slightly more at ease as he sat in the soft leather chair facing Davenport's desk.

Davenport leaned forward on his elbows. "Alright Mike. What's going on? They've got you pinned for stealing millions from BNL in illegal trading and to top it off you murdered Melvin Barry. You know as well as I do that it looks bad."

Mike swallowed hard. There was no easy way to say it. "How have you felt about the deals that BNL has been involved with over the years?"

"In general they're pretty solid. I always let you know when you bring me something I don't like. What are you getting at here?" He didn't like to beat around the bush.

Mike didn't hold back. "I think BNL has been involved in major illegal activity. I can't prove it but I believe that they've been manipulating stock prices. I've been set up for Melvin's murder and they threw in seventy-five million in a secret account to make it more believable." Mike felt a weight lift off his chest as soon as the words left his mouth. He decided not to bring up the fact that he had copies of wires and the information he got from Melvin Barry. He'd let Davenport come to his own conclusions.

"These are serious allegations Mike. Who do you think is behind this?" Davenport sounded pissed off and rightfully so.

"It has to be Philip Layden. If he's been facilitating something illegal through BNL, he's got a reason to set someone else up. The whole goddamned Street is being investigated right now and maybe he got word that the authorities were getting close."

Mike was trying hard to keep the fact hidden that he learned most of his information from Barry the night before he was killed. "I looked back at a few deals that we brought out in the past and noticed that the stocks were wavering until a few small firms pumped money into them."

Mike leaned forward in his chair. "I'm at a loss here Tony. I've got no one to turn to on this."

Davenport just stared at Mike. He was taking all the information in but had no response. Mike wasn't sure if he was starting to boil under his serene appearance.

He finally broke his silence. "You did the right thing, Mike. If Philip is running something illegal up there then you've got to somehow separate yourself from them."

Mike was visibly relieved. He finally had an ally.

"I'm going to need some more information if I'm gong to be able to help you. Have you been able to do any in depth research?"

"I haven't been back to the office since Melvin died…," Mike paused and corrected himself, "I mean murdered. I did some quick work on the internet." He kept Jack's name out of it. It was just a matter of time before he became the number one suspect in Jack's murder as well. "Are you familiar with companies called Prometheus Holdings and Atlas Consultants?"

Tony paused again as if thinking. "I don't recall the names. Were they deals that BNL did?"

"No. I was looking through some public records and found that they were big investors behind Layden and Dowd, Philip's father's financing firm. I don't know if it means anything but I've got nothing else to latch onto right now."

"The names don't ring a bell but I'll run it by Wilson."

"I'd really appreciate it if you left Wilson out of this as long as possible."

Davenport's expression became stern. "I've got a lot at stake here, Mike. I'll handle this my way. You're a wanted man and I let you into my place of business. If the FBI finds out about this meeting I could be taken down for aiding and abetting." There was concern in Davenport's powerful voice. Mike knew it wasn't concern for him but for Davenport's own skin.

Mike answered truthfully, "I understand how you feel and thank you for listening to me. Before long, the truth will come out and you'll find out that I'm innocent. If you think of anything that could help me, please call my cell phone. If I'm right about Layden, I'll be lucky to survive until trial."

"The magic words there are 'if you're right'. How the hell do you think you can prove any of this if it hasn't been uncovered already? Are you prepared to be wrong and is it even a possibility?"

Mike thought about Davenport's words for a moment. This enormously wealthy man sitting across from him could be caught in the rubble if BNL fell and Mike felt responsible to an extent for Davenport's involvement.

"I know I'm right Tony. There's no way some of these deals would have survived without some well placed trades. Someone made the right calls at the right time." He used Barry's words.

"We need more to go on than what you've got. Why don't you think about this tonight? Go through all the deals that BNL has done and we'll do an analysis tomorrow to see if we can figure something out." Davenport stood and walked toward the door. "Where are you staying?"

"The Ambassador. Do you know it?"

"Yeah, nice place. I guess you didn't register under your own name?"

"I couldn't. I'll be under John Simon."

Davenport nodded. "You work your magic tonight and get back here bright and early. We'll get a hold of this mess. I'll call you a car." He picked up the phone and told his secretary to call the car service. He hung up and walked toward the door. "They'll be here by the time you get downstairs."

"Thanks Tony, I'm glad I brought this to you."

"I'll see you in the morning."

After Mike left, Davenport picked up his phone, punched a few numbers, and waited through a series of beeps and clicks.

"Yes?" a voice answered.

"It's Tony. Why the hell didn't you tell me that Brennan knows?" his voice was raised.

"Calm down," Philip Layden said from the BNL offices. "We weren't sure how much he knows. We're in the process of finding that out."

"Did you know he came down here to tell me all about it?"

"He's in Atlanta?"

"He just left my office. He also knows about Prometheus and Atlas."

"How could he possibly know?" Layden was angry.

"I don't think he knows details but he knows there's a connection to BNL. My company's name is on the corporate resolution for Prometheus and Browning is on the hook for Atlas. How the hell did he find out about them?"

"I don't know but there's nothing to worry about. We've come up with a plan to guarantee his cooperation. In the meantime, get someone to watch him while I make some phone calls." Layden slammed the phone down.

Davenport knew that if this was made public he'd be investigated and his real connection to BNL may be uncovered. He wasn't about to let that happen. He picked up the phone and dialed his chauffeur and bodyguard, who spent most of his time waiting for Davenport in a room off the lobby.

"John, there'll be a man coming off the elevator wearing a blue sport coat, white shirt and red tie. Follow him to the Ambassador Hotel and let me know if he stops anywhere along the way or leaves once he checks in. I'll get further instructions to you shortly." Davenport was as calm as if he were ordering a ham on rye.

CHAPTER THIRTY-SIX

"Thank you for seeing us so early Ms. Brodworth. We appreciate it." Agent Reynolds and Special Investigator Battaglia followed Sam Brodworth down a couple steps to the sunken living room.

Sam looked at the two security men that her father hired to protect her. "You guys can take a break for a minute. I'm okay for now."

"We'll be in the kitchen." The men eyed the two visitors in suits and walked slowly to the kitchen. They sat on stools at a counter out of earshot but were still able to keep Sam in their sight.

"Do they come with the penthouse?" Battaglia asked before sitting on the leather couch.

Sam smiled. "I've only been here a few hours and I'm finding that I don't like to be watched. Daddy is very protective."

"Do you have reason to believe you're in danger?" Reynolds asked.

"Nothing concrete."

"Are you afraid of Michael Brennan?"

Sam tried to hold back her laugh but was unsuccessful. Before she could reply, one of the guards returned with a carafe of coffee and cups and placed them on the coffee table in front of Sam.

"Thank you, Joe." Sam poured three cups without asking if they wanted any.

"Ms. Brodworth, your boyfriend is in a lot of trouble. As an attorney, you know that it would be much better for him in the long run if he turned himself in. Do you know his whereabouts?" Reynolds poured cream into his mug and stirred.

"I don't know where he is, Agent Reynolds. The last time I saw him was the morning after the Plaza fundraiser."

"Do you have a means of contacting him?" Battaglia asked.

"No."

Reynolds took out his notepad and a pencil. "You were together the night of Melvin Barry's death?"

"Why are you wasting my time? I've already answered these questions. You know I was with him at the Barry's. You know I was with him at the Plaza. Are you expecting me to slip up and tell you he's hiding in the closet?"

Reynolds continued without acknowledging Sam's outburst. "There were reports that Brennan left the fundraiser and returned sometime later with a black eye."

Sam folded her arms across her chest. "He slipped on the stairs."

"Are you aware that another coworker of his was murdered at the hotel? Jack Darvish's body was found yesterday morning stuffed in a laundry bin. His neck was broken."

Sam was unfazed. "I heard about Jack."

Reynolds raised his voice slightly. "Ms. Brodworth, your position with the mayor's office will not help you in any way to avoid prosecution."

Sam stood up. "Don't threaten me. I didn't have to grant this meeting. If you opened your eyes you'd see that Mike is innocent. Instead, he's out there doing your job for you."

"What do you mean by that Ms. Brodworth?" Reynolds asked.

Sam walked to the door and the two men followed. She opened it and made a sweeping motion with her hand. "I'm sure you'll find out soon enough."

Sean Sullivan parked his rented car in front of a fire hydrant along Forty-Eighth Street just east of Second Avenue. He looked across the street to see the awning of William Brodworth's building. Two well dressed men came out the door and got into a dark blue sedan. One of the men, the taller and thinner of the two, was a bit better dressed than the other. He carried himself with confidence and Sullivan thought to himself that he looked like he didn't belong in a Chevy. Sullivan couldn't help his thought process. He got paid to notice things. Very well paid.

Sullivan got out of the car and crossed the street. He approached the building and tapped on the glass door. The doorman looked up from his paper but was obviously hesitant to come to the door. Sullivan didn't expect to be allowed to walk upstairs without a question so he came prepared. He removed his wallet and held a badge up to the glass which resulted in the doorman putting his paper down and slowly opening the door.

"I need to see Ms. Brodworth," Sullivan said.

The doorman eyed the badge. "You guys were just here. Can't you leave her alone for a while?"

"It'll only take a minute."

The doorman gave in. "Okay. I'll let you up."

Sullivan followed him to the elevator and rode up to the penthouse alone. On the top floor, he stepped into the small hallway and knocked on the Brodworth's door.

"Hold on," came an irritated male voice from inside the apartment.

He knew that there would be a security team. A man as wealthy as William Brodworth wouldn't allow his daughter to sit at home alone when she could be in danger. He now needed to find out quickly how many and how well trained the guards inside actually were. He listened as the locks turned and the door finally opened to reveal a large man with an obvious bulge under his suit jacket.

"Can I help you?"

Sullivan held up the badge. "I need to speak with Ms. Brodworth briefly."

"Where are your two friends? They couldn't have left five minutes ago." He opened the door wider but didn't move out of the way.

Sullivan smiled. "Those guys are from the New York office. I just got in from D.C. and I need to ask Ms. Brodworth about some new developments."

Sam walked up the two steps from the living room and looked around the guard at Sullivan standing near the door.

"Let him in, Joe. It's okay."

Sullivan held up his badge for her to see. "I'm Special Agent Doran. Actually Ms. Brodworth, we'd prefer if you came down to Federal Plaza."

The second guard approached from the kitchen and stood next to Sam as she stood strong. "I've already been through this with Agent Reynolds. I'm not going anywhere with you. I'll consult my attorney and get back to you. Now please leave."

The first guard started to close the door but Sullivan reacted quickly. He pushed the door in, hitting the guard in the face. He fell to the floor unconscious and bleeding from the nose. Sullivan had his gun out before the body hit the floor and pointed it at the guard standing next to Sam.

"Slowly. And I mean slowly, remove your weapon and slide it to me."

The man removed his 9mm from his shoulder holster, held it with just two fingers on the handle, and placed it on the wood floor.

"Kick it to me." The guard kicked the weapon, causing it to slide down the short hallway.

Sullivan leaned down, picked up the gun, and placed it in his waistband.

"Now put your hands on top of your head, turn around and walk backwards toward me. Ms. Brodworth, please do the same."

Sam slowly complied, looking at the guard on the floor, blood leaking out of his nose. "I'll have your badge for this."

"I'll worry about that later." Sullivan replied.

When the guard shuffled backwards to the doorway, Sullivan put his hands on his back to stop him. "Now, say goodnight."

"What?" The puzzled man removed his hands from his head and started to turn around. Before he made the full rotation, Sullivan slammed the butt of his own weapon against the base of the guard's skull. He dropped on top of his partner with a sick thud.

Sam froze as she looked at her protectors lying unconscious on the floor. She looked at Sullivan who now had his gun pointed at her and stated the obvious. "You're not FBI, are you?"

"That's right. And we're not in Kansas anymore, Dorothy."

Sullivan grabbed her arm and pulled her through the door. As they waited for the elevator he holstered his weapon and grabbed her face with one hand. He looked into her scared eyes and said through clenched teeth, "Stay calm. You're going to come with me downstairs and through the lobby. If you try to even look at the doorman, I'll shoot you both. I don't plan on hurting you, but I will if I have to. I just need to speak with Mr. Brennan and you're going to help me do that."

Sam didn't see any other choice but to follow the stranger's instructions. In the lobby, she kept her head turned from the doorman and went through the front door with Sullivan close behind. When they got outside he put his arm around her and guided her to his rented car across the street. He opened the front passenger door and she got in without an objection.

He quickly walked around the car and got in the driver's side. "You're a smart girl, Ms. Brodworth." Sullivan flashed his smile. "Now tell me where Michael Brennan is." The smile vanished as quickly as it appeared.

"I don't know."

"Bullshit. I said I wouldn't hurt you and I won't if you cooperate. Now where the hell is he!" He screamed.

"I'm not lying. I really don't know. He didn't tell me where he was going."

"Have it your way, Ms. Brodworth." He started the engine and pulled away heading west on forty-eighth street.

CHAPTER THIRTY-SEVEN

Bryant Park had become a hot spot in New York City when Mayor Giuliani cleaned it up years earlier. On warm summer evenings, it fills up with young people having drinks at the pricey establishments behind the library. On occasion, movies are shown on a massive screen for couples sprawled out on blankets drinking wine and eating cheese.

It also happens to be a popular location for fashion shows. A tremendous tent is set up on the lawn to house a runway, spectator's section, dressing area, the works. This year's big show was being partially sponsored by Claire Cosmetics and several big name designers were showing their latest. Not just anybody got invited to shows that involved Albert Claire. You had to be good.

Philip Layden worked his way through the crowd and was impressed by the number of celebrities and press that were in attendance. As he made his way toward the rear of the tent, he slowed his pace. There were too many scantily clad women to admire.

A trailer, the kind you'd see on a construction site, was set up behind the staging area and served as the brain center for the show. Albert Claire was deep in conversation with a man wearing headphones and a microphone when Layden knocked on the open door. The surprise was obvious on Claire's face.

He quickly regained his composure. "Will you excuse us for a few minutes, Roger?"

"Show starts in fifteen minutes, Mr. Claire," the stage manager huffed.

"I'm painfully aware of that fact. This shouldn't take long." He physically took the man by the shoulder and walked him to the door past Layden.

Layden smiled at the display. "A bit rough, don't you think Albert?"

Claire closed the door. "I really don't have time for this Philip. What is it you need now?" He was obviously flustered, not expecting the visit.

"Oh, it's nothing really." Layden took a sheet of paper from his pocket. He unfolded it slowly as he smiled at Claire. "You don't often see a CEO sell off a hundred thousand shares of his own company. This is the second block in less than a week. What the hell are you trying to do?" He held up the trade confirmation for the other man to see.

The previously regained composure disappeared. "How the hell did you get that? It was executed just before the close today."

"It's public information, you stupid bastard." Layden was angry.

"I know that, but not until tomorrow."

"There's really not much we don't know, Albert."

"That's becoming apparent."

"Are you good pals with your former broker?" Layden took a few steps forward. "Did you and Brennan discuss this transaction at your party?"

Claire was speechless. He didn't think anyone knew Mike had been at his house but it somehow got back to Layden. He struggled to get his words out. "He had no idea about the trade and I'm allowed to sell my own stock Philip. It's perfectly legal." Claire tried to stand firm but knew it was a futile effort.

"Didn't you know he was wanted by the FBI for murder?" Layden moved closer and pushed Claire against the wall of the small trailer. "We have an agreement, Mr. Claire. First of all, when you plan on selling a block this size, you let me know first. Secondly, if I hear that you speak to Brennan again, I'll kill you."

"I was going to tell you tomorrow but I've been busy with the show."

"Bullshit." Philip came a little closer. "This is your last chance Mr. Claire Cosmetics. If you want to stay in the game you play by our rules."

"Fine. Just get the fuck out and let me get on with this." Claire walked around the larger man and opened the door for him.

Layden was growing tired of the man's defiance. "I don't usually give out more than one warning. I wasn't kidding the other night when I said I liked you Albert. Don't end up like your broker's boss."

Claire's jaw dropped slightly as he thought of Melvin Barry. "Are you saying…?"

Layden cut him off. "I'm not saying anything Albert. Have a good show." He walked out of the trailer and back through the staging area. Claire looked after him until he lost sight of him in the crowd. He closed his eyes tightly and again wished that his life had turned out differently than it had. He took a deep breath and tried desperately to concentrate on his current tasks.

Before he got a chance to close the door a woman approached from the side.

"That didn't look like it went well," she said.

Albert looked at her and then back toward the crowd where Layden had disappeared seconds before. "Get in here. He can't see me talking to you."

She moved quickly up the stairs and he closed the door behind her. Albert spoke into a small handheld radio. "Roger, I need another fifteen minutes. Have the girls ready to go."

Roger's voice came back through the radio. "But Mr. Claire, we..."

"Just do it." He shut the radio off.

Cynthia Highsmith was already sitting by the small coffee table with her pad and tape recorder set up in front of her.

Albert looked at the tiny machine. "Shut that thing off. We do this on my terms."

She smiled. "You're a lot tougher than I thought Mr. Claire. I give you a lot of credit for doing what you're doing."

"I don't need to be stroked Ms. Highsmith. I'm not doing this out of some sense of nobility."

"I think we'll need more than fifteen minutes."

"This will have to be a slow process. Today, I'll give you an overview of what I believe to be true. After that, if I feel I can trust you, I'll name names."

"Will you do it on my show?"

"Listen to me, Ms Highsmith." Albert began pacing the small open area inside the trailer. "I've been answering to someone else for more than two decades and I've reached my boiling point. If I decide to go public with what I know, I'm going to need more than the witness protection program." He stopped pacing and looked directly in her eyes. "Are you prepared to hide me and my family for the next thirty or forty years?"

She didn't reply.

"I didn't think so."

CHAPTER THIRTY-EIGHT

In the large entrance hall of the Browning mansion on Park Avenue in Manhattan, five Secret Service agents sat drinking coffee as Vice President Browning met with his brother on the second floor. In the library, a room that was swept for listening devices on a daily basis, Joseph Browning leaned back his chair. He looked through the cigar smoke to his brother sitting across from him.

"Can you please explain to me again why this Brennan was allowed to leave the Plaza if you knew he was there?"

Ernest Browning took a puff on his cigar and let the smoke out slowly. "Maddux must have let him out the back door. He's tight with Brennan's girlfriend, Samantha Brodworth."

"I'll make sure the mayor doesn't get off easy. We'll see how much federal funding comes his way in the next budget. I'll have to stop by City Hall before I leave for Washington to have a little chat." He smiled, showing his perfectly white politician's teeth. "Is this girlfriend the daughter of William Brodworth?"

"One and the same."

"That's interesting." The Vice President raised his eyebrows.

As often happened when the brothers met, there were long periods of silence. They puffed on their cigars and waited for the other to speak.

It was Joseph Browning who broke the silence. "Father would be sick to his stomach to know what you've allowed to go on with his life's work."

Ernest knew it was only a matter of time before his younger brother brought this up. "He left it in my hands, not yours. You've been in Washington most of your adult life and have no idea what it takes to manage this enterprise."

"I have no idea? Are you kidding? As Senator, I supported legislation time and again that padded the families' bank accounts with millions."

"But as Vice President you sit on your ass attending funerals and making meaningless speeches."

The younger Browning stood up, leaving his cigar in the ashtray. "I've dedicated my life to this family and I'm a heartbeat away from the oval office. After the election next year, our power will increase exponentially." He walked to the door and turned back at the opening. "Now if you'll just do your part, you old fool, we'll be back on track."

Ernest Browning sat watching the line of smoke rise from his cigar. He'd never admit that his younger brother was right. Not to his face. He knew Brennan was the key to getting things back to normal. If he failed, the plan his father put in place almost three quarters of a century earlier would be at risk of collapse for the first time. He didn't want to be known as the man to let that happen.

CHAPTER THIRTY-NINE

After checking in at the Ambassador Hotel in Atlanta, Mike made a list of companies he felt could have been problems over the years. He was relieved that his visit to Tony Davenport was a success and he finally had someone on his side. He worked his way through a few hours of analysis and was too mentally drained to stay awake. He stretched out on the bed and it didn't take long for him to fall into a deep sleep.

Hours later, the incessant ringing of the phone on the nightstand pulled him back to semi consciousness. Night had fallen and the room was pitch black with the shades drawn. Disoriented, it took a few seconds before he understood where he was. He fumbled for the lamp next to the bed and the bright light stung his eyes.

"Hello?" His voice was raspy with sleep.

"Hey it's Tim. Were you sleeping?"

"I guess I was. What time is it?"

"Almost nine o'clock. How'd it go today?"

Mike paused as he struggled to remember what happened earlier in the day.

"Are you there?" Tim broke the silence.

"Yeah, I'm still half asleep. I met with Tony Davenport and let him know what's going on. He took it pretty well considering the impact it could have on him."

"Are you sure this guy's a straight shooter?"

"He's all I've got at this point. I need someone with his expertise to help me dig into the details. I think he's my ticket."

"I hope you're right because you're all alone down there. Will you let me call my friend at the Bureau to back you up?"

"Not yet. Let me see what happens tomorrow and I'll keep you updated."

"Please be careful little brother."

"I will." Mike hung up the phone and picked up his notes, continuing his list. He was struggling with his memory when the phone rang again.

"Yes." He thought it was Tim again.

"Brennan, it's Louis Wilson."

"Wilson?" Surprise was evident in his voice.

"We need to meet right now."

"Now? Can't it wait until tomorrow?"

"Listen closely. I know why you're here and I have information you'll want to hear. I'm not saying any more on the phone. Meet me at the bar in the lobby in twenty minutes." He hung up without waiting for a reply.

Mike pulled the phone away from his ear and stared at it. He sat in silence for a moment, thinking about how Wilson could have known why he was there. Tony probably went against his wishes and brought his underling in on the news. He took a quick shower before heading down to the bar to meet Wilson.

Stepping off the elevator into the lobby, Mike could see the entrance to the bar on the other side of the reception desk. The lobby was done in beautifully finished oak accented with polished brass. It looked expensive and was. The doorway to the bar was bracketed by large leafy potted plants. The bartender looked up from drying a glass as Mike walked in.

"Good evening sir. What can I get for you?"

Mike looked around the room. The place was empty except for an older couple occupying one of the booths. He took a seat at the bar facing the door. "I'll have a bottle of Fosters."

Mike placed a fifty on the bar as the bartender poured the beer into a large frosty glass. He was just about to take a sip when Wilson walked through the door. He was about Mike's height but with a slight frame and dark hair mixed with some gray. He looked out of place in warm up pants with matching jacket and a baseball hat pulled down almost covering his eyes. *He looks ridiculous*, Mike thought.

Walking by Mike at the bar, he motioned for him to follow to a dark booth toward the back. Mike slipped into the opposite bench. "What's going on Louis? Just finished up a tennis match?"

Wilson didn't smile. "Did you know you were followed here, Brennan?"

Mike stared at him blankly.

"I know why you're here and if you don't listen to what I have to say you'll be heading back to New York in storage instead of first class.

Mike's mouth suddenly went dry. He raised his glass to take a drink.

"Listen to me you arrogant New York bastard. I've known for years that Davenport has been involved in shady deals. Much like yourself, I found out much too late for anyone to believe my innocence."

The bartender walked up to the table to ask Wilson if he wanted a drink. He declined in his usual abrasive manner, then continued. "Do you know anything about my family?"

Mike shook his head.

"My blood line started in this country well before the Revolutionary War. They came over here with money and each generation significantly increased that wealth. After the stock market crash in 1929, the family took a huge hit and never quite recovered. We certainly still had money but we never got back to the same level."

Mike interrupted. "I appreciate the history lesson, Louis, but why the hell are you telling me all this?" Mike couldn't concentrate. He was thinking about the possibility that his one hope, Davenport's help, was just shot out of the sky.

"I'm trying to tell you that the same people who kept my family from returning to their privileged lifestyle are part of the same group who are manipulating the market through BNL." He struggled to keep his voice low.

"I'm very confused."

Wilson opened his mouth to speak when his cell phone rang. He quickly answered it and listened for almost thirty seconds.

"Right now?" he asked whoever was on the other end of the call. He abruptly stood from the booth and put the phone back in his pocket.

Mike looked up at him. "Where are you going?"

"Not me. Us. We've got to get the hell out of here fast because Davenport's goon is about to enter the lobby." He turned and walked to the back of the bar where a door led to the kitchen. Mike thought he had no choice but to follow. The cooks and busboys ignored them as if strangers walked through the kitchen regularly. At the back, behind a tall walk in refrigerator, was a hallway that led to the alley behind the hotel.

Wilson paused at the back door. "Stay close behind me and don't look back. The alley leads to a street on the back side of the hotel where I parked my car. I'll take you out to Dekalb Peachtree where you can charter a plane back to New York."

"Hold on Wilson, you're talking too fast."

"Listen to me and listen good Brennan. Davenport is not acting alone. I've always suspected collusion but I couldn't determine who it was. I'm not sure if it's one person or many, but I know he's not alone."

"Davenport is a part of this organization you're talking about?" Mike was shocked.

"That's what I've been trying to tell you. His grandfather somehow shut my grandfather out. I've given it a lot of thought and there's only one way to find out who else is involved. We've got to get inside and seize their records. Find out who the hell is behind it."

"Get inside where and behind what?" Mike asked.

"Exactly. Therein lies the mystery. I've spent the better part of a year trying to come up with something that I could hold onto in case they tried to pin something on me and I've got nothing. I think it all starts in New York."

"In New York?"

"Let's go. I'll tell you more on the way to the airport."

As Wilson was talking Mike realized that there was no way to know if he was telling the truth or part of a bigger plot with Davenport. He'd have to trust him.

Wilson seemed to read his mind. "You can trust me, Brennan. If I were in on this shit I wouldn't be standing here talking with someone whose level of involvement is unknown. To be honest with you, I normally wouldn't care less if you made it out alive but I need you to keep myself out of jail."

Wilson pushed open the door into the dark alley. Mike followed closely and the door closed behind them. The stench of garbage was overwhelming in the humid evening air. The only light in the area was a small uncovered bulb hanging above the doorway. It was just enough light to cast faint shadows.

Mike heard rustling behind a dumpster and looked to his left. A man dressed in a dark suit stepped from the darkness and pointed a gun at Wilson.

"Going somewhere Mr. Wilson?" It was a large man who looked like he didn't need a gun to handle both Wilson and Mike.

"Hello John. Any reason why you're lurking in the shadows behind a hotel?" Wilson said in a surprisingly composed voice.

"You know him?" Mike asked, barely able to get the words out.

Wilson nodded. "This is John. Tony Davenport's bodyguard."

"Security Consultant," John said.

Wilson smiled. "Of course. Security consultant."

Mike remained quiet as the two men carried on a calm conversation.

"Mr. Davenport told me you might meet up with our visitor."

"And your instructions are?"

"He wants me to bring you both to his place out in Druid Hills. He'll explain when you arrive."

Wilson was obviously uneasy going anywhere with this man. He was looking back and forth between Mike and the gunman and after an uncomfortable silence he said, "Whatever he's paying you I'll double it." His tone was suddenly desperate.

The security consultant smirked. "It's not only about the money, Mr. Wilson. I thought you knew me better than that."

Wilson turned to Mike. "It was worth a try, don't you think Brennan?"

Mike was caught off guard by the question. "Well, uh…"

Wilson cut him off with a loud yell as he charged their unsuspecting captor. The man tried to move to one side to avoid the hit but Wilson caught him with a shoulder in the mid section. Mike was impressed with force of the tackle.

The goon fell to the ground and rolled over backwards only to end up on his feet in a crouching position. He was stunned but kept his composure. Wilson started to run at him again when the man raised his gun. Mike heard one shot and knew that Wilson was going down. As Wilson slipped to his knees holding his stomach, Mike heard four or five more rapid shots. They weren't coming from the man in front of him, but from the kitchen doorway.

Mike dove quickly to the ground and rolled to the side of the ally. He picked his head up in time to see John, the gunman, jerk back with shot after shot to his chest. He ended up sprawled on the ground with his eyes wide open, his head lying at an odd angle against the dumpster.

Mike looked to the door to see four men in suits holding their guns in outstretched arms. One of the newly arrived gunmen walked slowly toward the dead man and kicked the gun out of his hand. Another turned Wilson over to uncover a large pool of blood. He looked back to the others and shook his head. Wilson was dead.

Mike hadn't moved from his prone position on the side of the alley, not knowing what to expect next. One of the men walked toward him and grabbed him under the arm to help him up.

Surprised, Mike looked at the man and asked, "Who the hell are you guys?"

The man reached into his inside coat pocket and flipped out a wallet holding it up to Mike.

"FBI. Are you Michael Brennan?"

"That's right." Mike's voice was shaky.

"My name is Paul Schmidt. I'm a friend of your brother's."

Mike tried to smile as he shook his head. "How the hell did you know where I was?"

"Tim gave me a call a couple of hours ago. When he told me a little about your problem and what you'd planned on doing, I knew you'd be in danger. We've had Davenport under investigation for some time and he's suspected of some pretty serious crimes. Not only financial. Since the news broke about you and what you're suspected of doing, the investigation has intensified."

Mike was sorry that he'd brought his information to Davenport but he had nowhere else to go. He needed a starting point and this couldn't have turned out worse. The only thing that would bring him down further is if Special Agent Schmidt arrested him along with Davenport.

"Are you going to arrest me?"

"Your brother told me everything and I have no reason right now not to believe him or you for that matter. Tim and I go back a long way."

"Thanks." Mike turned to look at the bodies sprawled on the ground. He still didn't believe he'd be allowed to walk away. "So am I going to jail?"

"I'm not going to bring you in. We never saw you." He pointed into the darkness. "Head out through the alley and grab yourself a cab. You can hire a charter at Dekalb Peachtree if you've got the cash. The screening will be minimal and you can slip back to New York undetected."

Mike thanked him and didn't wait another moment to get away from the scene. He started down the alley and after just a few steps Schmidt called out, "Hey Brennan."

Mike turned back and said, "Yes?"

"If your friends at BNL are anything like Davenport, you'd better be careful."

The cab let Mike off at the main terminal. It was only big enough to house four or five counters servicing a few small commuter airlines. Just inside the door, he stopped at a payphone against the wall and dialed information. Earlier that morning, as his plane landed, he had seen a hangar with a sign hanging on it for a charter service. He'd known for years it was there but never had a reason to make the trip from New York. Now he hoped that the owner of the charter was there this late at night and that his request for help would fall on sympathetic ears.

"Blake Charters please."

He wrote down the number and hung up. He dropped a quarter into the slot and dialed. It was five rings before someone answered.

A woman answered. "Blake Charters. Can I help you?"

"Can I please speak with Lisa Blake?" Mike asked.

"Speaking."

"Lisa, it's Mike Brennan."

There were a few seconds of silence. "Mike?"

He got right to the point because he didn't want to stay exposed in the terminal.

"I'm in trouble and I need your help."

Again, silence followed by, "What kind of help?"

"I need you to fly me New York."

"When?"

"Now."

"You've got to be joking."

"Let me explain in person. I'll be there in five minutes." He hung up quickly, not waiting for an objection.

The terminal was nearly deserted at this time of the evening as he followed the signs for the private charters. He was still sweating and his heart was working double time as he walked along the terminal walkway. He was surprised to be allowed to leave the building to access a path that led to several small hangars. Security was nearly non existent. A guard was posted at the front door of the terminal but he hadn't seen another since.

Outside, most of the hangars were dark. The second to last structure closest to the runways had its door open and Mike could see a sleek Lear jet with its lower hatch open. A pair of legs in coveralls and boots was all Mike could see as a mechanic worked on the engine.

Mike stepped through the large doorway. "Excuse me. Is your boss here?"

No reply. Mike stepped closer and raised his voice to make sure the mechanic could hear him. "Excuse me sir, is Lisa Blake here?"

This time he was heard. The mechanic quickly ducked out from under the hatch and still facing away from Mike, grabbed a cloth off a rolling tool bench. "I've been called a lot of things in my life but 'sir' isn't one if them." Lisa Blake took off her baseball cap and turned to Mike, letting her shoulder length blond hair spill over her shoulders.

"Sorry, I didn't expect…"

"Me to be fixing my own plane?" She put her hands on her hips.

"Yes ma'am." Mike was embarrassed.

"Now that I'm used to," she said, still wiping the engine oil off her hands. "It's hard to get good help around here." She took a step closer and they hugged. "It's been a long time."

"I know it has." Mike noticed the hug lingered a couple of seconds too long.

"It took a while to get over you."

"It wasn't easy for me either, Lisa."

"Are you still happy you left the Corps when you did?" she asked.

He thought for a moment before replying. "I was very happy until recently."

"I still regret signing up again." She looked into his eyes knowingly. "We were good together."

Lisa had piloted many missions that Mike commanded during his years as a marine. She was one of the best flyers he knew who earned the respect of her peers not only due to her talent but also because of her lack of bravado. She simply had a job to do and she did it well, which was obvious by her rank of major at retirement.

"We were great together but let's not dwell on the past." Mike was slightly uncomfortable talking about a relationship that ended so many years ago. When Mike was offered his discharge papers he was ready to marry Lisa and settle down. Unfortunately, she wanted the military to be her life. She outranked him and it was a difficult relationship to maintain especially when they were deployed on different sides of the world. When she finally left the service, Mike had already met Sam and it was too late to salvage their past.

"You're becoming famous. I've seen your picture in the papers. Why are you here, Mike?"

"I wasn't kidding when I said on the phone that I'm in trouble. If you've been reading the papers I hope you realize just about everything you've read is a lie."

"I knew it didn't sound like you but people change."

"Well I haven't changed. I came down here to try to enlist the help of a client I thought I trusted but it turned out he's involved with the scheme that they're trying to blame on me. I barely made it out and now I'm sure they're looking for me again. Unfortunately, I can't run to the FBI because they're after me as well. I can fill you in on the details on the way because we're running out of time. Can you fly me to New York tonight?"

She thought for a moment. "I usually like some advance notice but I'm willing to make an exception for you." She unzipped her coveralls to reveal her pilot's uniform consisting of a white collared shirt and grey slacks. She stepped out of her boots and slipped on a pair of shiny black loafers. At a desk against the wall, she picked up her flight log. "I'd usually need to call in your name, rank, serial number, etc… in order to get clearance from the tower."

"Do you often take solo flights?" He didn't want to broadcast his whereabouts, for his protection as well as hers.

She closed the book and leaned back against the table. "I think that can be arranged. I often head up north to pick up fares. What's different about this? Can you afford the fee?"

Mike smiled. "I knew I could count on you. Name the price."

She smiled back. "Five grand is the usual bill to New York."

Mike reached into his inside coat pocket and took out a wad of bills. He counted off fifty one hundred dollar bills and handed them to her.

She walked back to the Learjet 40 and closed the hatch making sure it was secure. The stairs leading to the cabin were already folded down.

"This is some machine." Mike looked up and down the length of the sleek aircraft.

"I got it second hand and I'll be paying it off for the rest of my life."

She let Mike climb on board first, then followed him in and activated the mechanism that folded the stairs in and sealed the cabin.

"We don't have time to bring in an attendant so you'll have to settle for me. Welcome aboard Blake Charters." They were now ready for the flight.

CHAPTER FORTY

Special Agent David Reynolds walked quickly through the hallway on the eighth floor at 26 Federal Plaza to meet with his boss and Attorney General Jacobs. After the search for Michael Brennan came up empty, they decided he may have tried to leave the country so Reynolds sent his task force into the field. They scoured all points of exit and came up with some interesting clues.

Battaglia was already inside the office with Jacobs and the Agent in Charge of the New York region, Jake Holloway. Reynolds didn't knock upon entering. He and Holloway went back a long way. When Reynolds joined the Bureau and was paying his dues investigating bank robberies and kidnappings, he had reported to Holloway. They moved into financial crimes together and had become close over the years.

Jacobs was leaning against Holloway's desk. Although he liked to stay involved, he was trying not to interfere with the task force's investigation. He was only there to make sure that everything was being done to bring Brennan in and get him talking.

Jacobs asked, "What's the latest?"

Reynolds placed a folder on Holloway's desk and pointed to it. "Take a look at those. The wonders of face recognition technology. We pulled the tapes from Kennedy, LaGuardia and all the smaller local airports. Our guys have been running them through the program since early this morning."

Holloway opened the folder and laid the grainy black and white photographs flat for all of them to see. There were only about five people in the shot of a small airport terminal and one man's face was circled in red. It was Michael Brennan.

"Where is this?"

"Republic Airport out in Farmingdale," Reynolds answered as he sat across from Holloway's desk.

"How long did it take the techies to find him?" Jacobs asked.

Battaglia took this one. "The better part of the day. He was last seen in public at the Democratic Party fundraiser at the Plaza two nights ago. It was a lot of hours of tapes to analyze but these guys did a great job."

Reynolds jumped in. "After the positive ID, we sent a couple of agents out to Republic to grill the charter owners. They were cooperative and it turns out that our guy Brennan is now known as Mr. John Simon."

Holloway leaned back in his chair. "Where did they fly him?"

"Atlanta. He landed at about five this morning."

"I think it's safe to assume the Atlanta boys haven't located him, correct? Otherwise you would have come in here telling be about the takedown."

Reynolds nodded. "You've got it. I just got off the line with the Atlanta AIC and there was a homicide involving employees of a firm that's a large client of BNL. One that Brennan handled personally over the past few years."

"So he went down there to kill some more?" Holloway asked.

Reynolds shrugged. "That's one theory, and the obvious one, but you know I don't like to jump to conclusions."

"You're scouring the Atlanta area airports?" Holloway already knew the answer.

"We've got them all covered including the small ones in the outlying areas. We've had some positive IDs within the last hour from Dekalb Peachtree, which was where he landed this morning, but no photos or video. They're pretty far behind in security. We're monitoring several charters that left from various places close to the city shortly after the shootings. Two are headed to the New York area, one to L.A., and another to Houston." Reynolds read off his list.

"Passenger manifests?"

Reynolds continued. "We've got six on the flight to L.A., looks like a family headed to Disneyland. Three to Houston, all female. One of the New York flights has one male passenger landing in Westchester County Airport and the other coming our way has the pilot flying solo into Islip, out on the South Shore. This last one left from Dekalb so if we're to believe the workers who recognized his picture, this is the one to watch. We've got teams waiting at both New York airports and the pilots have already been instructed to hold off deplaning until we're out on the tarmac."

"If he's got millions in those offshore accounts that we found, he's probably got more somewhere else and another identity. He could have easily disappeared on a commercial flight or bought his own plane and vanished into oblivion." Holloway looked at the photo one last time and closed the folder.

Reynolds stood. "I've still got a feeling about this guy, Jake."

Battaglia laughed. "This guy and his feelings."

"I'm serious Pete. He's on one of those charters coming home. He's not the kind of guy to leave loose ends and I don't think he's finished."

"Where's his girlfriend?" Holloway asked.

Battaglia lost his smile. "We talked to her this morning at her father's penthouse on forty-eighth. She contacted us through the mayor's office and offered an interview. She's a legal advisor to Maddux and obviously a good attorney because she kicked us out after five minutes. A report came in a few hours later that she left with a man who said he was FBI and didn't return. The doorman got suspicious. He went up to the residence and found her bodyguards in a heap on the floor. They were beat up badly but they'll live."

Holloway looked at Reynolds. "So now we've got someone impersonating agents and kidnapping people involved in this investigation?"

"It appears that way, sir."

Holloway rubbed his chin. "Do you think Ms. Brodworth is involved with Brennan's scheme? She comes from a long line of money, doesn't she?"

"She's loaded but maybe it's the excitement of the game." Reynolds walked to the door. "I'll be out in Islip waiting for that solo flight. He's too smart to land at a bigger airport with tight security like Westchester."

CHAPTER FORTY-ONE

Sam sat on a bed in a well appointed apartment. She didn't know exactly where she was but she knew it was in Manhattan. When the phony FBI agent forced her out of her father's apartment and into his car, they didn't drive for more than ten minutes. He made her get on the floor of the car and keep her head down on the short drive. As the car turned left and right she tried to keep track of the route visually in her mind but after a few turns, she gave up.

The door opened and the man entered the room. "Are you comfortable Ms. Brodworth?"

"Oh yeah. I feel like I'm vacation." Sam lifted her right arm as far as she could, showing her captor the handcuffs that he used to attach her to the wrought iron bed frame.

He smiled. "You're a feisty one. I can see why Brennan likes you."

The man looked different than he had earlier in the day, Sam thought. His hair had been slicked back and darker. Now his shoulder length blond hair hung around his shoulders. The suit he wore was replaced with jeans and a tee shirt. She didn't realize until that moment that this was more than likely the man who attacked Mike at the Plaza. As he took a step closer, she noticed that the skin under his eye was slightly bruised.

He picked up her cell phone that sat just out of her reach on a bedside table.

"Every good girlfriend should have their boyfriend's number on speed dial. Wouldn't you agree?" He pressed a couple buttons, found what he was looking for and hit the auto dial.

"You're a good girlfriend Ms. Brodworth."

"Fuck you."

"A good girlfriend with a foul mouth. I can deal with that. Now please be quiet while I talk."

Mike sat in the co-pilot's seat next to Lisa Blake. They were talking about their lives since they parted ways years earlier. He still felt comfortable enough with her that he let her in on most of the details of his current situation.

Mike's cell phone vibrated in his pocket. "My phone's going off. Can I take it without interfering with your instruments?"

"Absolutely. Try to make it quick." She turned her concentration to the sky.

Mike looked at the incoming number. "Sam?"

"This is quite an honor Mr. Brennan." It was a voice he didn't recognize.

"Who the hell is this?" Mike struggled to keep his composure.

"Someone who has a great interest in your whereabouts," Sullivan answered.

Although Mike had no idea who he was speaking with he knew what was happening. "Why do we have to bring her into this? Let's settle this without anyone getting hurt."

"I have no plans to hurt her Mr. Brennan, but I had a feeling that she could get me what I want. And that's you. Make sure you're in New York tomorrow morning."

"Let me talk to her."

After a pause, Sam got on the line. "Mike?"

"Are you okay?"

"I'm fine but…"

Another pause and the man's voice returned. "Don't attempt to locate us. I'll be in touch bright and early."

Sullivan ended the call and cut the power to the phone. He reached over without warning, grabbed Sam's free wrist and attached it to the bed frame. Sam was now lying on the bed, her arms above her head, feeling very vulnerable. She instinctively tugged on her restraints.

He saw the look of fear in her eyes. "I'm not a savage, Ms. Brodworth. I just need to make sure you don't try to get away from me while we rest. Tomorrow's a big day."

"What are you going to do?" Her tough exterior was slowly crumbling.

"We're going to meet Mr. Brennan."

"He got the better of you once. This time he'll kill you if you hurt me. You know that don't you?"

He smiled and replied, "He won't have the chance."

Mike dialed his brother to let him know what happened. Tim had already spoken with his friend Paul Schmidt in Atlanta and heard about the shootings.

"According to Schmidt, you're at the top of the FBI's list."

"I think I knew that. The pilot just got instructions from the New York tower to hold on the tarmac and await further instructions."

"Shit." Tim said. "He told me about a task force that's been investigating your company along with a lot of others in the business. The combination of Barry dying, Jack Darvish turning up dead and you disappearing has them in a frenzy. You're the number one suspect."

"Any ideas?" Mike knew if they landed anywhere in the metropolitan area, they'd grab him immediately.

"Do you remember that place we used to visit as kids on the North Shore, not far from Barry's place in Cove Neck?" Tim asked.

"I remember. We used to watch that guy fly his homemade planes." Mike remembered visiting cousins out on Long Island when he was young. There was a wealthy family nearby that was somehow related to the Vanderbilts. They inherited a large estate and one of the eccentric sons would build his own light aircraft and fly them off his property. "Is that place still there?"

"Nassau County cops busted a drug runner flying in and out of there about six months ago on seventeen-hundred feet of runway. What kind of plane are you on?" Tim asked.

"It's a Lear. Seven passenger." Mike was looking around the cabin.

"Is the pilot willing to help?"

"I think so."

"Ask him how much runway he needs to land that thing."

"Her." Mike corrected.

"Her? Are you serious?"

Mike turned to Lisa. "How many feet of runway do you need to land?"

"I'm supposed to have almost twenty-seven hundred but I've done it in fifteen. Why?"

"Are you willing to divert to a landing strip about thirty miles northwest of Islip?"

"The FAA will be all over me for that but that's the least of my worries. If I divert from the course I've logged in New York airspace, they'll have F-16s on my ass in minutes."

Mike understood but continued to drive his point home. "If we land at Islip, I'll be arrested and will never get the chance to prove my innocence. I think these people I'm dealing with are too rich and powerful to let anything happen to them in the courts. I need the chance to dig up evidence before I get tossed in jail or I'll spend the rest of my life behind bars. You've got to help me," Mike pleaded. "Please."

She closed her eyes and shook her head. "God damn it! Why did I say yes to taking you up here in the first place?"

Mike didn't reply and gave her a moment to think about it.

"Now I know why you've been so successful in sales. I can only pray that you're telling me the truth because I don't want to see you hung out to dry. I'll divert."

"Thank you. I'll make sure you're compensated for your trouble." Mike put the phone back to his ear and worked out a meeting place with Tim near the landing strip and then put the phone back in his pocket.

"Here's what we've got to do," Lisa said, a plan forming in her head. "They've already instructed me to loop around and come in over the Long Island Sound from the North. I'll call in an emergency and tell them I can't make it to Islip. If I come in wobbly and put it down on your strip, we can probably avoid being shot out of the sky. Are you sure the runway is in good condition?"

"All I know is that someone was using it six months ago."

She quickly calculated the risk in her head. "I can always abort if I see something wrong."

CHAPTER FORTY-TWO

Reynolds sat in his unmarked vehicle with three other agents outside the main terminal at Islip Airport. They were parked just inside the security gate next to a van filled with heavily armed agents that were going to take Mike Brennan off the plane when he landed. He knew his guy was on that plane because there was no way he'd let it be known he was on an easily traceable private charter. He must have paid off the pilot to not report a passenger.

He was monitoring the control tower's transmissions with the incoming flights when he heard it.

"NR2352 inbound from Atlanta, do you read?"

The female pilot answered with her tail number. "NR2352, I'm experiencing engine trouble. I just made landfall on the North Shore but I can't hold my altitude. I'll never make it to Islip, I've got to put down up here. I've got less than a minute air time."

The air traffic controller replied, "NR2352, can you make it to Republic? They've got enough runway for you."

"I'm losing it tower. I'm going down now, in control but can't maintain altitude. There's a strip dead ahead that looks long enough, I'll put down there."

The controller remained calm. "That's probably the Vanderbilt estate in Old Westbury. I'll dispatch emergency vehicles immediately. Good Luck."

"Thank you tower. Out."

Reynolds slammed his hand on the dashboard startling the agent in the passenger seat. "That son of a bitch!"

"What?" The agent was puzzled.

"That's our fucking plane! It's going to land up on the north shore while we're sitting here like idiots. Call Nassau County PD and tell them to get as many units as they can spare out to that Vanderbilt estate. He's on that plane."

Lisa Blake felt guilty about misleading the air traffic controllers but thought that she was performing a noble act in helping Mike with his pursuit of the truth. It didn't hurt that they had a past and could have had a future if she had made different decisions a few years back.

"Hold on tight now. This is going to be bumpy and I'll be stopping in half the distance stated in the manufacturer's specs."

"Are you sure you want to go through with this?" Mike was worried about what the authorities would deduce from this incident. His name didn't appear on her log so if he got out of the area before any of the emergency response team arrived, she'd be clear.

"We've reached the point of no return. I'm not giving up now." She rolled the wings back and forth to make it look like the plane was having difficulty staying on course. She dropped her altitude to less than a hundred feet and came in over the tree tops bordering the strip. The ground came up faster than Mike expected and he braced himself for a hard landing but was surprised by the light touch when the wheels made contact with the concrete. The engine whined as Lisa enabled the reverse thrusters and the plane came to a stop with no more than a hundred feet to spare.

"Thanks for flying with Blake Charters. I hope you enjoyed your flight." She quickly removed her seat belt. Within moments she was opening the side door.

"I can't thank you enough, Lisa. I'd probably be dead if you didn't get me out of Atlanta."

"Now don't make an ass of me. Go and find something to prove you really are a good guy. If I find out you swindled me, I'll hunt you down." She smiled before she quickly went down the three steps to the ground.

Mike took a wad of bills from his coat pocket, followed her out, and handed it to her. "Here, take this. Pay off some of the mortgage on this beast and then take a vacation."

She looked at the roll of hundred dollar bills in her hand. "I can't accept this." She moved to hand it back to him.

"You don't have a choice." He backed away from her and then turned and started running for the trees. He could hear sirens in the distance and he had to move quickly to get to the rendezvous point to meet Tim. When he reached the edge of the pavement he turned back to give Lisa a wave but she was already inside the engine hatch. She needed to make it look like there was engine trouble and she had to work fast. The NTSB and the FBI would be there in minutes.

The layout of the property hadn't changed much since Mike was a kid so he easily followed a path around the mansion and down to a service road. The sirens were getting louder but they were now behind him and probably on the scene already. He continued jogging down the road to the gated entrance. Just inside the wrought iron fence sat the same SUV that Tim had rented the night before.

As Mike got closer, Tim lowered his window. "Push the gate open and then close it when I pull out."

Mike did as instructed then hopped into the passenger seat. Tim sped out to the main road and turned south toward the Northern State Parkway. Several police cruisers past them heading in the opposite direction toward the landing site. Just before they turned onto the entrance ramp, an unmarked dark blue sedan came skidding around the corner toward the air field. The light on the dashboard was flashing but there wasn't a scream of a siren.

Tim looked in the rearview mirror as the car sped down the road. "Those are feds. It seems you're pretty popular right now."

"Let's get as far away from here as possible."

"Did you have a nice trip?" Tim asked.

"Just lovely, thanks," Mike said as he took out a notepad.

"Before we go on I need to know how the hell you got that lady to land on an unmarked strip."

"I told you I'm a good salesman but it didn't hurt that we dated when I was in the Corps. She flew my team all over the world and I think she still trusts me."

Tim could only shake his head and smile.

"My main concern right now is getting Sam back unharmed. If she gets hurt in any way, I'll never rest until I find every single person involved and make them suffer."

"I don't completely disagree but I'll say this one last time because the cop in me is screaming. Let's bring what we've got to the authorities and let them help get Sam back. We can go straight to Manhattan and I'll call some friends on the NYPD. They'll make sure you're treated well."

"Thanks for the concern but I need to do this alone. After finding out that Davenport is involved I'm beginning to understand that the scale of this operation is far reaching. Who knows what law enforcement agents are involved as well? I can't trust anyone but you right now." He held up his notepad. "I've been doing some thinking but I can't come up with anything. I can't get past those companies that Jack found that are behind Layden and Dowd, Prometheus Holdings and Atlas Consultants. They're somehow involved with all this and I'm thinking that maybe they control the process that Melvin started to tell me about before he died."

"He didn't go into detail?" Tim asked.

"He alluded to the fact that there was one central entity controlling various firms. He didn't know how many were involved but knew it was more than BNL. This guy Wilson in Atlanta was shot before he finished telling me about a theory he had that someone is out there who controls BNL. Unfortunately, he never got the chance to finish." Mike looked out the window at the trees flying by. "I think there's a reason Jack hit a dead end when he tried to find their corporate resolutions. We've got to find Prometheus and Atlas."

Tim pulled out into the middle lane of the parkway. "Let's get to a hotel and catch some sleep before these assholes contact you again."

CHAPTER FORTY-THREE

Reynolds pulled in beside a fire truck on the edge of the landing strip. The small Lear jet looked much larger than its actual size, sitting on the short strip surrounded by tall trees. There were several agents surrounding the aircraft while the pilot was standing off to the side with the Nassau County cops. She was leaning against a squad car drinking a bottle of water. The cops thought she had just been through a traumatic experience and were trying to make her comfortable.

Reynolds thought differently. "Can I have a word with the pilot alone officers?" He was holding his badge out for them to see. The cops backed off reluctantly, not liking the fact that a fed was infringing on their turf.

When they were out of earshot Reynolds spoke. "Had some mechanical difficulties did you?"

"That's right, Special Agent who?"

"I apologize for not introducing myself. I'm Special Agent David Reynolds with the FBI. I've reason to believe that you didn't have engine trouble tonight."

"That's ridiculous. You think I'd drop my very expensive plane on a strip of concrete more than a thousand feet too short? I've got my life's savings buried in that thing."

"I've got another idea for you Ms. Blake." He already knew her story. Battaglia, back at the office, pulled her service record while he was speeding toward the landing site from Islip Airport. "A fellow marine asked you to do him a favor tonight and not report him as a passenger on a flight up to New York. When he found out we were looking for him, he asked you to make an emergency landing far enough away from the airport so that he'd have time to escape."

If she was surprised by the accuracy of his description of the evening's events, she didn't show it. "I don't know what you're talking about."

"Did he tell you that he killed his boss and another young man from his firm?" He raised his voice slightly. "The kid's neck was broken and he was left to die in a goddamned laundry chute in a hotel." He looked at her with contempt. "What got to you? Was it money or just his good looks?"

"You're a jerk Agent Reynolds. If you had anything solid on me I'd already be in the back of your car heading wherever it is they take federal prisoners these days."

He looked at her for a few seconds and turned to walk away, disgusted.

"I love being right," Lisa said, mostly to herself.

Reynolds heard her and turned back quickly. "I'll take you down Ms. Blake. Distinguished service record or not. If you aided and abetted a criminal and filed a false flight plan, you're going to jail."

She stared at him expressionless. He left her leaning against the police cruiser and rounded up his agents. He'd leave this part of the investigation to the local police and the NTSB, not wanting to waste any more of his time on her.

CHAPTER FORTY-FOUR

Mike was awakened from a fitful sleep in his hotel room on the side of the Grand Central Parkway near LaGuardia Airport. His cell phone was ringing on the nightstand. He grabbed it quickly and looked at the number display. It was Sam's.

"Yes."

"Mr. Brennan? Or should I say the infamous Mr. Brennan?"

Mike knew who it was. "What is it you want? I'm prepared to pay you anything you ask."

Sullivan ignored the offer. "Have you been watching the morning news for the past hour?"

Mike looked at his watch. It was 7am.

"You look great on T.V." The connection was cut.

"Turn on the news," Mike said to Tim who was sitting on the other bed in the room listening to the quick conversation.

Tim hit the power on the remote and the network news appeared on the screen. Across the bottom of the screen were the words *Special Report* with Mike's picture in the upper right hand corner. It took him a couple of seconds to realize it was his own image. He tried to concentrate on the words of the news anchor.

"Michael Brennan of Manhattan, Executive Vice President at BNL Securities on Water Street, is suspected in the murders of one of the company's founders, Melvin Barry and a technology expert at the firm, Jack Darvish. It's also believed that he embezzled millions of dollars from the company."

Mike moved to the edge of the bed and turned up the volume.

The anchor continued. "The FBI has been looking for Mr. Brennan since the Nassau County Medical Examiner changed the ruling of Mr. Barry's death from accidental to homicide."

The image shifted to Davenport's building in Atlanta. "In an odd coincidence, an employee of a firm in Atlanta, Davenport and Associates, was shot and killed this afternoon at a hotel in the business district by a coworker. The gunman was then shot and killed by a team of FBI agents that had them under surveillance. Mr. Anthony Davenport, a longtime client of Michael Brennan and BNL, was unavailable for comment."

The screen cut to a shot of Philip Layden in his office at BNL. He was shaking his head and saying, "I find it very hard to believe that Mike Brennan would be involved in anything like this. I know he's been having personal problems but nothing that could lead to…"

The on scene reporter, Cynthia Highsmith, cut him off mid sentence. "What do you make of the allegations that Mr. Brennan was behind the incidents of market manipulation that have now been made public?"

Layden answered calmly, "Ms. Highsmith, these are new charges that the FBI and the Attorney General have brought against our firm and we are cooperating fully in resolving the issue."

Highsmith chimed in again. "This is more than an 'issue' as you call it, isn't it Mr. Layden? The FBI has reported that Michael Brennan, a senior officer at BNL, has offshore accounts totaling close to a hundred million dollars. Is this all part of Mr. Brennan's personal problems you mentioned?" She was tough.

The camera cut back to Layden and Mike looked at his smug expression. "I have no further comment."

Cynthia looked directly into the camera. "This is Cynthia Highsmith reporting live from the offices of BNL on Water Street where federal agents have been on scene tearing through the companies records. Watch my special report tonight at eight o'clock to hear more. Back to you in the studio, Mark."

Mike stood and slammed his hand into the television, shutting off the power. "That bastard is hanging me out to dry. I knew they were going to do this after they went so far as to kill Jack. Seeing Layden say it live is just surreal."

His cell phone rang again and he grabbed it quickly.

"Yes."

"Did you get a good feel for your predicament, Mr. Brennan?"

"I'm beginning to get the picture."

"Meet me at Grand Central Station, alone and unarmed, under the clock at the information center in the middle of the Grand Concourse."

"When?"

"One hour. Now here's the deal you can't refuse. I'll let your beautiful girlfriend go the minute I have a hold on you. We'll go to a safe place where you'll sign a confession stating your guilt in the market manipulation and insider trading and we'll make the murder accusations disappear."

"I'll be there in an hour."

"Remember, if I feel that you're not alone, the deal's off and you don't get a second chance." He paused. "And neither does Sam." The line went dead.

They gathered the few things they brought with them as he quickly told Tim about the conversation. They left the hotel and got onto the Grand Central Parkway which took them over the Triboro Bridge to upper Manhattan. When they got off the FDR Drive at the Forty-Second Street exit, Mike stopped the car to let Tim out. He had to follow the instructions and pull up to the terminal alone. He drove the remaining few blocks alone and parked the car illegally on Vanderbilt Avenue on the west side of the station.

The taxi stand was crowded at this time in the morning and the line of cabs went a hundred yards down Vanderbilt Avenue. He weaved through the commuters and made it through the entrance to a balcony overlooking the vast concourse. He wanted to get a view of the meeting place from above so he slowly approached the railing and peered over the side.

The main concourse of Grand Central Station is one of the largest open indoor areas in Manhattan. The number of commuters and tourists walking through at any given time was overwhelming. There were hundreds of people walking in different directions and more than twenty were loitering around the big clock in the center. Some were in pairs and others alone. Unfortunately, the information center was a popular meeting point because it was so easy to find. He had no idea which of the men could be the one who was holding Sam.

Whoever was looking for him knew what he looked like and how to contact him so he decided to move to the center of the floor. His heart pounded loudly, blocking out the noise of the crowd as he descended the stairs. His eyes moved back and forth and up and down struggling to focus on the other balconies that topped the east and north side of the concourse.

As he drew near the middle, a cop came into his peripheral vision. He realized then that not only was the goon holding Sam looking for him but the NYPD had a bulletin out on him. He quickly turned his face away and continued forward. Circling the clock, he eyed the strangers standing around but no one was holding his eye contact for more than a second. He looked at his watch, thinking he may have missed the meeting but he was exactly on time. The cell phone in his pocket rang and he pulled it out and put it to his ear.

"I'm glad to see you can be trusted Mr. Brennan. Look toward the west side of the concourse. See the sign for the Forty-Fifth Street Passage?"

Mike found the sign on the side of the main stairway.

"I see it."

"Walk to the right of the stairs and continue to the shoe shine stand. Hop up on the chair and get yourself a shine." The connection was broken.

Mike again scanned the crowd for anyone on a cell phone and found too many to pinpoint his man. He walked as instructed, passing a coffee shop on the right and a candy store on the left. Ahead, next to the entrance to the Forty-Fifth Street Passage was the shoe shine stand. Mike climbed up into an empty chair and looked at the people passing by. Again, nobody looked at him for more than an instant.

When the shoe shine man was finished with Mike's second shoe he looked up and said in heavily accented English, "Mr. Brennan?"

Mike stood up. "What the hell is going on?"

The man cowered as Mike got down from the stand and walked toward him. He backed up a few steps and pointed behind him. "Walk slowly down the passage."

Mike looked beyond the man, down the long hallway. "God damn it."

He ignored the other customers who put down their papers to watch the short exchange. He walked at a deliberate pace down the passage looking intently at the people coming toward him. Occupying the left wall were two shops that were more like large windows with counters. The first was a tennis shop where the man behind the counter was busy restringing a racket. The next sold and repaired watches and the lone shopkeeper sat with a jewelers monocle engrossed in his work.

Mike continued toward the end where the tunnel broke off in two directions. To the left, a smaller hallway led out to Forty-Fifth Street near the Roosevelt Hotel. To the right was a metal gate pulled across what looked like an extension of the passage. He peered through the gate into the darkness, struggling to see where it led. He was concentrating so hard that he didn't hear someone walk up behind him.

"Looking for someone Mr. Brennan?"

Mike spun around to see Sam walking arm in arm with her captor. He recognized him as the man in Jack's room at the Plaza Hotel.

"Oh Mike," she said almost inaudibly. Tears were welled up in her eyes and she was visibly shaking. She tried to move toward him but Sullivan held her tightly. Mike could see the gun in his waistband.

"Take your jacket off and turn around slowly," Sullivan instructed.

Mike did as he was told, satisfying the man that he was unarmed. Sullivan moved past Mike toward the metal gate, still holding Sam close. Mike stepped in front of him. "Let her go," he demanded.

"I told you I'd let her go when you're in my grip. Patience, Mr. Brennan. Patience." Sullivan said. He stepped around Mike and slid the unlocked gate open. "After you, please."

Mike walked into the darkness of the hallway and heard the gate close behind them. The man said, "Keep moving. Your eyes will adjust to the darkness."

Twenty yards down the tunnel Sullivan stopped walking. "Stop here and give me your hand."

The long haired man grabbed his wrist and handcuffed him to a drainpipe hanging from the wall. Sullivan turned to Sam. "Go back through the gate and keep walking. If you call the police I'll kill your boyfriend and then find you and kill you too."

Sam reached out to touch Mike's shackled hand but her arm was pushed away by their captor. "Leave now before I change my mind," he growled.

"Go Sam. I'll be fine." Mike tried to sound brave but had no way of knowing if he'd ever see her again.

She turned and left the two men in the darkness. Mike watched as she pushed back the gate and stepped into the lighted hallway. He knew she'd call his brother immediately but could only hope that the crazy man holding him was acting alone and didn't have someone back there waiting to grab Sam again.

"You enjoy intimidating women?" Mike needled the man.

"You keep your fucking mouth shut. You're god damned lucky she's walking away right now because I could have done anything I wanted to her. Show me a little respect," Sullivan said as he was removing the handcuffs. "Let's move. If you try anything I'll put a bullet between your eyes. I owe you for the lamp to the head the other night."

Mike believed him and began walking. "Where are we going?"

There was no reply. The deserted passageway had a dim light bulb every thirty feet, barely illuminating the space to the next light. The damp air in the tunnel was musty. They continued forward and past several doors, all shut tight with padlocks.

Sullivan stopped at a door. "Here we are."

A terrifying thought entered Mike's head at that moment. This man could easily kill him in the depths under Grand Central and his body would never be found. The man stuck a key in the door, waited a moment for the door to slide open, then pushed Mike lightly through the opening.

Sullivan seemed to read Mike's thoughts. "Don't worry Brennan, I'm not going to kill you." He followed Mike through the doorway, stuck the key in the wall, and the doors slid shut. Mike hadn't realized that they had stepped into a dingy freight elevator.

"When these doors open again we'll walk through the lobby and out the front door. On the street you'll see a blue BMW. Get in on the passenger side and slide across to the driver's seat. I'll be two steps behind you with my finger on the trigger." He took the weapon from his pocket. It was a 9mm automatic with a silencer attached. Mike looked at the gun and swallowed hard, his expression unchanged. He couldn't show this maniac that he was the least bit scared.

The elevator slowed to a stop and the doors slid open. As they entered the bright lobby, Sullivan moved his head close to Mike's. "I wouldn't feel bad burying a couple of hollow points in your back."

Mike was looking straight ahead and continued walking toward the door. He immediately realized where he was because a client had an office in the building. The front doors led to Lexington Avenue between Forty-Fifth Street and Forty-Sixth Street. The structure had an atrium that rose several floors in the center with artwork being displayed all around the perimeter. He felt helpless as they crossed the wide open lobby, bathed in sunlight from the massive skylight above. He had to squint after having been in the darkness of the bowels of the building.

The guard at the desk didn't look up from his newspaper as the two men walked by him. When they reached the revolving doors leading to the street Mike toyed with the idea of breaking into a run as soon as he hit fresh air. He decided to wait for a better opportunity. Knowing the reason hollow point bullets were known as 'cop killers', he pictured himself getting only a few feet away before he felt his back explode from the projectile fired from the madman's gun. He'd be left sprawled on the sidewalk with people gathering to gawk at his bloody remains.

The BMW was directly in front as promised. Mike crossed the sidewalk, opened the passenger door and slid behind the wheel with Sullivan immediately following. The car was pointing south on Lexington Avenue with the keys in the ignition.

Sullivan turned in his seat toward Mike with the gun in his hand pointed directly at Mike's abdomen. "Start her up and stay in the center lane," Sullivan ordered.

Mike started the car and pulled into the heavy mid morning traffic. His heart was now beating slower as he calmed down slightly and was able to gather his thoughts. He made a quick mental list of his options, at the top of which was the least attractive choice; letting this madman reach their destination. Would the people behind this massive market manipulation scheme be happy with a confession? Knowing that Melvin Barry and Jack Darvish were murdered, he had serious doubts about what the real plans were for him.

The second option was equally as unattractive. He could try to open the door and jump out of the car but he fully believed he'd be shot. *Unless I could create a diversion*, he thought. *But what kind of diversion could be made inside a car?*

Mike looked ahead half a block. There was a delivery truck double parked in the left lane and Mike's plan developed over the course of three seconds. He accelerated slightly, almost imperceptibly. When he was less than ten yards behind the truck he pressed the gas pedal to the floor. The powerful engine made the car leap forward as he turned the wheel to the left.

Mike was braced for the impact but it caught his captor off guard and he didn't have enough time to prepare. The airbags exploded from the steering wheel and the dashboard on the passenger side. Mike looked over at the stunned man who looked like he sustained a broken nose from the force of the deployment. Mike had his arms in front of his face before the car made contact so his face was spared any damage. His arms were aching but he could move them freely.

Mike's door was open and he was out of the car before the man had the chance to recover from the initial shock. The passenger side airbag was covered in blood but Mike didn't wait around to find out the extent of his injuries. He dodged cars as he crossed to the west side of Lexington Avenue and ran south toward the back entrance of Grand Central Terminal. He ignored the pain in his arms and picked up speed on wobbly legs.

Mike heard a sharp ping from the wall of the building on his right. He turned his head slightly toward the noise to see a small chunk of concrete fall to the ground. Another ping and more chunks went flying, stinging the back of Mike's neck. He turned back toward the accident scene to see the madman thirty yards behind him covered in blood, running down the center of Lexington Avenue with his gun held out in front of him.

Mike now knew that he had to get some cover before taking a direct hit. A few more steps and he was at the glass doors marking the entrance to the terminal. He heard a loud bang and expected the doors to shatter. Instead, he heard only the screams of pedestrians on the street. He figured his pursuer removed the silencer or switched guns.

He turned again quickly toward the street expecting to see the man at full speed heading toward him. Instead he saw a police officer bent over the trunk of his cruiser, leaning on his elbows. His left hand still supporting the weapon held in his right. The cop's partner was already running to where the gunman was laying on the ground writhing in pain. All Mike could hear now were sirens and the shouts of onlookers.

People rushed past him as he stood in the doorway, trying to get a closer look at the action outside. He quickly regained his composure and decided to keep moving away from the scene. Chances were that someone saw him running from the man and they'd start pointing the cops in his direction.

He pushed his way against the rush through the doors and saw five uniformed cops running toward him. He hesitated a moment before he realized they were running outside to back up their fellow officers. He kept his head down and continued toward the main concourse, the place where this ridiculous circle started not more than twenty minutes earlier. Once he was back in the crowded terminal his first thought was to find Sam. He pulled out his phone and dialed Tim's number.

"Mike?"

"Yeah, it's me. Is Sam with you?" He held his head down, walking quickly toward the next train out. He figured the best thing would be to get out of the city as fast as possible.

"She's right here with me. I have my police scanner on and I thought that was you dropped by the NYPD out on Lexington."

"That was the asshole who took Sam."

"Where the hell are you?"

"I'm back in the main concourse and it's crawling with cops. I need to get out of here while they're still concerned with the activity outside. I'm getting on the next train out." He quickly scanned the departure board.

"Can you pick me up in White Plains?"

"We'll be there."

"I'll see you in a little while." Mike ended the call and got on the train, settling into a seat in the rear.

CHAPTER FORTY-FIVE

David Reynolds was back in his small office at Federal Plaza. He had spent most of the day at the BNL offices with his agents. He wouldn't admit it to Battaglia, but he was being consumed by the case. His social life had been nearly non existent for the past year, mainly because of this investigation. The chain of events of the past week, beginning with the death of Melvin Barry, had kept him on the job for close to twenty four hours a day.

His chart of suspects and companies was in the same place hanging on the wall but he rearranged the tags. Michael Brennan and BNL were now squarely in the center with all others arranged around them. The latest tool he was working on was a timeline. He found them useful when working through an investigation to plot when major actions took place.

He had a long and a short term line. The long one graphed a span of many years and had events like company start dates, hiring of employees, and revenues. The short line started with the deaths of Barry and Darvish, then the discovery of Brennan's offshore accounts followed by his disappearance, the murder in Atlanta and finally the charter flight that had to make an emergency landing out on the island.

The short term line all pointed to Michael Brennan but it was too obvious. It was never this easy to connect the dots. BNL and several other brokerage houses, large and small, had been under investigation for a hell of a long time and Brennan all of the sudden falls in his lap. There was no doubt in his mind that Brennan was the key to the puzzle but what Reynolds would find out when he caught him was another story. He had to bring him in if he wanted answers. Brennan knew something that made him run the way he did. Reynolds knew he wasn't going to get the answers from the remaining partner of BNL. His only answer was to find Brennan.

CHAPTER FORTY-SIX

"He's fit to go officers." The doctor scribbled something on a clipboard. "You're a lucky man." He patted Sullivan on the shoulder then turned and left the private examination room.

Sullivan stood and held his arms up to the uniformed patrolman standing nearby. The cop put a cuff on one wrist and turned Sullivan around to connect his wrists behind his back. Sullivan winced slightly in pain, not wanting to show the police any signs of weakness. His chest was badly bruised where the cop on the street put a bullet into his Kevlar vest. The shock of the impact caused some damage but that was minimal compared to the fact that he'd most certainly be dead right now if he didn't have that thing on.

They rode the elevator in silence to the lobby where another bunch of uniforms were waiting to escort the prisoner to his next stop. Sullivan knew this was all just a formality because his employer would pull some strings shortly to have him released.

They left St. Vincent's Hospital through the emergency bay and piled into three squad cars. Sullivan thought it a little much to have three cars and eight officers in the caravan to Bellevue Hospital. What he did was slightly off the wall but was a psychological examination really necessary? He'd been trained well on how to deal with interrogators which he could easily adapt to deal with psychologists. Sullivan would have them believing anything he wanted them to believe.

Bellevue was the main hospital in New York City where extensive psych services were available and was always the first stop for anyone who commits a crime and is deemed potentially unstable. The fact that Sullivan was so cool and collected after the incident on Lexington Avenue was what prompted the doctors at St. Vincent's to recommend the trip downtown.

The cops tried to pull into the emergency dock at Bellevue but found it jammed up with ambulances. They were forced to drive around front to bring the prisoner in. This hospital was famous for its ability to attract reporters which was something the officers wanted to avoid. A photographer would snap their picture on the way in without even knowing who they were, or what crime was committed, hoping it was potential news.

The three marked cars double parked a half block from the main entrance. Policy dictated they couldn't take the cuffs off the prisoner which unfortunately would immediately attract the attention of the news hounds. As they neared the entrance, they heard a truck backfire. It was loud enough to make the two cops in front turn toward the noise. They immediately realized there was no truck in the direction of the noise and assumed gunfire. In the split second it took for them to come to that conclusion, Sullivan dropped to his knees and then fell hard on his face. The officers alongside and behind him had seen his head jerk immediately after the noise and drew their guns and took defensive positions.

The sergeant in the group immediately grabbed his radio off his belt and yelled into it. "Unit 2-5-6. We've got shots fired in front of Bellevue. Our prisoner is down."

The radio crackled back, "Backup is on the way."

The sergeant first looked to see that his men were accounted for and after being satisfied that they were alright and safely behind parked cars, he looked at the body of the prisoner face down on the sidewalk with his hands cuffed behind his back. The hole in the back of the man's head was exactly in the middle and there was so much blood flowing from the front of his head that his face must have been blown clear off. He put the radio to his mouth again, "We need SWAT here. Possible sniper in the area."

CHAPTER FORTY-SEVEN

The air was crisp and clear on the shores of Lake George, just north of Albany. Sam's parents had purchased some lakefront property before the real estate and tourist boom hit the area. They eventually built a house that they visited infrequently. It was the perfect spot for Mike, Sam, and Tim to regroup without fear of being found by whoever was looking for them.

Mike and Sam were sitting on a bench near the shore as Tim approached.

"I just spoke with my guy at the NYPD and Paul Schmidt at the F.B.I."

"How is my new friend Special Agent Schmidt?" Mike asked.

"He's not a happy guy. He still believes that you're innocent but it's becoming increasingly harder for him to keep up the story that he didn't run into you."

"I owe him for that."

"That's exactly right. He wants to be in on anything we uncover."

"He's got a deal. That's a small price to pay for what he did for me."

"What's the news from the NYPD?" Sam asked.

Tim continued. "The long haired maniac that was chasing Mike was wearing a vest when he took a slug to the chest on Lexington Avenue."

"Have they found out who he works for yet?" Sam continued her line of questioning.

"That's going to be somewhat difficult," Tim said hesitantly.

Mike grimaced. "He escaped?"

"Not exactly." Tim paused. "His head exploded as he was being transferred from St. Vincent's to Bellevue. He got out of the back of a squad car and a sniper placed a bullet in the back of his head and removed his brain and face."

Mike shook his head. "I assume the shooter got away clean?"

"No trace whatsoever. All they know is the bullet probably came from a hotel down the street. They've got no leads right now. I think it's safe to say, nothing will turn up either."

Mike closed his eyes and rubbed his temples, trying to figure out his next step.

"It looks like whoever is running this show is methodically eliminating anyone who might know something and is about to talk." His eyes remained closed.

Tim agreed, "That sounds right and unfortunately your somewhere near the top of that list."

Mike opened his eyes to look at his brother. "Have you got any good news?"

Tim shrugged. "I don't know if this is helpful but Schmidt gave me something else. I gave him your list of stocks that you thought were being manipulated in the market and he found a couple firms that seemed to pop up more than others.

Mike asked, "Who are they?"

He took a sheet of paper out of his pocket and read from it. "Duncan and A.C. Conklin. You know them?"

"Yeah, they're a couple of tiny shops. They were respectable back in the seventies but went downhill when the market boomed. They operate in that gray area that investigators have a hard time prosecuting."

Tim looked at his notes again. "They were brought up on charges a couple of years ago for having mob connections."

"Was it ever made public?" Sam asked.

Tim shook his head. "The charges were dropped before the case made it to the grand jury. Mob cases have a funny way of falling through the cracks."

Mike was silent for a few seconds as he processed this new information. He finally gathered his thoughts. "This could be the answer."

Sam looked at him, not quite understanding. "The answer to what?"

"Two things. On the night before Melvin died he told me he felt there were a number of firms involved."

"And?" Tim prodded.

"And he always had the feeling that they were being controlled by a central entity. Down in Atlanta, Wilson was alluding to a similar pattern just before he was killed."

"What's that?" Sam asked.

"He told me he thought the same people who tried to keep his family from regaining their lost wealth during the Great Depression might be the same bunch who are controlling BNL and working with Davenport."

Sam interrupted. "This just gets better and better. The same gang of crooks that's been running the bookmaking operations from Manhattan apartments for almost a century could be the same people controlling one of the largest brokerage houses in the country."

"Was the mafia that big back in the thirties?" Tim asked.

"You ever hear of a guy called Al Capone?" Sam's expression twisted slightly as she continued. "But then again, he was a common thug. Does the mafia really have the expertise and knowledge to manage such a broad scheme involving something as complicated as the stock market?"

Mike nodded and replied, "I know what you're saying. You usually read about a two bit gangster who ropes a broker into a scam to make a few hundred grand before the broker gets his license pinched."

They sat in silence for a moment when an idea came to Mike and Tim at the same time. Mike looked at his brother. "I think it's worth a try, don't you?"

Tim nodded, understanding the question. "He's as good a place to start as anything I've got."

Sam, not following the conversation, was getting frustrated. "What the hell are you two talking about?"

Mike answered, "We grew up in a part of Queens that for some reason had a pretty high percentage of gangsters. Have you heard the name Frank Martelli?"

Sam nodded. "As in the Martelli crime family? They're on the top of the mayor's list but unfortunately, Frank Martelli has an incredibly adept legal team. Maddux has been trying to put that guy away since he got elected."

"I went to school with his son Joe," Mike stated.

Sam raised her eyebrows. "You never told me you knew them."

Mike smiled. "You never asked."

"Did you know him well?"

"We played baseball together from little league until we were eighteen years old. I had many a Sunday dinner at the Martelli household before they moved out to the North Shore. He and Melvin Barry were practically neighbors."

"Didn't the son go on to law school?" Sam asked.

"Columbia Law. Joe's a smart guy and has his own practice now but he's almost solely retained by his father and his businesses. He's part of that talented legal team you're talking about."

Sam was visibly surprised by this recent revelation. "Interesting," was all she said.

Tim chimed in. "Have you kept in touch with him at all?"

"We've spoken a few times over the years and I ran into him at a Yankee game last season. We had dinner afterwards at a restaurant in the old neighborhood."

"Do you think he'd talk to you about this?" Tim asked.

"It's all we've got right now. I have to try." Mike declared. "Unfortunately I can't do it by phone."

Sam confirmed Mike's supposition. "I'm sure all their lines are bugged. They've been under investigation for years."

"I have to go there. I know he'll meet with me."

CHAPTER FORTY-EIGHT

In the press room in City Hall, a reporter stood from his seat. "Mr. Mayor. Is it true that the man who was shot by officers near Grand Central Terminal was the same man killed outside Bellevue?"

"Yes, that's true," the mayor said into the microphone.

"And he was wearing a bullet proof vest at the time of the first shooting?"

The mayor looked back to the police commissioner who was standing behind him with the rest of his entourage. Maddux was surprised that this bit of news already got out. The commissioner nodded. It would come out sooner or later.

Maddux turned to the reporter. "He was wearing a vest."

Another reporter stood. "Was he a member of law enforcement?"

"His identity has not been confirmed," Maddux answered quickly.

The mayor looked around at the crowd of reporters gathered at City Hall and reluctantly called on Cynthia Highsmith, who earlier in the day interviewed Philip Layden at the BNL offices.

She stood up at her seat. "Your honor, there have been reports that the deceased man was pursuing an individual on Lexington Avenue and was firing a silenced weapon when the officer shot him. Has this been verified?" She sat back down.

"The police department has pulled security tapes from stores along Lexington and they're being reviewed as we speak." The mayor scanned the room for another question but before he could call on another reporter, he was interrupted.

"A follow-up sir, if you don't mind." Highsmith stood again.

Maddux had purposely moved quickly to avoid a second question from her but wasn't fast enough. "Yes Cynthia, go ahead."

"One of your legal advisors, Samantha Brodworth, is in a long term relationship with Michael Brennan, the man accused of killing a partner of BNL and also embezzling millions of dollars from their clients. Have you spoken with her about this and is there any connection between today's shootings and BNL?"

Maddux expected the questions about Sam and was prepared. "I'll make no further comments regarding an ongoing investigation."

The mayor's press secretary stepped up to the podium and Maddux moved aside.

"That concludes the press conference for today folks. We'll keep you posted as the investigation continues. Thank you."

Maddux and all the people who were standing behind him turned and exited the press room as reporters continued to yell out questions. They entered a large office the mayor often used after meeting the press. Waiting inside the room with his own entourage of aides and Secret Service agents was Vice President Browning. As soon as the door was closed he spoke up, "What the hell Maddux? Haven't you got anything solid yet?"

The mayor didn't reply directly but turned to the police commissioner, Dan Healy. "Dan, will you please update the Vice President?"

"The commander of Midtown North called me just as the press arrived and told me they confirmed that this maniac was chasing someone down Lex this morning."

"How the hell did Cynthia Highsmith know that?" The mayor was angry.

Healy answered the rhetorical question. "I guess she's got a source within the department."

"I suggest you look into that, Dan," Maddux said.

"Unfortunately, I've got more news that no doubt will appear on Ms. Highsmith's program tonight and you're not going to want to hear it."

"I don't have time for games Dan. Spill it," Maddux said.

"The guy the perp was chasing was Michael Brennan."

Maddux let it sink in for a few seconds. "You mean the guy who's dating one of my legal advisors and the guy who I spoke with at the fundraiser?"

"We've already informed Agent Reynolds from the special task force that's leading the charge on BNL."

"What did Reynolds have to say?" the mayor asked.

"I'm headed there now to talk to the AIC, Jake Holloway and the rest of the team."

"My ass is on the line here Dan. Make sure those guys at 26 Federal know how important this is."

Healy headed for the door as he said, "They know how big this is, but I'll let them know how you feel."

Maddux had hoped that the Vice President would follow Healy's lead but he had no such luck. He remained seated and even had the nerve to put his feet up on the desk. The mayor was having a tough time holding his tongue.

"Comfortable, Joe?"

Browning motioned for his staffers and Secret Service agents to wait for him outside the office. When they shut the door he spoke. "I was at that fundraiser too. I saw you talking to Brennan and his girlfriend."

"It's all coming back to me now." Maddux sat across the desk from the Vice President and lit a cigar. "What the hell do you want me to do about it? Did you come all the way over here to tell me to get my best men on the case?"

Browning removed his feet from the mayor's desk and leaned forward. "I'm on my way to Albany to meet the President for another fundraiser so I thought I'd stop and impress upon you how important this is to me. If what they say about this Brennan guy is true, I need to be able to remove myself from any involvement with him. That's where you come into the picture." He took one of the mayor's cigars from the humidor on the desk and lit it before finishing his thought. "I want you to work a statement into your next news conference that says I had absolutely zero contact with this Brennan guy at the fundraiser or anywhere else as far as you know."

Maddux returned the request with a blank stare. He wasn't one to take political favors and wasn't about to grant one.

"Are you enjoying your political career, Maddux?"

Still no reaction so Browning decided to change course.

"Let me refresh your memory about the way things will probably go next year at the end of President Thompson's second term." As if they were good friends, Browning smiled as he said, "I will run for the Presidency and most likely win. I know I can use you in a top spot in Washington."

Without waiting for a reply, Browning stood and stuck out his hand. Maddux reluctantly shook it and the Vice President left without another word.

CHAPTER FORTY-NINE

The fancy conference room at 26 Federal Plaza was always used when the top brass from the NYPD made an appearance. The room had long tables set up in the shape of a horseshoe with the open end facing a large screen used for presentations. There were microphones set in the table to pick up voices around the room for all to hear through the many speakers in the walls.

David Reynolds was atypical in that he believed sharing as much information among different law enforcement groups was beneficial to any investigation. He made some great contacts within the police department over the years, which was why they called him immediately when they had information for him concerning the investigation.

Reynolds was in the front of the room standing next to the screen. "Thanks for coming Commissioner Healy. Let me bring you up to speed on what we've got."

The lights in the room were dimmed as the screen came to life. The black and white video was slightly grainy but still very valuable. The first image that appeared was of a BMW driving on the street. The film stopped for a second and the next store's video began to play. The car picked up speed suddenly and rammed the back of a large truck. The airbags exploded and within seconds the driver got out and ran out of the frame.

"Here's your shooter." Reynolds pressed a button on a remote and a red box framed the passenger's face as he struggled to get out of the car. His face and shirt were covered in blood. "As you're aware, one of your officers shot him as he ran down the center of Lexington Avenue. A few hours after that, he was shot and killed on his way into Bellevue. Someone was afraid he was going to talk and shut him up pretty damn quick. We're running his prints and face through our systems as we speak."

The video continued with the driver running on the sidewalk. Reynolds hit the remote again and a box framed the face of the running man. One more click and it came into focus alongside Mike Brennan's BNL ID photo.

Reynolds continued. "This, ladies and gentlemen is Michael Brennan, our alleged murderer and embezzler."

Commissioner Healy spoke up from the darkened room. "What are your theories?"

"We've only got two choices right now, sir. The easiest of which is that the long haired gentleman was an accomplice in Brennan's scheme who somehow felt slighted. Maybe he was forcing Brennan to drive somewhere he didn't want to go and Brennan thought better of it."

"What's number two?" Healy asked.

"It's unpopular but needs to be explored. Brennan could be innocent in this whole mess and is being set up."

Healy stood from his seat and said loudly, "Reynolds, I don't think I need to tell you how important it is to the mayor and this city that we resolve this quickly. It's my recommendation that you focus on Brennan as the guilty party and bring him in ASAP."

Jake Holloway, who was not one to be cowed, stood from his seat. "We'll take that under advisement Dan. We've been on this case for close to a year and it's reached the boiling point. We'll come out with the answers but we need to make sure that they're the right answers."

Reynolds turned the lights on. "This is a joint effort that includes resources of the NYPD. We'll get it done together, sir."

"I don't doubt that Reynolds. Just keep us informed."

"Understood."

CHAPTER FIFTY

Everything was the same as Mike remembered on One Hundred and First Avenue in Queens. The auto repair shops, plumbing and electrical supply stores, and Italian delis still lined the busy two way street. He parked the rented Navigator a few blocks away from his destination knowing the Feds had cameras set up all around to film the wise guys coming and going.

Joe Martelli got his father to agree to a meeting and then gave Mike instructions on where to park and what to wear. He had on sweat pants, a matching zip up jacket, and a baseball cap pulled low over his eyes. He kept his head low as he approached the door of the Martelli crime family headquarters known to outsiders by the sign hanging over the door, *Lodge 101*.

Although Mike knew Frank Martelli for years, his heart began to beat loudly in his chest and a light film of sweat coated his forehead. The barred windows were frosted, preventing anyone from seeing inside. The door had only a tiny hinged opening at eye level for the people inside to get a look at any visitors before opening the door.

Mike stepped into the recessed doorway and knocked on the door. Within seconds the small flap opened and a pair of dark eyes appeared. The flap slammed shut and Mike could hear the locks start to tumble from the inside. The door swung open and Mike stepped slowly inside. As soon as he was over the threshold, the man closed the door and locked it without a word to his visitor. Mike now got a good look at him. He was a good six inches taller and had him by at least a hundred pounds. Mike figured he wasn't kept around for his accounting skills.

Mike looked around the main room. It had tables and chairs set all around like a small café and a bar against the side wall but no decorations of any kind on the wall. He heard footsteps coming from the back of the building and turned toward the sound.

Joe Martelli came into the room. He was a few inches shorter than Mike, dressed sharply in a sport coat and mock turtle neck. "Nice to see you Mike. Welcome to the Lodge."

"We were never allowed in here as kids. It's not what I expected." Mike walked toward his old friend. They shook hands and gave each other a half hug that Mike felt was less than sincere. He hoped it wasn't a sign that Joe wouldn't help him with his problem.

"Things aren't always as they seem, Mike. We're not kids anymore."

"Your dad was generous in allowing me to come today."

"Out of all my friends growing up, he always liked you the best. He would say that you only had one fault." Joe smiled and Mike knew what was coming.

"My Irish blood," Mike answered for him.

"You got it."

"I'd tell you what I used to tell you years ago but I'll think better of that right now." Mike pointed over his shoulder at the giant guarding the door.

Joe peered over Mike's shoulder and smirked. "You're worried about Louie? He's a lamb."

Mike looked back to see the man's crooked smile and then shook off the chill that swept through his body.

"Come on back. Pop's waiting."

Joe went back through the door he entered minutes earlier and Mike followed. The back room was as sparse as the front. For some reason Mike expected more from the lodge. It was always a mysterious place as a kid and his imagination had developed a very different picture of the interior that included a juke box, pool table, and heads of stuffed deer and moose hanging from the wall. After all, it was a lodge.

Frank Martelli had aged well but Mike had not seen him in many years and the changes in the man were drastic. He seemed smaller and slightly frail sitting at a large round table surrounded by other aging Italian men in expensive suits. He still looked very distinguished with his thinning grey hair combed straight back.

He stood when Mike entered the room and put his arms out to him. Mike was surprised by the warmth of the welcome and walked around the table and returned the hug willingly. The old man held him at arm's length and looked him up and down. "Little Mikey Brennan ain't so little anymore, huh?" He reached up and slapped him lightly on the cheek and smiled, showing perfectly straight, white teeth. "It's nice to see you, my boy."

No one else in Mike's life ever called him Mikey. Or at least never called him that twice. When it came out of Frank Martelli's mouth, in his Queens Italian accent, it just sounded natural.

"It's great to see you too, Mr. Martelli. Thanks for taking the time to talk with me."

"You did the old neighborhood proud by going over there in Desert Storm. I used to tell Joe here that the yellow ribbon around my tree was for you."

Mike was flattered. "Thank you, sir."

The old man lost his smile and his face became stern. "Now what's this I'm seeing on the news? It can't be true, can it Mikey?" He sat back down in his seat.

Mike hadn't noticed during the greeting that the men who were seated at the table had slipped quietly into the front room to leave them alone. The old man motioned for Mike to take the seat next to him as Joe sat on the other side of his father.

"That's exactly why I'm here, Mr. Martelli. I'm being dragged through the dirt by my firm and I can't prove that I've got nothing to do with any of it."

"If you tell me you're not involved, that's all I need to hear." The elder Martelli poured three glasses of red wine. "Salute!" He raised his glass to touch Mike's and Joe's. They each took a sip.

"If the F.B.I. felt the same as you do, I'd have no problem." Mike tried to smile.

Martelli again turned serious. "How do you think I can help you?"

Mike prepared his words while driving down from Lake George. He knew that Mr. Martelli may easily be offended by his assumptions and he needed to be as delicate as possible.

He took another sip before answering. "Please understand that I mean no disrespect in my request. I've come to you because I've known you my whole life and I've got nowhere else to turn."

Martelli didn't speak but nodded his understanding.

Mike continued. "There were a couple of firms that my company has dealt with that have been known to have ties with the mafia. I don't know the details but I do know that the indictments fell through the cracks and these companies are still in operation today."

"What are the firms?" the younger Martelli asked.

"One is Duncan and the other is A.C. Conklin. Do you know them?"

Joe looked at his father briefly, then turned back to Mike. "That's the Salvatore family. We have nothing to do with them."

Mike couldn't let it end there. "Let me tell you some things I've found out in the last few days." He looked both men in the eye. "Someone who I hired uncovered evidence of suspicious activity in the company's main accounts. He was actually trying to scam the firm out of millions when someone found out about it. A few nights ago, someone took a shot at him inside the building and nicked his shoulder. Unfortunately for me, he came to me with his problem and now they believe I'm involved with him."

Mr. Martelli interrupted. "Where is this man now?"

"He's dead. They killed him and will probably try to pin that on me as well."

The Martellis only nodded and remained silent.

Mike took this as a sign to continue. "My boss told me before he died that my company, BNL, was controlled by a central entity that he believed controlled many other firms. When I heard of the possible mafia connection, I thought they could be the entity behind the market manipulation."

Joe spoke again while his father remained silent. "Why don't you bring this to the authorities?"

"Because I need more to prove I wasn't involved. On top of that, the F.B.I. claims to have proof of accounts in my name holding millions of dollars."

"Is that true?" Joe asked.

Mike shook his head. "Someone planted that. I had no knowledge of any wrongdoing until my boss told me just a few days ago."

The elder Martelli broke his silence. "What else have you learned?"

"I went to Atlanta to bring what I know to a client I thought I could trust and I came within inches of being killed. Turns out this client's involved and a guy who tried to tell me that he knows something ended up in the morgue."

"They killed him for talking to you?" Joe asked.

Mike nodded. "I would be dead now too if it weren't for the FBI showing up at the last second."

"Where's this client now?" Frank Martelli asked.

"He conveniently fell off the face of the earth."

Joe looked at his father again before saying, "I'm sorry we can't be of more help, Mike."

He wouldn't give up yet. "Is there a possibility that the Salvatore family is sophisticated enough to control a number of trading firms?" Mike was desperate.

Mr. Martelli smiled and replied, "Mario Salvatore couldn't find his face in the mirror."

Joe leaned forward and finished his father's thought. "What Pop's trying to say is that the Salvatores muscled their way into those two firms and squeezed someone's head until they paid them. There's no way they have the brains to actually manipulate the market."

Mike was disappointed. "I'm sorry to have bothered you both. I need a starting point and I'm having a difficult time finding one." He stood from the table and the younger Martelli stood with him. The old man didn't move.

"Sit down Mikey." The old man said.

"Pop?" Joe asked.

"Take it easy Joe. I'm an old man and Mikey's an old friend. He deserves our best effort."

Joe Martelli raised his voice slightly. "That's exactly right. You're an old man who won't have to live with the consequences. Leave it to my generation." Mike had never heard Joe speak to his father with such disrespect.

The don's eyes were like daggers holding his son's. "Your generation would be nothing without mine. We were the money makers and you are now the spenders."

Mike was uncomfortable. "Maybe I should leave."

"I said sit." The older man pointed to Mike's recently vacated chair.

Mike did as instructed and took his seat again.

Martelli went on. "I know of this central entity your boss told you about, but it has nothing to do with La Cosa Nostra. It makes us look like children compared with their wealth, power, and influence."

Mike was very surprised. "Who are they?"

"I don't know who they are but I know what we call them. The Blue Bloods."

Mike sat back, taking it all in as the elderly mafia kingpin continued. "Have you ever noticed that the mafia is not involved in high level politics or even your world of high finance?" He wasn't looking for Mike to answer and he didn't. "You hear about a stock scam here or there but never anything more substantial. Do you think it's because we don't have the brain power?" Again he paused, not expecting Mike to answer. "My beautiful son, Joe, went to law school at Columbia and do you know how he got there? It wasn't because of my influence. I have no influence at an Ivy League school. He got there because he was a smart kid and now he's grown into a smart man."

"Pop, please," the younger man pleaded.

"Joe, I'm not saying anything that isn't known by every made man in our organization." He turned to face Mike. "There are just some businesses and people that are not to be messed with and if they are, the consequences are severe."

Mike had remained silent since he sat down again and wasn't about to break the old man's concentration. He pointed his finger and went on. "Who do you think put Kennedy in the Oval Office in 1960 and then had him killed three years later? Have you heard that it was a conspiracy involving the mafia?"

"There were many theories. The mafia, vote fixers in Chicago, communists." Mike answered.

Mr. Martelli spoke in a hushed tone as if he didn't want to be overheard. No one spoke openly about this, not even the don. "It was these fucking Blue Bloods and I think there's more."

"More?" Mike asked.

"Like Nixon's resignation and that kid shooting Reagan. I can't prove it just the same as you can't prove you're innocence."

The information was rolling way too fast for Mike's brain to keep up. He never thought that the same people who wanted JFK to be President could be the same ones who wanted him out just a few short years later. He'd never heard any credible conspiracy theories involving Nixon or Reagan.

"How do they operate?" Mike finally asked.

Joe was now resigned to the fact that his father wanted Mike to know more details and decided to join in. "Nobody really knows. They have influence in many industries, at all levels. They allow us a piece of the action, but as soon as someone oversteps a boundary, they're gone."

"Gone?"

"I hate to be the one to break this to you old friend but you're living on borrowed time right about now." Joe said with a touch of sadness in his voice.

"Can you tell me anything else about them?" Mike pleaded.

The old man finished off the last of his wine. "I've heard that the man who's behind it all is a well known figure running a company that every American knows. No one ever speaks his name. I'm afraid you're on your own from here on out, son. We don't know any more to tell but if you can find a chink in their armor, I'll be eternally grateful."

Mike wasn't exactly concerned about improving the mafia's business but he couldn't think that far into the future right now. "How do I find them?"

"Don't worry. They'll find you." The old man lowered his voice again and leaned in. "But remember this. Once a Blue Blood, always a Blue Blood. Have you ever heard that a man must have pure Italian blood running through his veins to become a made man?"

Mike nodded as the don continued, "You need blue blood to be a member of their organization. If you don't have it, you will only be used, chewed up, and spit out." He stood and pulled Mike out of his seat with amazing strength for his apparent frailty. He held Mike's hands in his own and looked him directly in the eyes. "Go with God, Mikey. I'll pray for you." He turned and walked away.

Mike stared after him until he disappeared into a side room. Joe brought him out of his daze. "I'm sorry we couldn't do more for you Mike. My father really feels bad about it." Joe led Mike to the front door.

"Tell him I said thanks." Joe nodded as he shut the door leaving Mike in the small doorway outside the lodge. He heard the locks turning immediately.

He thought back a few short days when Sam's father didn't show up to his Man of the Year ceremony. He jokingly called his girlfriend a blue blood. The woman he loved came from an incredibly wealthy family but Mike had a hard time believing that her parents would be involved in anything like he just heard from the Martellis. He'd give her a call to ask her what she thought and if she'd be willing to talk to her family about it. He realized now that he had to get some backup and there was only one place for him to turn.

CHAPTER FIFTY-ONE

Long Island City was one of the few flops in New York City's rebirth over the last two decades. It was promoted by the city and development corporations as the perfect lower cost business location because of it's proximity to Manhattan. It turned out that not many companies were willing to move. The few that did found themselves in desolate, undeveloped areas that were extremely unappealing.

The one thing that large businesses did find the area useful for was warehouses. Tractor trailers packed with goods poured off the Long Island Expressway at all hours of the day and night. As Mike waited for a truck to pull out of a docking bay at one of these warehouses, he punched a number into his cell phone.

"Mike?"

"Hey, babe. How's it going?"

"Don't worry about me. How did it go with the Martellis?"

"They didn't offer me too much help, but at least now I know my situation is more grim than I originally thought." Mike was disappointed with the level of detail they were able to give him.

"What did they tell you?"

Mike did his best to summarize. The truck he was waiting for to leave the warehouse was getting ready to depart. "They think there's this kind of undercurrent organization of the super rich that secretly controls everything from businesses to politics."

"I thought that was the mafia's job," she stated.

"Crime families are allowed to operate within certain limits and if they step over their bounds, they're simply taken out."

"Taken out?"

"They're gone." Mike used Joe Martelli's words.

"This all sounds too unbelievable to me."

Mike felt the same way. He needed more information and Sam could help. Her dad, William Brodworth, certainly qualified as someone who was familiar with the kinds of people the Martellis were talking about. The Brodworth name and money were attached to so many schools, charities, and foundations that Mike couldn't keep track of them all.

"How do you feel about running this past your dad?"

"Do you really believe what they told you?"

"I don't have many options right now. If anything, maybe your father could offer me some advice."

"I'll give it a shot. He's coming up here tonight."

"Perfect. Thank you."

"Are you coming back now?"

"I'm making one more quick stop. I'll try to keep you posted."

"Please be careful."

"I will." Mike cut the line.

With the entrance now free, he pulled the SUV all the way into the building as he was instructed and the aluminum gate rolled down behind him, enclosing him inside a large open area. Men were driving forklifts carrying payloads from the loading dock in the front of the building and stacking them in various isles. Mike turned the engine off and got down from the Navigator.

He looked up a set of metal stairs to an office about twenty feet up the wall overlooking the entire warehouse. Before he closed his door two men came out of the room and started down. The man in front had the worn face of someone who worked outdoors his entire life. Underneath his loose fitting shirt, his muscles were rock hard. The only sign of Grady Wessler's forty five years were slight crow's feet and a little bit of grey in his crew cut.

Wessler put his finger to his lips as he approached. The second man was Hispanic and about the same age and build as Wessler. He stepped up to Mike and motioned for him to raise his arms. Grady watched with his arms folded as his partner began an expert pat down that ended with the removal of Mike's Sig Sauer P226 9mm from the small of his back. The man removed the clip and the chambered round and handed the gun back to Mike by the handle.

Wessler stepped forward with his hand extended. "Sorry for the precautions but you never know. I must admit I'm surprised you asked to come here, Captain Brennan."

"I can't say I blame you." Mike shook his hand.

"Where'd you get the piece?" Wessler asked.

"A going away present when I left the Corps." Mike smiled. "Have you been watching the news?"

Wessler nodded. "You're in trouble, sir."

Mike never got used to people older than he was calling him *sir*. From the day Mike earned his commission, Grady Wessler was the sergeant heading up Mike's platoon. They were on the beach in Panama together when Mike took shrapnel in the leg. Sergeant Wessler carried him to the medevac chopper before getting back to the platoon and leading them deeper into Panama. In Desert Storm, Mike got to return the favor and carried Wessler on his back for more than a mile after the sergeant took fragments of a B-52 payload that went off target. That earned Mike the Silver Star.

Wessler was one of the most decorated marines still on active duty at the time of his retirement a few years earlier. Mike got along well with him because he realized from day one that Wessler was the key to making the platoon run as a well oiled machine. The young lieutenant understood that he was an inexperienced officer and made it known to Wessler that he was willing to learn.

They kept in touch since parting ways and even saw each other a few times when the platoon got together every couple of years. After the previous year's reunion Mike and Wessler were the last ones in the back room of the bar that they rented on Third Avenue on the Upper East Side of Manhattan. After reminiscing some more about their service together and more than a few shots of tequila, Wessler told Mike about his new profession.

Mike heard of people working as mercenaries after they left the service but he never knew any of them personally. Grady Wessler hired himself and his team of former military men out for security, surveillance, and more. Mike believed him when Wessler told him he would never kill anyone for money. His jobs were mostly very rich people who wanted to snoop on a competitor or feared for their lives from various anti-American groups.

"Please drop the 'sir', Grady. We were always equals no matter what it said on my collar. If anything, I looked up to you." Mike had a great deal of respect for the man.

"Old habits die hard."

"Can I speak openly?" Mike asked.

"Sorry for being rude. This is my partner, Benito Gomez." Wessler pointed to the man who conducted the pat down. "He was a jarhead himself for nineteen years and you can say anything you please in front of him."

Mike shook the man's hand and continued. "Your first observation was correct because I'm in serious trouble. The thing is that everything that you've heard on the T.V. is bullshit and I need your help. I've got absolutely no idea where to start but I know in the end I'm going to go down fighting. That's why I need your services."

"You name it."

"Can you outfit me with this list?" Mike handed him a list that he made out while waiting outside. It contained flak jackets, silenced MP-3 rifles with night vision scopes, side arms, infrared cameras, a directional microphone and a shit load of extra ammo.

Wessler looked quickly down the page. "Who are you planning to take out?"

"I don't know yet, but when I do, I want to be ready."

"If you need someone to watch your back, you just say the word Cap. You know as well as I do that some things are easier when you've got a point man." He returned to military jargon and Mike followed suit.

"Thanks for the offer, Sarge but I'm trying not to bring anyone else down with me. I may need you soon enough and I know where to find you."

"Take a seat over there and we'll pack you up. Don't worry about paying me now. When things calm down you can send it to me."

"Thanks Grady, but I like to pay as I go. They've frozen my accounts but luckily I've got a pretty good support system."

"How is you're beautiful support system doing through all this?"

"Her career is going to suffer but she's doing all right." Mike turned and sat in a chair near the foot of the metal stairs. He hadn't taken the time to think about how Sam's career in politics was as damaged as his in finance. He would have to make it up to her somehow but he needed to make sure they both made it out alive before he thought about the future.

Wessler pulled out a handheld radio and spoke into it. Within a minute someone brought a large storage bin and placed it on the floor near the tail gate of the Navigator. Mike sat back and watched as the men packed up the items from his list. Rifles, flak jackets, radios. Memories of the Gulf War came flooding back.

He and his men were dug into fox holes near the Kuwaiti-Iraqi border that they had spent most of the cool night digging. With the sunrise came a heat that would only add to their fatigue and overall discomfort. Sleep was a luxury that they couldn't afford as thousands of Iraq's Republican Guard troops were less than two miles away, speeding toward their position.

Captain Brennan looked up and down his line of men and thought they looked more like something out of Star Wars than his elite troops. They were in full desert camouflage with some added extras to help combat the sand storms that would sometimes whirl up from nowhere. Only their heads were visible above ground level with their shaded goggles along with a special lightweight mask that kept the tiny grains of sand out of ears and mouths.

"How long do we wait?" Sergeant Wessler asked as he approached his captain from behind.

Mike lowered the powerful binoculars from his eyes and looked at Wessler. The wind was already whipping up particles of sand in a relentless onslaught on the men and the equipment. He could only recognize his sergeant from his distinctive deep voice because his face and eyes were covered like the rest of the soldiers. Camos were absent of any insignia that would distinguish rank. Although the chances were slim, they were at the highest risk of being captured by the enemy and it would be safer for the officers to keep rank from their captors.

"Can you mark their location yet?" Mike asked. He wanted to know if his navigational specialist was able to obtain the exact coordinates of the enemy formation that was speeding in retreat toward the Iraqi border.

"Parker says he's got them within five feet," Wessler replied.

"Let's have a look." Mike followed Sergeant Wessler about twenty yards behind the network of foxholes to the only above ground position they were manning. With the sand blowing in their faces, the well camouflaged tent was hard to make out in the distance. When they arrived, Wessler moved the flap aside and let Captain Brennan enter the command and control center.

Inside the tent, which measured only ten feet square, was a technical specialist monitoring an advanced radar and global positioning tracking system. Sticking out the top of the tent was a small dish that was communicating with a satellite a hundred miles above the Persian Gulf. It was sending them coordinates of the massive amounts of tanks and trucks that were trying to make a mad dash back into Iraq, ahead of the U.S. military who weren't far behind.

Mike glanced at a screen showing a map with hundreds of small red dots moving slowly along. Each dot represented an enemy tank, truck, or armored personnel carrier. He shifted his eyes to the next screen which showed a series of hollow green triangles moving in a very slow circular pattern. Each triangle represented a B-52 holding formation, twenty thousand feet above them, waiting for Mike's command to start bombing.

Captain Brennan's mission was to identify likely routes that the enemy would take on their way back to Iraq so the B-52's could be prepared and in position. They had been patrolling the area for two days before the Allies first entered Kuwait.

"Call it in." Mike said quickly and left the tent. Within thirty seconds of reaching his command foxhole, he heard the unmistakable screech of the bombs heading for their targets. Although the destruction was more than a mile away, the explosions were deafening. He was just about to call in a report to his commander when he heard a loud whistling noise. It was different from the screech of the bombs and he couldn't place the sound.

He realized a split second later that it must be a bomb heading off target and toward his position. He stood and yelled, "Get down. Incoming!"

The explosion that followed was more than deafening. It was numbing. When he picked his head up from the bottom of the foxhole he was dizzy. The concussion of the powerful blast shut down his hearing momentarily and all he could hear was ringing. He tried to focus through his goggles but the detonation lifted more sand than any storm he'd witnessed so far and it was hard to see his hand in front of his face.

The first sound he heard seemed far away. At first it was a faint call but soon grew to an all out yell.

"Medic!" the voiced screamed.

Mike turned to look at the tent he had been in just minutes earlier and saw nothing but shreds of canvas and chunks of smoking metal that used to be his command center. Sergeant Wessler was on his knees leaning over what looked like a pile of clothes but Mike knew it was the specialist who'd been tracking the enemy formation.

"Medic!" It was Wessler, yelling again.

Mike got out of the hole and ran beside the Navy Corpsman up to the smoldering crater. The young man lying on the ground was looking straight up with unfocused eyes, moving his mouth trying to form words. The only sound coming from him was a gurgling sound from his chest.

"Do something for him, man." Wessler pleaded with the medic.

The Navy corpsman looked at Mike with an expression that said more than words. The kid's legs were blown clear off along with half his abdomen. There was nothing he could do. The medic grabbed a syringe of morphine and was about to jab it into the man's arm when he convulsed and stopped breathing. He was gone.

"God damn it," Wessler growled. "He was twenty years old."

"What the hell happened?" the corpsman asked.

Mike looked around to make sure his men were still low in the holes and replied, "Looks like one of the bird's payloads fell off target."

"Fuck them!" Wessler got up and started to walk toward the rest of the men.

"Sergeant, wait," the corpsman said.

Wessler turned. "What?"

"You're bleeding."

Wessler looked down at his leg to see it drenched with blood.

"Shit!" Mike said as he ran up to him and helped him down to the ground. The medic was on him within seconds, cutting Wessler's fatigues off his bloody leg. He poured a small bottle of saline cleanser over the thigh to clear the blood and get a clear look at the wound.

The medic spoke. "Shrapnel. Looks like it nicked the femoral artery. He's losing blood fast."

Mike motioned to his field radio operator.

"Get a medevac chopper in here now."

Captain Brennan turned his attention back to Wessler who was still surprisingly lucid for all the blood he was losing.

"We'll get you out of here in a few minutes, Sarge."

The radio man approached and waved Brennan over. He stepped a few yards away from Wessler and the medic. "They said they can't land because there are still hostiles about a half mile away."

"Can't they get an A-10 to strafe them and get one in here?" Brennan asked, angry.

"I asked. The A-10s are a hundred miles west and they can't get here in time."

"Give me the radio."

The radio man complied.

"This is Captain Brennan of First Recon Marines."

"Copy," the voice came back.

"I've got a wounded man here who needs more medical attention than we have available out here. I need a chopper now."

"We can't do that sir."

Mike knew the man behind the voice was following procedure and held back a tirade that would only serve to piss off the air traffic controller. "How close can you get to us?"

There was a pause on the line. "Two clicks, due east."

Mike thought for a moment and replied, "Go there now. We'll be waiting."

"Copy."

The corpsman approached as Mike finished the call. "I've got him tied off but he's losing blood. He needs surgery within the hour."

Mike looked east and saw the rise and fall of the dunes. About two kilometers away was a short rocky hill that he knew the medevac would use to shield itself from shoulder fired heat seeking missiles that the Iraqis were known to have.

"Harris! Greenberg!" Mike yelled to his men. Two men leapt from their holes and jogged over. Mike pointed to Wessler. "Help me lift him."

Wessler was getting groggy and didn't fight the process. When they had him standing, Mike leaned down, grabbed the sergeant around the knees and folded him over his shoulder in a fireman's carry.

"Harris, you take point. Greenberg, you've got our back."

"Yes sir," they replied in unison.

Mike turned to the men who still had their heads just above ground level and said, "Lieutenant Johnson, round up the men and follow at twenty yard intervals. We've got to get Sarge to the other side of those hills."

"Yes sir," came the reply from one of the holes.

Mike turned to Harris and Greenberg. "Move out."

Mike's legs felt like they'd give out way before they arrived at their destination but he wouldn't allow another one of his men to die if he could help it. He struggled up and over the hill where the two men helped him lay Wessler gently on the ground.

They heard the medevac before they saw it. It came in low from the east hugging the ground and looked as if it would pass their position. The pilot banked sharply toward them at the last second and put the flying ambulance down with a gentle touch. A corpsman and a surgeon jumped out with a stretcher and immediately went to work on Wessler, taking his vitals and hooking him up to an IV. Mike and his men helped carry the stretcher to the chopper and then stood back and watched as the pilot lifted off and followed the same route he took on the way in.

Wessler pulled through and Mike got the Silver Star for his actions but never thought of himself as a hero. The sounds of the chopper and the sand storms were still in his ears when he heard someone talking to him.

"You're all set." It was Wessler.

Mike didn't know how long he had been sitting in the warehouse and was surprised when he looked at the clock on the wall and realized only ten minutes had past and the crate was filled to the top with his grocery list.

"Seeing all that equipment really brings back memories," Mike said.

Grady closed the lid and locked it while two of his men grabbed a side each and lifted it into the back of the SUV. "The scenes never go away, Captain."

"You got that right." Mike walked over with a few stacks of neatly packed bills. "Will this cover it?" he asked.

Grady flipped through the bills. "This is too much, I can't take this."

"Think of it as a retainer."

He smiled. "We'll be waiting for your call."

CHAPTER FIFTY-TWO

Mike pulled the recently loaded SUV out of the warehouse in Long Island City and drove along the uninhabited streets. He was about to check in with Tim and Sam when his cell phone rang. He looked at the incoming number but didn't recognize it.

"Hello?"

"Is that you Michael?" a man asked.

Mike didn't know the voice and was in no mood for any more games. "Who is this?"

"It's Albert Claire."

Mike was initially surprised to hear from him. Then he remembered his visit a couple nights ago and the promise Claire made to call him when he had some information

"We need to meet. I have what we talked about at my house."

"I don't think that's a good idea. Every law enforcement agency in the city is looking for me right now and I wish they were the only ones."

"I know you're in trouble but I think I can help you. I know a place they won't expect you to be where we can meet"

Mike was wary.

"Can you get to St. Patrick's Cathedral?" Claire asked.

"I think so."

"I'll be in the first confessional on the left."

"How do I know this isn't a trap Albert?" Mike couldn't trust anyone at this point.

"I can't say much on the phone, but I'll tell you this. I want to put Layden away as much as you do. This will help us both."

Mike calculated the risk briefly in his head and figured it was worth it. "All right Albert. I'll trust you. I'll be at St. Pat's in an hour."

Mike knew the Midtown Tunnel would be heavily guarded as it had been since the terrorist attacks on the city so he headed over to Queens Boulevard and crossed the Fifty-Ninth Street Bridge into Manhattan. Heavy traffic was heading out of the city at this time of the day. He made it to his destination with enough time to leave his vehicle in a parking garage a few blocks away from the cathedral. There was no way he could park it on the street with the stash of weapons and equipment Wessler packed up for him. He self parked on the first floor of the garage with the rear of the vehicle against a wall to make it harder for a snooping parking attendant to get a look at his supplies. He removed some items from the crate and stuffed them in a backpack before walking out onto the street.

He approached the tremendous cathedral from Fiftieth Street to avoid the larger and more open Fifth Avenue. His baseball hat was pulled down low and he tucked his chin toward his chest. He also tried to change his walk slightly in an effort to further alter his appearance. Anyone who knew him wouldn't recognize him unless they were a few feet away.

Mike was counting on large numbers of tourists walking in and out of the main doors on Fifth and wasn't disappointed. He latched onto the end of a group and followed them through the entrance. Inside the dimly lit cathedral, it took a few seconds for his eyes to adjust to the light. Mike broke away from the group and went up the left isle to the confessionals.

He opened the first door just beyond a side altar and entered the tiny box. It was only large enough to fit a chair and a padded kneeler. The only light came from the connected box that would normally be occupied by a priest waiting to hear a list of sins. Again his eyes had to adjust to darkness as he struggled to make out the form of the man sitting on the other side of the screen.

"Albert?" Mike whispered.

There was no answer so Mike spoke slightly louder, "Is that you Albert?" Again no reply. Mike took a tiny penlight from his pocket, slid open the screen between the booths and shined it through. He saw Albert Claire sitting calmly in the priest's chair with his eyes open. The only unusual thing about his face was that there was a dark red hole the size of a dime between his eyes and a trickle of blood running down the side of his nose.

Mike shuddered at the sight and immediately removed his 9mm from the waist band at the small of his back. Whoever did this could be right outside the door, Mike thought to himself as he tried to formulate an escape plan. Unfortunately there was only one way out of the confessional and he'd be in plain sight of anyone waiting outside.

After a few seconds of thought he put the gun back in its hiding place and quickly pushed the door open.

As soon as he stepped into the isle he screamed, "Help. Somebody please help me. Oh my god, the priest is dead."

Most of the tourists turned and ran toward him as he made his way down the isle toward the Fifth Avenue exit. People were drawn in his direction as he hoped and a small crowd soon formed around him. He made eye contact with one man whose emotionless expression made him stand out from the crowd. The man started pushing his way through the crowd toward Mike but was forced to stop when an NYPD officer who had been posted at the side entrance came running up the isle.

The cop caught his breath. "What's the problem?"

Mike stayed at the back of the crowd and let the tourists speak, keeping an eye on the possible killer. An Englishman took the lead. "A man was yelling something or other about a dead priest. We saw him by the side over there." He pointed toward the confessionals.

The cop put his radio to his mouth and screamed above the noisy crowd, "I need backup at St. Pat's. Possible assault on a priest."

He pushed his way through the crowd and ran up the isle. Mike turned and walked quickly to the exit. Out of the corner of his eye he could see the same man across the pews in the next isle keeping up with him. He broke into a jog and the man did the same. Mike picked up speed, dodging tourists, and made it to the large bronze doors at Fifth Avenue.

He just got through the threshold and down the steps as three police cruisers skidded to a stop on the street. Six officers ran up the steps and created a perimeter, closing off the exit.

Mike quickly crossed Fifth Avenue and half turned to look at the Cathedral. The cop on the inside must have called in the fresh corpse in the confessional because more cruisers sped up on both Fiftieth and Fifty-First Streets and cops emptied out. He saw the man who had been tracking him inside the church being held back with the crowd. He was holding his wrist up to his mouth. Mike knew the guy wasn't working alone and was probably radioing his people on the street.

Mike looked around and saw the expensive clothing stores that lined Fifth Avenue around the cathedral. He decided quickly that they would serve a dual purpose. First, he needed to get off the street to avoid being seen by the cops and whoever just murdered Albert. Second, he needed a change of clothes. He pushed through the glass door of the first boutique he hit and was immediately approached by a salesman.

"Can I help you sir?" He looked at Mike's sweat suit as if it were covered in bugs.

Mike tried to remain calm and spoke slowly. "You sure can. I'd like to see what you've got in sport coats and casual slacks. Unfortunately my luggage never left L.A. this morning and I need to get some things to hold me over."

The man's eye's lit up. "My pleasure sir. Come this way."

Within twenty minutes, Mike had changed into a navy blue blazer, khaki pants, and a hat that he normally wouldn't be caught in public wearing but would make an exception for today. He paid the man and asked him to dispose of his cheesy sweat suit and went back out to the street. The Cathedral was now taped off and crawling with cops. Mike pulled his hat down low and walked toward Fifty-First Street.

He wasn't paying attention to the crowd on the sidewalk and bumped into a woman, knocking some things out of her arms. He bent to help her pick them up and apologized. As he stood from his crouch he was facing a large stone pedestal, about fifteen feet high, in a recessed area of an office building. He took a couple of steps back to see what was sitting atop the massive stone block. There, standing thirty feet high was a colossal statue of Atlas holding the world on his shoulders.

All the information from the past few days came rushing back through his mind and stopped on the two companies behind Layden and Dowd. Atlas Consultants was the name of one of them.

Mike said out loud, "This is it." The woman who he just bumped into looked at him strangely. She started to back away from the crazy man as he continued talking to himself. "This has got to be it."

He realized that another piece of the puzzle was sitting just a block away and started running south on Fifth Avenue, passing Fiftieth Street. About thirty yards in on the right was the promenade that led to the Rockefeller Center skating rink. The walkway, filled with beautifully manicured bushes and flowers, was bordered with expensive shops and as with most of the area, was jammed with tourists. The stone fish in the fountains down the center of the walkway were spitting water into pools. Mike had to stop running because of the crowd and pushed his way through toward the rink. During the summer months, the rink shut down and the surrounding restaurants offered outdoor seating on the flat surface.

As he got closer he saw the shiny gold top of a statue. He struggled to see more but it was sunken down one level with the rink. He finally made it to the end of the promenade and peered over the side and saw the statue in all its glory. It was another Greek God. This one was Prometheus, floating on his side, appearing ready to soar over the diners at their tables. Mike read the engraved wall above the statue: *Prometheus, teacher in every art brought the fire that hath proved to mortals a means to mighty ends.*

Mike thought back to the first time Jack brought up the names of the two companies, Atlas Consultants and Prometheus Holdings. He knew there was a connection outside Greek mythology and this was it. He'd seen these statues a hundred times before and never thought twice about them. Philip Layden had smaller versions in his home office and this was too much of a coincidence.

His eyes left the inscription and rose to the top of the skyscraper towering over Rockefeller Plaza. He struggled to see the uppermost floors in the haze to make out the letters on top of the building. Although the letters were unclear, he knew the name that was plastered up there for all of New York to see. It was Browning Aerospace, the company that owned most of the buildings around Rockefeller Center. Mr. Martelli had told him that the company behind the Blue Bloods was one that was familiar to all Americans. This had to be it. Mike had always known that most criminals were cocky and liked to flaunt their crimes in public, but this was outrageous.

He still had no proof but at least now he had a theory. Something bothered him about the firms named for Greek gods and now he knew why. He'd have to get someone to do some research on Browning but he needed to get out of the area first. He was pushing his luck walking around the city when someone was bound to recognize him from the news reports. Now, on top of Barry's and Darvish's murders and embezzling millions, he would be connected with Albert's murder after they pulled the tapes from the security cameras in the cathedral.

He thought it best to leave the Navigator where it was for now with the trunk full of weapons. Again thankful for the crowds, he latched onto a pack and walked north toward Central Park. He'd come back to the area after nightfall when the police presence died down.

CHAPTER FIFTY-THREE

The medical examiner stepped out of the confessional and removed his rubber gloves. Agent Reynolds approached him and flashed his badge.

"What's the word?" Reynolds asked.

"My preliminary assessment is a .22 between the eyes. Close range."

"How long ago?"

"No more than an hour. Right about the time the officer called in for backup."

"Thanks." Reynolds turned and walked up the main isle of the cathedral toward the altar.

"Dave." Reynolds turned to see his partner entering through the west entrance. "This guy certainly gets around doesn't he?" Battaglia asked.

"He's been busy. Let's get a look at those security tapes," Reynolds said.

Behind the main alter and the organ in the northeast corner of the building was the usher's office. It doubled as the security center where the video surveillance equipment was stored. Thousands of people come in and out of the cathedral every day and security of the patrons is a top priority. Cameras are set up at all the entrances and also scattered around the inside. The man in charge of security was Tom Damica, a former NYPD detective.

The door to the room was opened as Reynolds and Battaglia approached. Reynolds knocked on the door jam as they entered the cramped office. Damica was in front of a monitor, running through the video. He turned when he heard them come in.

Reynolds already had his badge and ID out. "Mr. Damica?"

"That's right," he said as he stood.

"I'm Special Agent David Reynolds and this is Special Investigator Pete Battaglia."

"I've been expecting you boys. I've got the tapes set up and ready to go. Have a seat." He hit the play button and the black and white image showed a small, older man walking nervously up the side isle. Every few feet he would turn and look behind him as if he knew he was being followed. He was wearing a light colored suit and carried a thin briefcase.

Damica paused the film. "Here's your stiff. Mr. Albert Claire. Is it true he's the guy from Claire Cosmetics?"

Battaglia answered, "One and the same."

Damica pressed play again and continued his narrative. "The camera's on an arm that automatically sweeps back and forth. You can see him open the door to the confessional but we can't see him actually go in. Right here the camera sweeps back again to show the door closed."

The equipment squealed again as the tape sped forward, this time a little slower. "Now here's your perp, about three minutes lapse time."

A man in a sweat suit and a baseball cap is seen walking up the left isle and entering the same confessional. The camera sweeps away and returns twenty seconds later to the scene. The man in the sweat suit opens the door, steps back into the isle and looks like he yells something before walking quickly to the center isle.

Reynolds looked at Damica and asked, "Can you freeze it and magnify on the guy's face?"

"No problem." Damica pressed a few buttons and Mike Brennan's face came into focus as the image enlarged. "You know him?"

Battaglia nodded. "It's Brennan."

Reynolds looked at the security man. "Do you have any more angles?"

"Not of the confessionals, but we got him leaving down the center isle. I need to put in the tape from the rear camera. It'll just take a second." He popped out the tape, replaced it with a new one and cued it up.

He pointed to the screen. "Here comes Johnson." They watched as the officer posted at the rear of the church ran up the center isle to the crowd that had formed around the man in the sweat suit. The cop says something, lifts his radio to his mouth then runs out of the frame toward the confessionals.

Brennan can be seen backing away from the crowd immediately and then running for the doors at Fifth Avenue. Damica stopped the video. "That's it guys. We can have a still shot of the perp blown up if you want."

Reynolds leaned forward in his seat. "Can you roll this last one back slowly?"

Damica did as requested and Mike jogged backwards into the frame.

"Pause it." Reynolds said quickly. "Look at that."

"What?" Battaglia asked.

"The guy with the briefcase on the edge of the crowd. It looks like Claire's briefcase. Run it forward now. Watch him pick up speed down the side aisle as Brennan does."

Battaglia was puzzled. "You think he's working with someone?"

"No. I think that guy's tailing him."

"You're unbelievable."

"Anyone could have gone into that confessional and popped Claire before Brennan showed up. And that's not the only thing that bothers me." He looked at the security man. "Can you roll it back slowly one more time? Just to the point where our guy turns to run down the aisle."

"You got it."

The machine whistled quietly as the tape rewound. On the screen, Brennan was pulled backwards to the edge of the crowd.

"Stop there." Reynolds s put his hand up. "Can you run it forward now frame by frame?"

The image shifted from image to image as Mike Brennan looks across the aisle and then starts to slowly turn toward the back of the cathedral.

"Pause it."

The image froze as Brennan's sweat jacket flips up as he begins his turn.

"What do you see there?" Reynolds asked Battaglia, pointing at the screen.

"I see the murder weapon stuffed in his waistband," Battaglia answered.

Damica leaned in, his trained detective's eye studying the frame. "No you don't. I see a 9mm. If that guy was shot with a 9mm, half his head would be gone."

Reynolds looked at Battaglia. "The M.E. says it's probably a .22 caliber."

Battaglia refused to give in. "So he's got a .22 strapped to his leg?"

"All I'm saying is that we need to keep an open mind about where this guy fits into the puzzle."

Battaglia didn't deny it. "You could be right but the only way we'll know is if we bring this god damned guy in and get him talking."

Reynolds stood. "He's in the area. Let's clamp down and maybe we can flush him out."

"He moves fast," Battaglia said. "He could be anywhere by now."

"We've got to try. Let's rally the troops and head underground and search the tunnels. He could be sitting down having a nice dinner at the Sea Grill right about now."

"You think it's going to be that easy to find him?"

"Wishful thinking."

CHAPTER FIFTY-FOUR

Grady Wessler fully expected to hear from Mike but not quite so soon. Just hours after his former commander left the warehouse in Long Island City, he got a call.

"Hello."

"Grady, it's Mike."

"Hey. Everything okay with your order?"

"It's fine. I said earlier I was going this alone but I've come to the realization I need help. The kind of sophisticated help that you and your men can offer."

"I think I understand."

"Can you be ready to move within an hour?" Mike asked.

"When the hell did it ever take me an hour to suit up? We'll be out the door within twenty minutes," Grady said proudly.

"Dress code is business casual here. Do you understand?"

"Absolutely. Are you within fifty miles of our last meeting?"

"Yes."

"Do you have the two-way with you?"

"Yes." The small radio was one of the items Mike grabbed from the supply trunk before heading into the cathedral.

"On the back of the two-way is a switch, do you see it?"

"I see it," he said.

"Switch it to the right and it will act as a homing device. We'll find you within sixty minutes. Are you in immediate danger?" Grady needed to know what he was getting into without saying too much over the phone.

"I'm fine but the place is swarming. I'm well hidden."

"Stay put. We'll be there."

After the brief conversation Wessler packed up his own SUV with supplies. He then changed into a collared shirt and khakis and left the warehouse with his point man, Benito Gomez and a third man, Arthur Haas, his communications expert.

Wessler was at the wheel listening to Haas' directions from the rear. "According to this reading he's right smack in the middle of Rockefeller Center." He had a small laptop computer opened on the console between the two front seats.

Gomez spoke up from the passenger seat. "That's a little crowded, isn't it?"

"Hell yeah it is," Wessler replied. "But it's probably thinning out at this hour."

"That's not good. We need the crowd." Gomez knew with a lot of cops around it would be hard to slip through with the country's most wanted man.

"Do you think he popped that guy in the cathedral?" Haas asked.

They had been monitoring police transmissions as they did regularly and Grady's ears perked up when they broadcast an APB for Michael Brennan in the vicinity of St. Patrick's Cathedral. He thought about Haas' question for a second before responding. "It doesn't sound like him, unless it was self defense. But a bullet between the eyes doesn't sound much like self defense."

"We can trust this guy?" Gomez already knew the answer but he had to voice his concerns. His boss wouldn't be on his way into the middle of a possible hornet's nest if he didn't think Brennan was worth it.

"With my life," Wessler answered quickly.

As promised, within an hour of Mike's call, the three former marines were outside Thirty Rockefeller Plaza, directly above the skating rink and the monstrous statue of Prometheus that Mike had seen a short time ago. All three had packs on their backs and could have past for tourists themselves. Haas carried a video camera that doubled as a portable homing device. He actually could record about forty minutes of digital footage but he was saving the battery for the more important purpose of locating their target. Wessler carried a camera around his neck and was taking pictures of the area as any visitor would.

Hass moved close to Wessler and pointed at the revolving doors. "He's inside the building, below ground level."

"Let's move out." Wessler replied. Gomez would normally take the lead but since Haas was tracking at the moment, they'd follow him in. There were several restaurants and stores in the lower level of Rockefeller Center so the trio wasn't alone in the area.

After entering the lobby and finding the down escalator Gomez said, "There aren't as many cops as I thought."

Wessler nodded. "I've got a feeling there are a lot of feds in plain clothes lurking about."

They got off the escalator a floor below and instinctively spaced themselves out, leaving about twenty yards between each man. Haas had a clear reading and was walking at a good clip heading west, away from the skating rink. The tunnel split into two sides, both lined with fast food joints, coffee houses, and drugstores. There were still plenty of people moving about with a good mix of tourists and business people.

About a hundred yards down the tunnel, Haas put his hand up in a fist. Wessler and Gomez stopped immediately and looked casually into the windows of the stores where they happened to stop. Wessler watched through a window as a girl dipped strawberries in expensive chocolate. He turned and looked ahead to Haas. The point man put up his five fingers and then put his hand to his ear signaling their mark was about five yards away and Wessler should contact him.

Wessler dialed the number and only waited one ring before Mike picked it up.

"Hey Grady. Are you in the area?"

"My guess is about fifteen feet away."

"Come on in. This place is empty."

Wessler walked to where Hass was standing in front of a store that was under construction. The windows were covered with brown paper, preventing them from seeing in. They looked up and down the tunnel to make sure no one was watching and then opened the door and entered the darkened space.

"Mike." Grady whispered.

"Over here." Mike turned on his small penlight showing them the way.

"Are you sure this place is secure?" Gomez asked.

"I watched the construction workers pack up and leave about an hour and a half ago. I easily clipped the small padlock on the door."

"Way to go, Captain," Wessler said. He removed the pack from his back and set it on the floor. "What's the plan? I thought you'd be long gone by now."

"I should be out of the city with all the manpower they've got looking for me but I think I realized who may be railroading me and I may not get the opportunity to be so close again. If you guys are willing, and please remember that I'll pay your going rate and then some, I need to get into the Browning Aerospace offices." Mike waited for their reaction to his idea.

"Can I ask why?" Wessler asked.

"They're the ones who kidnapped my girlfriend, set me up for murder and embezzlement, and tried to kill me."

Gomez spoke up. "That's some list. I guess you've got a right to be pissed but what do you think you'll find up there?"

"I'm not sure. I was hoping one of you guys was a techie."

Haas stepped forward. "Arthur Haas at you're service."

Mike shook his hand. "Nice to meet you, Haas." Mike knew he couldn't possibly go by his first name. "They've probably got some pretty sophisticated security. Do you think you could get us in?"

Haas smiled. "I can breeze through fingerprint or retina checks. Whatever they have, we'll get through it"

"Excellent. I'm hoping it won't be that advanced but I'm glad you're prepared. There's a freight elevator in the back of the store that goes all the way to the roof. I'd think that the tightest security is on the floors that house research and development. That's good because I don't really give a shit about their new technology."

"Where are we going?" Haas asked.

"Ernest Browning's office."

Wessler said, "Let's get moving. The quicker we move the quicker we're out of here."

Mike led them to the waiting freight elevator. When they were all aboard Mike slid the door across and said, "First stop is the office of the CEO."

CHAPTER FIFTY-FIVE

Ernest Browning sat in his study at the family's Cooperstown estate. He was preparing for his talk with the associates that would be attending the meeting. He was interrupted by a knock at the door.

"Come in." He didn't like to be interrupted.

One of his personal assistants opened the door and stuck her head in. "Mr. Browning, you asked me to let you know when all the attendees have arrived at the hotel."

He looked at her and nodded his head in response. His employees were used to his gruff behavior and never expected more from him. All the people in his inner circle were well paid and very loyal to him. They could live with the fact that he treated them like unwanted pets as long as he paid them and he would do so as long as they did as ordered.

"Send Hailey in," he said before she closed the door.

"Yes sir."

Five minutes later came another knock. "Yes."

Mark Hailey walked into the office. He was in charge of security for Browning Aerospace as well as Ernest Browning's personal security. The entire Browning empire was under twenty four hour surveillance, and was ultimately his responsibility. After taking a shot at Jack Darvish on the trading floor at BNL, he'd taken a backseat to the specialist that Layden brought in. Since that guy took a bullet outside Bellevue, he was once again in charge.

"You wanted to see me Mr. Browning?"

"All the guests have arrived at the hotel. Is everything set for tomorrow night?"

"Yes sir. I've got my best men here to monitor the controls and patrol the grounds."

"My associates are counting on the utmost privacy so there can't be anyone entering the grounds during my meeting. That means no photographers, no pizza delivery, and no sleeping on the job."

"Sir, I meant it when I said my best men are here. There are no slackers left on our security staff and I've chosen the best for this assignment."

"Where's Layden?"

"On the company jet heading to Aruba."

"Thank you," Browning said and returned his attention to his work.

Hailey took his cue and left the office. After the door closed Browning picked up the handset of the secure satellite phone. He pressed a speed dial number and waited for the beeps and clicks to stop before he heard a ring. The voice scrambler was now activated and he could speak freely.

"Yes." Philip Layden was sitting in one of the spacious seats on the company Citation, drinking a glass of wine.

"Is everything set for tomorrow evening?"

"Yes. I've spoken with Francois and he's got everything ready for the wire transfers. We just need to supply him with the dollar amounts and destination accounts."

"Everything's ready on this side so be ready for the call."

"I'll be waiting. Has anything been turned up at BNL by the investigation?" Layden asked.

"They've got nothing. They're focusing on Brennan."

"Perfect," Layden answered.

CHAPTER FIFTY-SIX

When the freight elevator stopped on the twenty-sixth floor, Mike slid the door open about an inch and stepped to the side. Gomez unrolled a tiny fiber optic tube, stuck it through the opening and slowly twisted it around. An image of the small lobby appeared on the screen on Haas' laptop. Wessler was looking over his shoulder to get an idea of the extent of security before they left the elevator.

As the tube turned up toward the ceiling, a wall mounted camera came into view. It was pointed down toward the elevator doors covering most of the vestibule. Gomez continued to slide the long tube upwards until it was next to the camera. He pushed on a small handle at the base of the tube and a wire extended from the end. On the end was a plug that he inserted into the camera in a receptacle that normally was used to connect to a monitor.

"It's attached," Gomez said.

"Give me a few seconds." Haas tapped away on his keyboard. "Got it. Remove the cord."

Mike turned to Wessler and said in a low voice, "What's he doing?"

Wessler replied, "He's freezing the camera on its last image. Anyone in a control center monitoring this camera will see nothing but an empty elevator bank." Wessler slid the doors open all the way and the men filed out.

Attached to the wall next to the entrance to the main offices was a small security panel. Haas stepped to the front and removed the plain black cover with a screwdriver. He attached another cable from his laptop to the circuit panel inside the wall and worked his keyboard for a few seconds.

He removed the cable, reattached the front panel, and pointed to Gomez who then took the fiber optic cable and shoved it under the door moving it slowly from side to side. The image on Haas' screen showed a reception area that was free of security cameras. Browning Aerospace was probably like most companies that had their surveillance equipment concentrated on the entrances and high tech areas. They figured that if anyone wanted to get in and steal from them it would have to be where they have a camera mounted.

Gomez opened the newly disabled door and led the way into the reception area. Across the large open space was a closed door that had a gold name plate attached, showing that it was the office of the CEO, Ernest Browning III. The door was closed but Gomez assumed correctly that it was locked. He turned the handle just to make sure before taking out a small black case from his pack. He inserted an instrument into the lock, twisted it around, and the handle turned within seconds. He pushed open the door and let the other three enter the expansive office. He stayed outside to monitor the area to make sure guards weren't patrolling the floors.

The lights in the office were off but the moonlight provided enough brightness to show the way to the desk near the windows. Mike led the men across the room and started a search. He didn't know what he was looking for but tried to keep in mind what the Martellis told him earlier in the day about the Blue Bloods.

Haas sat behind the desk and reached underneath for the computer. He turned it around to expose the ports in the back and inserted his cable to attach his laptop. When his screen lit up it asked for an ID and password. He exited the screen, entered some commands and bypassed the security system. Browning's e-mail program came up on the small monitor. He went to the calendar and looked at the current date.

Haas said to Mike, "It looks like your friend Ernest is at a conference up in Albany and he'll be staying nearby at his Cooperstown residence."

Mike came around the desk and looked at the screen. "Can you get a list of attendees?"

"It's probably here somewhere." He flipped through some e-mails and stopped on one that had the title *Albany Meeting*. "Here we go." He launched the file and read down the page. "This is a virtual who's who in the business world. Some of the names are written in red." He read further down the page. "According to this, some of them will be attending a meeting at the estate tomorrow night."

"Can you print that for me?"

"I'll save it on my hard drive and print it out later," Haas replied.

Wessler called softly from the other side of the room, "Mike, check this thing out." He had a closet door opened and was looking inside. Mike walked over to see a large antique safe standing five feet tall with a dial in the center of the door and a handle on the left.

"You think he keeps the crown jewels in here?" Wessler asked.

"Can we find out?"

"Gomez is the man for this. I'll send him in." Wessler walked toward the door.

A few seconds later Gomez was admiring the safe. "This thing's got to be a hundred and fifty years old. I'll bet it's still got the original mechanism."

"Can you open it?"

"Child's play."

"How long will it take?" Mike knew they were running out of time. Every second inside the Browning Aerospace offices increased the chances of getting caught.

"Ten minutes, tops." Gomez said with certainty.

CHAPTER FIFTY-SEVEN

Inside a coffee shop, in a tunnel under Rockefeller Center, Reynolds and Battaglia stood in front of a group of ten agents. They had just finished a sweep of the area above ground and were ready to go through the maze of passageways that spread out for many blocks in every direction.

"There's a lot of area to cover down here but most of the shops are closed at this hour so there can't be many places for him to hide. He was wearing a sweat suit earlier but could have changed into anything by now. Keep your eyes open and be careful, we believe him to be armed and extremely dangerous," Reynolds said to the agents.

Battaglia stood to give his input. "There was a corpse across the street who could attest to that. Brennan feels cornered right now so call for backup immediately if he's spotted. We've got the NYPD starting the search from the west side so if we meet in the middle without flushing him, we'll call it a night."

The agents split into pairs and fanned out in different directions. Battaglia started for the escalator to the street and said to his partner, "I'm going to check on the guys at the office to see if we got any hits outside the city. He may have slipped out across one of the bridges or tunnels. If we don't expand our area now we may lose him."

"Good thought." Reynolds removed his weapon and checked for a round in the chamber.

"Be careful down here, man." Battaglia wasn't a cop and didn't pretend to be. He was a good lawyer and a smart investigator but he left the dirty work to the professionals, which was fine with Reynolds. The FBI man understood completely.

Reynolds walked east down a deserted tunnel. A few restaurants were open but the majority had locked up for the night. He pushed on each door as he went down the row to see if any were unlocked.

Twenty six floors up, Gomez worked the mechanism on the safe. His headphones were connected to a device attached to the door, listening for the tiny clicks telling him to stop turning the dial clockwise and flip it the other way. Mike watched from a short distance as the man removed the listening device and smiled.

"Would you like to do the honors?" He pointed to the handle.

"Hell yes." Mike pushed the handle down and pulled the door open easily. He half expected to see mounds of cash or jewels piled high inside. Instead, he found neatly stacked files, each with a separate year handwritten on the tab. He pulled the first one off the pile and looked at the writing. It was for the current year. Inside were no more than ten sheets of paper with several columns of type written names of companies followed by a person's name, a series of numbers, ending with what looked like dollar amounts.

Mike recognized the majority of the companies and quite a few names of CEOs. The last page in the folder was different in that it didn't list companies. This last list started with a state, followed by names and numbers. After a brief scan Mike realized that it was a list of United States Senators, Congressmen, and Governors. Republicans and Democrats.

Mike had seen some of these people at the fundraiser at the Plaza a few nights earlier. He brought the scene back to his mind and pictured his conversation with Mayor Maddux being interrupted by Vice President Browning. He said the mayor needed to speak with some contributors and the image slowly unfolded in Mike's brain. The V.P. steered the mayor toward a small group of men standing nearby and Mike recognized one of the men. It was Ernest Browning III along with a couple other names on the list.

The grim picture was gradually falling into place as he looked at the stacks of files and realized that these were the lists of people on Browning's payroll. The people whose names appeared were quite possibly the Blue Bloods that Frank Martelli told him about.

Wessler came back in the room and looked over Mike's shoulder. "Have you found what you needed?"

Mike didn't answer for a moment. He ran his hand down the stacks of files. "I think I've found more than I bargained for tonight."

Wessler looked at the list in Mike's hand. "Are those routing numbers?"

"Yeah, and these numbers at the end are probably dollar amounts."

"Dollar amounts? Most of them look bigger than the GNP of some third world countries."

Mike handed Wessler the current year's folder. "Can you have Haas try to match any of these names with the list he pulled off the list of the Albany convention attendees?"

"No problem."

"Have him e-mail the names and account numbers to this address." He wrote down his brother's address. "Put a note in to have Paul Schmidt run them through his system." Mike knew that the names wouldn't be attached to the numbers anywhere because of the secrecy practiced in offshore banking but maybe the FBI database could at least identify where the accounts are held.

Mike reached down to the bottom of the pile and pulled out the first file. The year written on the tab was 1930 and the paper inside was slightly yellowed. The handwritten words were faded but Mike could easily read the names of some extremely well known businessmen from the early twentieth century. These were names that everyone knew from America's royalty. There were medical foundations, railroad stations, universities, and even cities named for the people on this list.

Next to the pile was an ornate metal box about two inches high by a foot wide and long. It had a clasp on the side but no lock. Mike opened it to find a few faded pages held together by a paper clip. In elaborate script it began, "A contract among gentlemen, the undersigned will abide by the terms for eternity and will reveal this secret to no man, woman, or child outside his bloodline. Like Prometheus and Atlas, we have been assigned the task to deal with the common people and will accept this charge for the betterment of our families and our country." Mike read on in amazement as this group likened themselves and their tasks to those of the Greek gods. He knew he'd found the Blue Bloods complete with signatures. These people were framing him for crimes they've been committing for nearly three quarters of a century. Browning had the nerve to have the statues of Prometheus and Atlas built outside his company's headquarters which just happened to be one of the largest tourist attractions in the country.

He thought of a commercial that airs around Christmas each year that has the on-air personalities for a major network news program, along with support staff, singing Christmas carols. They line up like a choir next to the ice skating rink in the Plaza with the statue of Prometheus floating behind them.

Browning was flaunting it in the faces of the authorities and of every American. The names of the companies that invested in Layden and Dowd and then BNL, were made into statues and placed in an area that would be viewed by hundreds of thousands of people. It made Mike angry to think that these bastards permeated the lives of honest business people and consumers and had the audacity to display it.

Wessler came back over to Mike. "Gomez radioed there's activity on the passenger elevators. We've got to get the hell out."

"I'm ready." Mike reached into the safe and grabbed the whole stack of folders and put them in his pack with the original contract and the folder from 1930.

"Don't you think they'll miss those?"

"It's too late to care about that. They're not going to know what hit them when I'm finished."

"Let's hope we get out of here so you can have the chance."

Mike closed the safe and the closet and looked quickly around the office to leave as little out of place as possible. Gomez was waiting by the freight elevator when they arrived. They packed on, closed the door and started the descent to the basement.

They went through the same procedure when they got to the bottom floor as they did when they arrived upstairs. The door was cracked open enough for Gomez to slip the fiber optic tube through as Haas watched the screen of his laptop. After a few sweeps of the device, Haas gave the thumbs up.

They headed toward a side door that Mike had scouted before the group arrived. They didn't want to go back out through the storefront. Before they reached the door, Mike stopped. "I left my cell phone up in the front. I'll meet you at the door."

Wessler shook his head. "No way. We've got to get out of Dodge. We could have tripped a silent alarm somewhere along the line and this place could be crawling with more cops and feds than we could imagine."

"I'll be fine. Give me a couple minutes and if I'm not back, get out while you can." He turned and ran to the front of the empty store near the passageway. He had spoken briefly with Sam and put his phone down in the dark, forgetting to grab it when Grady and his men arrived.

The front was dark but he had his small light to help him avoid the construction equipment. He looked where he had been sitting but didn't find the phone. As he turned around to head back he heard footsteps from the darkness to his right. He quickly moved the light in that direction expecting to see Wessler. He was surprised to see a man with his arms extended, pointing a gun directly at him, emerging from the darkness.

"Put your hands up, Brennan!"

He did as he was told. "Who the hell are you?"

"Special Agent David Reynolds, FBI. Hands on the wall."

Mike was slightly relieved that it was a fed instead of another of Browning's minions. Reynolds held Mike against the wall with one hand as he placed a cuff on one of his wrists, then attached the other behind his back.

Reynolds turned his prisoner around to face him. "I've been following your blood and money trail for the better part of a year." He did a quick body search and removed Mike's 9mm and his small handheld radio.

"*My* trail?" Mike asked.

"You sound surprised." Reynolds lifted his own radio to his mouth.

"Hold on. I didn't do anything illegal and I'll help you find who did." Mike sounded desperate.

"You can talk to the U.S. Attorney about cutting a deal." Reynolds answered.

"I'm not talking about a deal. I'm not about to take the fall for anyone."

Reynolds lifted the radio to his mouth again and was about to speak when he felt something hard touch the back of his head.

A voice said, "Put the radio down."

He leaned down and dropped the radio to the floor.

"Hands behind your back," Wessler said. He secured Reynolds' hands with a plastic flex cuff similar to the kind used by riot police.

Mike smiled, relieved. "I thought I told you to leave."

"Did you ever hear the saying, 'Leave no man behind'? I learned that somewhere a long time ago."

"How about getting these cuffs off me?" Mike asked.

Wessler pulled the key ring off Reynolds' belt and released Mike's wrists.

Mike frisked the FBI man and removed his weapon from its holster under his arm. Mike popped the clip out, removed the chambered round and placed the gun in his pocket. He found his own gun and radio and took them back.

"Agent Reynolds, you can either be a help to me or a hindrance. Which will it be?"

"You're giving me a choice?" Reynolds asked.

"I had nothing to do with what has been plastered on the news for the past few days. I was at Barry's house the night before he died but I left him there safe and sound in his study."

"What about the Grand Central Station incident?"

Mike wasn't surprised they knew he was there. "The guy NYPD brought in kidnapped my girlfriend and then took me in exchange for her. He told me that I needed to sign a confession admitting my involvement in the market manipulation and the murder charge would go away"

"And you obviously didn't believe him."

"That's right. If he was telling the truth that would mean he probably had someone in the law enforcement world on his side. But it seems the cops weren't very keen on keeping him alive if they allowed someone to take him out near Bellevue. Whose side are you on Reynolds?"

"I've got a clean record." He shifted the conversation back to Mike. "What about Albert Claire a couple of hours ago across the street? We've got you on video."

"You may have me on video going in and coming out but I would bet my life that you don't have me as the shooter. Claire was dead by the time I arrived."

"Come down to Federal Plaza with me and you can explain the whole story. You have my word you'll get a fair shake."

"You think I'm an idiot? This thing is much bigger than just BNL, Agent Reynolds. I'm now a marked man due to the fact that I know too much and they won't stop until I'm gone because I'm a danger to them. You've been on this investigation for a year and you've still got nothing?"

Reynolds shot back. "You've been at BNL for years and you claim you know squat about them breaking the law. Why the hell should I believe you?"

"Touché."

Reynolds figured he'd keep going while he had Brennan talking. "What made you choose this building to hide out in?"

Brennan smiled. "I think I've told you enough about myself. If things work out the way I plan, you'll find out soon enough why I'm here."

Wessler was silent up until this point and was getting uncomfortable with the length of the conversation. His men were waiting by the side door. "We've got to get moving."

Mike took Reynolds' gun out of his pocket and the FBI agent drew back slightly. Mike noticed his movement and said, "Don't worry Agent Reynolds. I may not like you but I'm not going to hurt you." He reached inside the man's jacket and replaced the gun in its holster and the clip in his pocket. "You'd probably catch hell if you lost that."

Reynolds was visibly relieved. "What are you going to do with me?"

"Give me your partner's phone number. I'll call him when we're out of here."

Reynolds gave him Battaglia's number. "If you really are innocent, why don't you let us help you instead of risking your life?"

Mike thought about the question for a moment. "Because I can count on one hand the people in this world I can trust, and no offense Reynolds, you're not one of them."

Wessler took another tie from his pack and attached Reynolds' wrists to a beam. They couldn't allow him to run out into the passageway and alert the rest of the search team before they got some lead time. They left him sitting in the dark.

CHAPTER FIFTY-EIGHT

Mike's rental was where he left it in a garage a few blocks east of St. Patrick's. He took the long away around on his way to the west side to avoid the heavy concentration of cops that were continuing the search near the cathedral. Once he was a safe distance away from the city, he'd make the call to Agent Reynolds' partner. Mike thought the guy would probably never live it down, but it was a hell of a lot better than the alternatives. When he arrived at his destination, Wessler and his men were waiting.

"Pop the hatch. The bird's waiting," Wessler said.

Mike watched the men grab the crate out of the rear of the Navigator and looked at the chopper sitting on its pad near the edge of the Hudson River.

"Just like old times," Mike said to his sergeant. He had to admit to himself that it was exciting to be back in attack mode once again. Years at a desk had made him soft and he wasn't sure now that he'd ever go back. That was of course if he didn't go to jail.

Gomez and Haas lifted the crate into the helicopter and followed it in. They had already packed a crate of their own gear leaving just enough room for themselves. Mike jumped into the copilot's seat and looked at the pilot in his baseball hat and headset.

"Ross, I owe you big for this."

"I've always had a soft spot in my heart for jarheads. I'm guessing that these guys aren't your buddies from the office?" Ross Bricker could obviously spot a military man a mile away.

"You could say that," Mike replied.

"I'm also guessing that they haven't been civilians their whole lives."

Mike nodded. "Very perceptive."

"Hang on boys. We just got clearance." Ross lifted the chopper off the ground and headed west briefly over the Hudson toward New Jersey. As he climbed through one thousand feet he banked north and plotted his course directly up the Hudson heading to their final destination of Albany, New York.

Before they leveled off, Mike turned to the men in the back and raised his voice above the noise of the rotors. "Ross flew in Nam in the last days pulling grunts out of the jungle."

Wessler smiled. "My dad was there at the end and said if it weren't for you guys flying like madmen, they'd never have made it out alive."

"Well I can't say I like that description, but thanks for the compliment," Ross replied. Wessler reached up and patted him on the shoulder.

When they leveled off, Ross pulled his headset off and looked at Mike. "You're in a shit load of trouble, man. I hope none of what I've been hearing is true."

"The only thing that you've seen on the news that's true is my name, rank and serial number. Other than that, it's a bunch of bullshit. I think I've finally got a bead on who set me up which is why we're heading upstate."

"I didn't want to believe it but that Cynthia Highsmith is very convincing. She's been running her shows almost every night with a focus on you."

"I've seen a couple of her broadcasts and she's helping to convict me before I even get to court."

"She's had some heavy hitting guests. Last night Vice President Browning was on bellowing about how you'll be brought to justice and you're the perfect example of what's wrong with business today."

"He mentioned me by name?" Mike asked.

"You were the main topic on her show man. The administration is going to crack down hard on corporate corruption."

Mike didn't say anything but thought about what he just uncovered in the Browning Aerospace offices and how deep this conspiracy has gone. There was a remote possibility that he alone could bring it all to a screeching halt but the odds were astronomical.

"It's all lies?" Ross asked, jarring Mike from his thoughts.

"One hundred percent. If it's this hard to convince you face to face imagine how I'd do in front of a jury. That's why I need to get to the guy at the head of this and cut the heart out of his organization. It's the only way I'll walk free when this is over." Mike made a mental note to make sure that Vice President Browning didn't slip out of this and is brought down with the rest of them. Whoever the hell *them* really was.

"All right, buddy. No further explanation needed. I'll take your word as a friend."

"Thanks." Mike tried to think about the next twenty four hours and how he needed to move quickly. "Are you willing to stay on and help us out?"

"This beats chauffeuring people back and forth from Southampton."

Mike smiled. He knew the old daredevil would take the challenge. "Can you arrange for a return trip for us tomorrow night?"

"No problem." Ross put his headgear back on and turned his concentration to flying.

Mike moved to the second row of seats next to Wessler so they could plan their next move. Surveillance of the Browning's Cooperstown estate, followed by a possible infiltration could be extremely complicated and dangerous depending on the level of security. Mike had a feeling that this was no ordinary meeting and gaining access to the grounds and participants would be particularly difficult.

As they were talking about the different ways to handle running the operation, Mike started to flip through the folders he took from Browning's safe. He was going year by year from the beginning. Some years the list was longer than others but most of the same names were repeated over and over. He got through the 30's and was now well into the 40's when a name he recognized appeared on the list. He put the folders back in his pack and leaned up toward Bricker.

"Slight change of plans, Ross. Have you got enough fuel to take us an extra fifty miles?"

Ross looked at his gauges. "No problem."

Mike went back up to the co-pilot's seat to give him the new landing coordinates.

CHAPTER FIFTY-NINE

"Monsieur Layden, it's a pleasure to see you again."

Layden removed his sunglasses and shook the hand of Francois Barrau, head of private banking for the Banque Internationale de Zurich. When hearing of Layden's need for an emergency meeting, he left Switzerland immediately. Barrau's employer made millions of dollars in management fees from Layden's accounts and he made sure he gave him the personal customer service that a man of his stature deserved.

"Monsieur Barrau, comment ça va?" Layden asked.

"Ça va bien, merci. You always speak such excellent French, Monsieur. I trust you had a comfortable trip?"

"Absolument."

Barrau was a Frenchman who was an expert in international banking regulations and although he held a very high position with the bank, he always handled the larger clients himself. Switzerland is well known for its banking privacy and Barrau's institution managed billions in assets that were next to impossible to trace back to the real owners.

Banque Internationale de Zurich's very private building was located on Hendrikstraat in the tiny business district in Oranjestad, Aruba's capital city. The gold nameplate attached to the door read simply *B.I.Z.* and the few windows that allowed the brilliant sunshine to enter the lobby were placed almost ten feet up the wall to keep anyone from peering in from the outside.

This was not an ordinary bank where you'd find velvet roped waiting lines, tellers and desks with loan officers. It resembled more a brownstone on Forty-Sixth Street in Manhattan's exclusive Turtle Bay. The lift to the second floor offices was directly ahead of the front door in the center of the building.

Barrau led the way into the small elevator. "Let's have a quick drink in my office before you review the instructions."

"Do you have any of that Dartigalongue Armagnac that I like so much?" Layden asked, knowing the answer.

Barrau smiled and replied, "I believe we do, Monsieur. Is 1900 an acceptable vintage?"

"Excellent." Layden appreciated the treatment he got from the Zurich people and after all, the thousand dollar bottle of brandy was a minor expenditure. The important thing was that Barrau knew what he liked and was well prepared.

Inside Barrau's office, they sat in comfortable arm chairs and slowly sipped the hundred year old brandy. The Frenchman knew well the code of offshore banking. There are no questions asked in the world of high finance when it comes to numbered accounts and privacy. The names on the accounts are recorded but are locked away so tightly that it would be a very difficult process involving too many people within the organization to uncover them.

The rebalancing of the accounts normally took place on an annual basis but this set of transactions was slightly different. Barrau didn't know it yet but billions of dollars were going to fly through cyber space, generating huge transaction fees for B.I.Z. With all the problems going on with BNL, Browning thought it necessary to shift money to accounts that would make it harder to pin down the owners.

For Layden, the last few days were almost a blur. After Sullivan failed to bring Brennan in, there was no way he could allow the man to roam the streets armed with knowledge of Layden's involvement. The reports of the Surfer's murder were almost as big on the news as those of Michael Brennan, good boy turned bad. He liked the spin the media took at first but now they were overdoing it.

The specific problem was the news exposure that Brennan and his alleged crimes were receiving from the nationally known correspondent, Cynthia Highsmith. Layden knew she was one of the smartest reporters in the field and was making connections that the police hadn't even thought of yet. The fear he had was her taking it a few steps further to make the link to Browning. Odds were low that she'd be able to do that but Layden needed to consider stopping her in her tracks before she made too many correct assumptions to lead her to the story of the century.

CHAPTER SIXTY

"A break in?" Browning fumed.

"Yes sir," Mark Hailey answered.

"What floor?"

"Twenty six."

"Twenty six?" Browning slammed his hands on his desk and stood up. "What the hell am I paying you for, Hailey?"

"My guys in the building say that nothing appears out of place, Mr. Browning."

Browning sat back in his chair and didn't speak for a moment. "You'd be out on the street if I didn't have this meeting tomorrow night. Do you think you can keep your head out of your ass long enough for me to conduct my business?"

"Your visitor's privacy will be protected, sir." Unfortunately for the head of security of Browning Aerospace, he had no way of knowing that he would end up eating his words.

CHAPTER SIXTY-ONE

Ross Bricker hugged the tree line of the rolling hills just north of Albany. The full moon was more than enough light for him to fly by sight. His chopper was relatively new but he didn't have much use in his normal course of business for the kind of terrain seeking technology that most military helicopters were equipped with these days. Farm after farm flew by beneath them as they stayed away from the more populated areas to minimize the chances of someone calling the state police.

The spot that Mike asked Ross to land the helicopter was a heavily populated tourist attraction that normally didn't allow flyovers. The only type of flying done at Lake George was parasailing.

"Thirty seconds, Mike." Ross said through the internal radio.

Mike gave the thumbs up, removed his headset, and stepped into the rear of the chopper.

Mike turned to the three men in the back. "Ross is going to put the bird down on the beach behind the house and we've got to be out with our equipment within ten seconds. He'll follow the same path back out over farm country and make his way back to Albany."

Mike looked out the side window and saw the trees end and the shimmering lake appear underneath them.

"Here we go boys." Ross yelled over the noise of the rotors.

He was so close to the water, Mike thought that Bricker miscalculated and they were going into the lake. Before he had the chance to brace himself, the chopper banked hard right and stopped on a dime. The skilled pilot set the machine down softly on the small beach, just twenty feet from the back of the house.

Mike slid the door open and yelled, "Go! Go! Go!"

Wessler and Gomez hopped out first and Haas and Mike handed them the two trunks packed with equipment. Haas jumped to the ground followed immediately by Mike, who turned and slid the hatch shut.

The helicopter lifted off as soon as the door was closed and quickly disappeared over the trees lining the lake. Mike turned to the other men and put his finger in the air in a spinning motion signaling them to pick up the crates and move toward the house. The noise of the helicopter was sure to have drawn some attention from the neighbors. Most would write the noise off as a speedboat too close to shore, but Mike didn't want to draw any attention to four heavily armed men being dropped on the shores of one of New York's largest lakes. As they stepped onto the deck, the back door of the house opened and Tim Brennan stepped out. He held the door open for the men as the supplies were carried in and set on the floor.

When they were all inside Mike closed the door. "Fellas, this is my brother Tim."

He then pointed first to his former Sergeant. "Tim, this is Grady Wessler, who saved my life in Panama. And these are associates of his, Benito Gomez and Arthur Haas." They shook hands all around.

"That was a quite an arrival. Was that Ross Bricker?" Tim asked.

Grady Wessler answered, "He's one talented son of a bitch."

"Where's Sam." Mike wanted to get to the point of his detour to Lake George.

"She's in the study with her father." Tim offered.

"You guys wait here for a few minutes. Get yourselves some coffee." Mike left the kitchen and walked toward the center of the house. He found the door to the study closed but didn't bother knocking.

Sam was happily surprised to see him. "Mike, I'm so glad to see you. Why didn't you call?" She stood and put her arms around his neck. Mike hugged her tightly and looked over her shoulder at William Brodworth.

Mike stuck out his hand and said, "Mr. Brodworth. Glad to see you're still here."

Brodworth shook his hand and his eyes were drawn immediately to Mike's Sig Sauer P226. It was hanging on his left side in a shoulder holster, ready to grab with his right hand. "You're in a lot of trouble, Mike."

"Thanks for stating the obvious, sir," Mike said sarcastically as he sat on the couch.

Sam was more taken back by the comment than her father. "Mike, Daddy was just telling me how concerned he's been for you."

Mike smiled and looked at her father. "Is that so? Does that mean you believe I'm being framed?"

Brodworth wasn't a man easily intimidated. "It's hard to know what to believe with all the things I've been seeing on the news."

"Cynthia Highsmith?" Mike asked.

"Mostly," he answered. "But it's all over the place, son. All the networks."

"Don't call me 'son', Mr. Brodworth."

Sam was puzzled by Mike's attitude and wanted answers. "What the hell's going on? Why are you talking like this?"

Mike opened his pack and took out a pile of manila folders. "I think you two should have a seat. I've got a few questions for you Mr. Brodworth."

Sam's father reluctantly sat on a chair across from the couch but Sam remained standing.

Mike looked up at her. "Did you get a chance to ask your father about what the Martellis told me?"

Brodworth laughed. "You mean what those thugs told you about a secret society of rich people that are ruthlessly controlling the country?"

"Something like that."

"It's absurd. Do you actually believe that fairy tale?"

Mike was trying desperately to remain calm as he opened the first folder. He looked Brodworth in the eyes. "Are you familiar with the Browning family?"

He paused a second too long before replying, "Of course. Vice President Browning comes from a famous family. Browning Aerospace is an American staple."

"Let me read you a little bit of information that I took from the office of Ernest Browning III earlier this evening."

Brodworth interrupted. "What do you mean *took* from his office?" His nervousness was now apparent.

"I mean stole, lifted, robbed…"

Brodworth shook his head and cut him off again. "Your rap sheet is growing as we speak."

"Let me finish. I've got here a contract signed in 1930 by the patriarchs of some of the most influential families in the country. The body of the document tells of how the individual families will work on behalf of the whole group to make sure they maintain the level of wealth to which they've all grown accustomed."

Brodworth spoke up. "It sounds to me like any other social organization. One hand washes the other. It's been going on since the beginning of history."

Mike shuffled the folders and continued. "That wouldn't be a problem if it ended there." Mike stopped at a folder. "Does the year 1948 have any significance for your family Mr. Brodworth?"

William Brodworth swallowed hard and looked at his daughter. He tried to retain his smooth façade. "I was ten years old. Maybe my first trip to London?"

Mike ignored the attempt at sarcasm. "That's not all." Mike looked at the papers in front of him. "It also happened to be the first year the Brodworth name appeared on Browning's lists."

"Lists?" Sam asked.

Mike handed her the folder. "There's a list of names for each year from 1930 through today with names, account numbers, and dollar amounts."

Sam scanned the sheet quickly and found her family's name. She looked up at her father and pleaded, "Daddy?"

William Brodworth's expression betrayed the fact that he knew he was defeated. "I was planning on never having to tell you but I promised myself that if you ever asked me directly about it, I'd tell you what you wanted to know. I'll be willing to bet if you look at the list from 1964, you'll see our name dropped off." Brodworth leaned back in the soft chair, looking strangely relieved to be telling someone a secret that he thought he was going to take to his grave.

Mike quickly moved his finger down the pile and stopped at the year in question. He pulled out the folder and handed it to Sam without looking. She opened it and looked down the list again, this time not finding the Brodworth name.

She looked at her father and asked, "What's special about 1964?"

The older man looked back and forth between Mike and Sam before replying. "There's nothing special about 1964. It was the year before that was important."

"1963?" Sam was at a complete loss.

"Can you think of any major events from 1963?" Her father asked. Mike answered him. "JFK"

Brodworth pointed at Mike. "Give the young man a cigar."

"What does JFK's assassination have to do with any of this?" Mike asked. Earlier that day, Frank Martelli told Mike his theory that the Blue Bloods put JFK in office and then decided to take him out of office. He didn't give it much credence until now.

"It might be easier for you to follow if I start at the beginning."

"Please do." Mike said as he pulled Sam's hand for her to sit next to him on the couch. He didn't let go of her hand, knowing what her father was about to tell them was going to tear her heart out.

William Brodworth spoke quietly but his voice was steady. "My grandfather was approached by the Browning group in 1930 in an attempt to get him to join their society. They intended to band together to avoid another crash like what happened a year earlier in 1929. The story went that Browning went on about how they had a responsibility to their families and their country. He went so far as to compare their power to that of some Greek Gods."

Mike interrupted. "Prometheus and Atlas?"

Brodworth was surprised. "How did you know?"

"Layden had the statues in his house and then I happened to be in Rockefeller Center today and noticed the two statues. That's how I finally put it together that it was Browning."

"You're a clever young man, Mike."

"Please continue with your story." Mike wasn't ready to accept a compliment from a man he thought was involved with Browning.

"Well, Granddad refused to accept their radical ideas. He turned them down. The Brodworth family had made their money in publishing. A lot of money. They owned many publications around the northeast and struggled during the depression but came out of it stronger and more powerful than they ever had been.

"When Granddad died in 1948, they approached my father who, for reasons I never quite understood, embraced the society with open arms. He'd heard rumblings of the organization but never anything concrete. When he heard Browning and his associates wanted to have some control over a major media company, Sam's Grandpa didn't have to wait long for them to come calling when his father died."

"Grandpa joined them willingly?" Sam asked sadly.

"The forties was a tough decade. Thinking back I guess he wanted some support after his dad died. Believe it or not, his confidence level was pretty low and he never felt himself worthy to run the company his family built."

Mike was getting restless. "Can we jump to 1963?"

"Patience, kid. I'm almost there." William Brodworth took a long drink from his scotch and water. "When Kennedy ran for the U.S. senate in 1952 he was neck and neck with his opponent. My father's endorsement in his newspapers put JFK's campaign over the top and he went on to win easily. Now, the presidential campaign was a whole new ball of wax." He paused for another sip. "Selling an Irish Catholic in New England was one thing but the rest of the country was proving difficult. That cost a hell of a lot of money which my father and the rest of the society put up.

They were happy for a few years until Kennedy tried to break his ties with them and actually do some work for the country. There was a major split in the society in 1963. Browning and a few of the others wanted JFK out of office and my father and the rest were willing to ride it out. I guess you can figure out who won."

Mike and Sam were momentarily speechless. When he regained his composure Mike asked very directly, "Browning was behind the JFK assassination?"

Brodworth shrugged his shoulders. "I've always believed it to be true. They felt they deserved more from someone who they helped into office. Of course I have no proof but I can tell you that everyone who sided with my father was shut out immediately and their businesses have been struggling since."

Sam was saddened by the fact that her father would have anything to do with an organization that would operate above the law and resort to murder to get what they wanted. She needed to know some things before she could go on. "Daddy, where were you when all this was going on?"

He looked at her with sadness in his eyes. "I've dreaded this day since the moment you were born and unfortunately, somehow I knew it would come." He shifted his weight in his seat and continued. "I graduated Yale in 1962. I knew about the organization before I went away to college but never really understood the immense meaning of it. But to answer the question I know you're going to ask, I had no knowledge of any plan to murder anyone."

"But you knew all these years that Browning and the rest of them probably had a hand in it." Sam stated.

"True, but to make a statement against them was a death sentence."

It was Mike's turn. "Do you know anything about Nixon and Reagan?"

Brodworth nodded his head knowingly. "We were out of it by then but I still heard things. I believe they had a hand in Nixon's resignation and the assassination attempt on Reagan."

"Anything else?" Sam asked.

"If you've got a few days to spare, I could tell you everything I've heard. I can't prove any of it, but maybe someone else can."

Sam looked at Mike. "So Vice President Browning…"

Her father answered before she finished her thought, "I think it's safe to assume he's heavily involved."

Mike needed to know more about his current situation. "Did you know about their involvement with BNL through two companies called Prometheus and Atlas?"

Brodworth was happy he could finally deny knowing a piece of the story. "No, Mike. I had no idea it was them that was putting you through this."

Mike decided in that moment to believe him. He stood up and said to Sam, "I think you two have a lot to talk about and I'm going to go finish this thing."

Before Mike made it to the door, Brodworth called out, "You'd better be careful. They've got support in all kinds of places."

Mike didn't reply. He knew it was going to be dangerous but had confidence in Wessler's men. He also was pleased with the plan that was developed on the trip up and had just been finalized in his head as Brodworth was speaking.

He went back to the kitchen to find the men drinking coffee and talking. He helped them carry the equipment to the SUV that Sam's parents left at the house to use whenever they stayed there. Mike then went over the information he just learned with Tim and gave him instructions on his part of the plan.

They set off toward the southwest in the dark hours of the early morning. The next destination could prove to be the most dangerous yet for Mike on the quest for his freedom. Although he now had concrete information about the secret society and details directly from a former associate, Sam's father, he feared the extent to which the tentacles of the monster had reached.

CHAPTER SIXTY-TWO

The overcast early evening sky provided perfect cover for Mike and his men to approach the Browning estate in Cooperstown without fear of being spotted from a distance. They rented a boat earlier in the day on the north end of Otsego Lake and motored slowly down to the southwest edge. Dusk arrived to cover the deployment of the infiltration plan. Wessler cut the engine of the twenty seven foot Regal and coasted up to the bank about a hundred yards from the Browning property.

After they left the Brodworth house in Lake George in the pre-dawn hours, the group drove two and a half hours and scouted the roads in the immediate vicinity of the Browning property. The front entrance of the mansion was well hidden from the main road by large maple and birch trees. The bordering houses and properties were almost a half mile away to the north and south down the shore. The property line was defined by a six foot wrought iron fence with motion sensors.

With the edges of the property programmed into a handheld global position monitoring system and some visual plot points, it was an easy destination to reach from the water. They tied the boat to a tree near the shore and strapped their well prepared packs to their backs before moving toward the property line. Gomez took the point and the men followed at ten yard intervals; Haas then Mike with Wessler bringing up the rear. They were highly trained professionals and although very well armed with silenced MP3 sub machine guns and 9mm side arms, they would try very hard to avoid harming anyone. They weren't killers for hire.

Once they left the shore and entered the forest surrounding the estate they blended in well with the vegetation and were immediately enveloped by the dense, sweet scent of trees and earth. Their eyes became accustomed to the dim light within a couple of minutes and could easily spot the man in front of them in line. Gomez skillfully led them through the thick underbrush to a point in the fence that he thought would be easiest to scale and held up his fist to signal the line to halt. There were motion sensors attached to the fence but they were placed too far apart to be a hundred percent effective.

The land was flat where they stopped and made the perfect base for the simple method they were about to employ to gain access to the property. Each man removed their pack and took out two foot sections of high impact aluminum and placed them on the ground in front of Gomez. He quickly unfolded the pieces and fit them together to form a ladder that had steps on both sides. He lifted the contraption above his head and put it in position straddling the fence. He made sure it was sturdily in place before he went up and over with each man following quickly. After Wessler made it over he removed the ladder, folded it down and covered it with leaves. It could be easily retrieved for the return trip if they needed to get over the fence quickly.

They stayed off the main paths and slowly moved closer to their destination. Up ahead, the lights of the mansion could be seen through the trees and the first obstacle presented itself to the point man just a few feet from the inside tree line. Mike saw Gomez hold up his fist and then point to Haas who crept silently to the front of the formation. He went down on one knee and was examining a device attached to a tree. He removed a small bottle from his pack and sprayed the air two feet above the ground. The mist revealed crisscrossing infrared beams that had been invisible a second earlier. If an object broke the connection of the beam from its source to its target, an alarm would certainly go off inside the house. This was a sophisticated monitoring system but was simple to bypass. What made it easy to get through was the fact that the beams were placed slightly above the ground to avoid being set off by every small animal that happened to scurry through.

Gomez gave the signal to the men to get down and crawl through to pass under the beam. When it was Mike's turn to go he removed his pack and pushed it along in front of him just as the first two men had done. He came out on the other side joining Haas and Gomez behind a line of hedges and waited for Wessler to catch up. Gomez put his binoculars to his eyes and scanned the grounds surrounding the house.

From their position on the side of the mansion closer to the front, he could see two guards posted at the entrance. Gomez brought the figures into focus and scanned up and down their bodies.

Wessler arrived at his side. "Armed?"

"Bulges under the blazers and both are wearing earpieces."

"How about the rear?" Mike asked.

"I caught a glimpse of one, but I'm guessing he's got a partner nearby."

"Let me have a look." Wessler held his hand out for the binoculars.

He examined the tree line next to them. Then he swept the house front to back including the roof before settling on the men posted in the front. "These guys are former military. They look sharp."

"Can we get past them?" Mike was concerned.

Wessler smiled. "They might look good, but we're better. We'll wait for the guests to arrive before we move. Trust me. We can handle this."

CHAPTER SIXTY-THREE

Reynolds' was tempted to take the morning off after having a rough night sitting in a darkened, empty store under Rockefeller Center, cuffed to a pole. Instead of staying home and brooding about what happened, he arrived at 26 Federal Plaza early in the morning after only a few hours sleep and spent the day digging up information on Browning Aerospace.

After the few minutes of interaction with their main suspect, he was now positive that Brennan was being set up for every crime that had been made public so far in the BNL investigation. There had to be a significant reason that Brennan would take such a large risk and stay in the area of Albert Claire's shooting. He could have easily slipped away on the crowded New York City streets and went back into hiding. That fact bothered Reynolds.

There were no other tenants besides Browning Aerospace at 30 Rockefeller Plaza. They owned the building. That's why the FBI database in Washington D.C. had been working since the early morning spitting out information on the many businesses the Browning family had been involved with over the years. He told his boss, Jake Holloway, that he'd need about fifty agents to sift through all the material and by noon, the conference rooms were buzzing. The lower level people were ferrying the paper from the printers in the basement to the more experienced investigators spread throughout Reynolds' floor.

He was getting updates every hour from the supervisors, but the shear volume of information had become overwhelming. The agents were trying to compare the data coming through about Browning Aerospace with the information gathered at the BNL offices. By five o'clock, Reynolds and Battaglia realized that nothing was going to jump out from the piles of paper coming from Washington.

"What do you think he was looking for at 30 Rock?" Battaglia asked as he put the top back on his last box of papers.

Reynolds lifted his eyes from the document he was scanning. "Brennan told me this was bigger than BNL. Judging by the tax returns I've been looking at and the number of companies the Browning family has been involved with over the years, it doesn't get much bigger than this."

"Can we bring Ernest Browning in?" Battaglia asked.

"On what grounds? That Michael Brennan, a suspected murderer and embezzler, accused him of being involved in something?" Reynolds shook his head. "Our problem is that we don't even know what that something is."

"What would Brennan and BNL have to do with a company like Browning Aerospace?" Battaglia flipped through his notepad to an entry he made earlier that morning. "Browning's company has been on the stock exchange since day one. They'd have nothing to do with a firm that started in the eighties, would they?"

"The eighties was one crazy decade in the business world." Reynolds thought back to the time when corporate raiding and takeovers were commonplace. He wrote more papers at Yale on the principles of mergers and acquisitions than he cared to count. He got up from his seat and walked toward the door.

Battaglia looked at him. "Where are you going?"

He turned and replied, "I've got an idea that's a little far fetched but maybe it could streamline the focus of the agents wallowing in the data pouring out of the basement."

"I'm afraid to ask what you're talking about."

"Venture capital."

"What?" Battaglia was puzzled by Reynolds' cryptic statement.

"BNL had to have startup cash." Reynolds was getting excited. He finally had the beginning of a theory and he was looking forward to finding some answers. "We need to find the source. Maybe that will lead us back to Browning."

CHAPTER SIXTY-FOUR

The steady stream of limousines dropping off guests finally died down. Wessler and Mike moved to the opposite side of the Browning property, working their way through the forest surrounding the house. They encountered several more sets of motion detectors and crawled under each of the sensors without triggering them.

Wessler spoke into his headset. "We're in position on the west side of the mansion, about twenty yards out. What have the guards been doing?"

Gomez replied, "We've observed three security teams. The same guys are at the front and back doors but now we have a pair that roam at fifteen minute intervals, taking the same route each time."

Mike joined in. "Are they moving past your position?"

"Within twenty feet. Should we relocate to be in a better spot to take them down?"

Mike replied, "Affirmative. How long until the next pass?"

"Four minutes."

Mike paused to think about the next step. "Can you neutralize them without lethal force?"

"I don't think these guys are as good as they look. We can have them cuffed and gagged within thirty seconds."

"Okay. Take them down, then split and take up positions toward the front and back. Let us know what's going on."

"Roger. Out."

On cue, the pair of security men came out the back door and paused briefly on the deck, speaking to the men posted in the rear. One man lit a cigarette before they walked down the stairs and straight toward the back of the property. Although the estate rolled on for acres, they seemed mainly concerned with the tree line immediately surrounding the house. Their route was pre-planned because the motion sensors would be set off as they past them and the man monitoring the controls needed to know it was not an infiltration.

Gomez and Haas were about ten feet apart, on either side of a path that would lead the guards to the open grass on the side of the house. They blended in well with their dark surroundings and the security men weren't paying much attention to anything but their own conversation. Even highly trained men became lazy after a while and the fact that an incident requiring them to use their skills rarely occurred worked against them. They seemed to forget the rule that when you least expect something to happen, expect it.

Gomez whispered into his mouthpiece, "On my call. Five, four, three, two, one, Go!"

Haas stepped from behind a tree at the same moment Gomez dropped from a low branch hanging over the path. They had their MP3 sub machine guns trained on the two guards. The red laser beams painted small dots on their foreheads.

"Hands up!" Gomez said calmly. "You scream, you die."

The men put their hands up without a word and Haas chimed in, "Face down with your hands behind your head." The men looked at each other in disbelief. "Now!"

While Gomez stood a few feet away with his weapon trained on the prisoners, Haas conducted a pat down and removed their side arms and radios. He attached plastic flex cuffs to each and then a piece of tape over their mouths. They helped them up and moved them off the path where they attached them securely to a utility pole.

Although Gomez had no intention of hurting them he said, "You guys stay here out of the way and you'll make it out alive."

Haas spoke into his mouthpiece, "We've got two, safe and sound."

Mike had been listening on the open line and replied, "Excellent job. Move into position for the next takedown."

The plan was now to hit the guards at the back and front of the house at the exact same time. With the two roamers out of commission, whoever was controlling these guys from the inside of the house would be alerted to a problem when they missed a check in. They had to move fast.

Mike and Wessler split up. Mike headed toward the front and within a minute called in his position. He heard confirmations come back through his earpiece from each of the men.

"On my mark. Three, two, one, go!"

The four men converged on the house from opposite sides in unison, two at the front, and two at the back. Mike and Haas were up and over the stone railing surrounding the porch within seconds. The guards were seated near the front door, in the middle of the porch.

Again, the red laser beams found their marks before a word was spoken.

Haas called out, "Freeze!"

They agreed to use police jargon beforehand to put the guards at ease. If these guys were former military as they thought, it would be a lot easier to take them down if they thought the well armed team was the police instead of a group of unidentified assailants.

The guard closest to Mike reached into his jacket but before he could bring his hand out, Mike was on top of him. He swung the short butt of the MP3 upward, connecting with the man's chin. He dropped like a sack of rocks. The other guard watched all this unfold and raised his hands above his head.

"Smart man," Haas commented as he splashed a red dot on the man's chest. "Turn around slowly and place your hands on top of your head." The man did as instructed and Haas secured his wrists with flex cuffs.

Mike leaned down to the unconscious man and felt his pulse. He'd wake up with a major headache and possibly a busted jaw, but he'd pull through. He was just turning him over to fasten the man's wrist when he heard a voice come over the radio.

"Rear entrance secured. What's your status?" Wessler asked.

"A little dicey but we're set. I've got one unconscious and one ready to give us a layout of the interior of the house."

Mike walked up to the guard that Haas just secured and turned him around. "If you cooperate, I'll make sure you get treated well downtown."

The man was still in a state of disbelief. He replied, "I have no idea what's going on sir, but I'll do anything you say at this point."

"That's what I figured." Mike now knew they were vets, no one else called a stranger *sir,* especially not one holding an MP3. "Before we walk into the house, you need to tell me how many guards are here tonight and where they're posted."

The young man thought for a few seconds before replying, "There are seven of us, not including Mr. Hailey."

"Who's Hailey?" Mike asked.

"He's the boss."

Mike filed that in the back of his mind. The man given the job to head up a security team for a man like Browning was probably very good at what he did. He was also going to be extremely pissed off when he realized his security had been breached.

"Where are the posts?"

Again the man paused. He wanted to get it right for the well armed men who just knocked out his buddy. "Two up here at the front, two at the back, and two to patrol the grounds. Inside there will be one guy manning the monitors next door to the Great Room. I have no idea where Mr. Hailey will be."

"Where's the Great Room?"

"Down the hall to the left."

Mike spoke into his mouthpiece, "Grady, we've got two on the inside. One stationary and the second unknown."

Wessler replied, "Let's remove the one we know about, then worry about whoever is left."

"Affirmative." Mike looked at his watch. "We'll hit in exactly two minutes."

"Copy," Wessler answered.

Mike turned to Haas. "Let's get these guys out of sight. We're going inside in two minutes."

With difficulty, Mike lifted the unconscious man over his shoulder and started down the stairs. Haas followed with the second guard to the side of the house where the prisoners were secured to a water pipe. When Mike went to put tape over the second man's mouth he noticed a look of fear in his eyes. He knew this wasn't the way cops operated.

Mike patted him on the shoulder. "You really are going to make it out of here, man. We're not the bad guys."

They went back up to the porch and set up on either side of the door. Mike looked at his watch, ten seconds to go.

CHAPTER SIXTY-FIVE

The FBI's New York office wasn't the only one buzzing. In Atlanta, Special Agent Paul Schmidt received the list of account numbers from Tim Brennan. Mike kept his word by giving Schmidt something he could sink his teeth into. He'd been running the numbers through their powerful system all night and much of the morning. They drilled down to the name of the bank, Banque Internationale de Zurich. Under normal circumstances they wouldn't need anything else to get a subpoena and confirm the name behind the number. Unfortunately, international banking laws were a hell of a lot more complicated those of the United States.

When they took it a step further and discovered that the transactions over the years originated at the B.I.Z. Aruba branch, Schmidt and his team immediately arranged to fly to Aruba and have a look at the downtown Oranjestaad location. Upon arrival in the small island country, they avoided the authorities for fear of the locals being too concerned with pleasing their big banking clients.

They conducted surveillance of the small building in the business district and didn't see any activity until mid afternoon. Sitting in a rented jeep across the street, the three agents were looking through the pile of information that they brought with them from the home office. They had printed out all available photos of all the names that came up in the search.

Two men turned the corner and walked slowly to the middle of the block where the bank was located. Schmidt didn't even have to look at the pile of pictures to help him put a name on the face of the man across the street.

"That's Philip Layden." Schmidt said.

"Who the hell is that?" Another agent asked.

"He's in the pictures in your lap. He's the lone surviving partner at BNL. Let's not give them the chance to send any wires. We'll give them a minute to settle in and get comfortable. Then we'll go in and see what kind of information they're carrying and what they're willing to tell us with the threat of a trip to a federal pen hanging over their heads." Schmidt watched as Layden and his associate walked up the five stairs to the front door. The other man took a key from his pocket, opened the door and held it open for Layden.

Inside the Banque Internationale de Zurich, the American and his French banker slowly sipped their expensive Armagnac in an office near the front of the building. They were interrupted by the phone on the desk ringing. Francois Barrau pushed himself out of his chair and leaned over to answer the phone.

"Please forgive me Monsieur Layden. I'll be with you momentarily."

Layden sat in the chair across the desk from Barrau and watched him on the phone. After a few seconds, Barrau began pacing and then moved the curtain aside to look out onto the street. He hung up abruptly.

"That was my private security team." He was obviously nervous. "Your American FBI is in the area. They've apparently been sitting down the street for the better part of the morning."

Layden didn't understand. "What does that have to do with us, Francois?"

"They've been watching this building."

Layden was confident in his organization's ability to stay one step ahead of the authorities. "I've got nothing to worry about. Do you?"

Barrau sat down and leaned forward on his desk. "Philip, my old friend. Let's not kid each other. No one moves money around among so many offshore accounts on a regular basis if there is nothing to hide."

Before Layden had a chance to tell Barrau that he was not afraid, there was a knock at the door that resonated through the empty building. Barrau flipped on his computer monitor and pressed a few keys. An image from the security camera in the front of the building filled his screen. He turned the display to Layden.

"Do you still feel they aren't here to see you?" Barrau asked and immediately saw the look on his client's face.

"I can stall them while you go out through our private exit."

Layden saw no other way. The FBI would not have made the trip to Aruba and been so bold as to approach him inside a bank if they didn't know something. The relationship with BIZ was primarily used for funneling money to associates so there had to have been a major breach. He didn't work as hard as he had over the course of his career to have it all end here.

He still would not allow himself to believe that the current problem with Melvin Barry, Albert Claire, and Michael Brennan had anything to do with the FBI following him. The status of Barry and Claire was known. The only problem was that Brennan remained an unknown. Layden's dilemma, though he had no way of knowing, was that he greatly underestimated the young former marine from Queens.

"Show me how to get the hell out of here."

"Follow me."

They went down a rear stairway that did not have an exit on the ground floor. One floor below street level a door opened to a dimly lit hallway.

Barrau held the door opened and said to Layden, "Walk a quarter mile to the end. The stairs will lead to a shop in the downtown area. When you come out of the storeroom, the shopkeeper won't even look at your face. Walk quickly to the street and take a cab to the airport. I will call ahead to your pilot and have your plane waiting. Good luck."

Barrau let the door close without waiting for Layden's reply. He turned and walked down the barren passageway. As soon as he was on the plane he'd get in touch with Browning to find out if their security had been penetrated.

CHAPTER SIXTY-SIX

Tim Brennan's involvement in his brother's problems was about to increase from simply aiding and abetting a wanted man. He needed to make two phone calls to put the second part of Mike's plan in motion. The first was to 26 Federal Plaza, FBI headquarters in New York City.

Since he knew they would trace the call, he bought a disposable cell phone at the convenience store in town. He knew they wouldn't be able to pinpoint his location so it really made no difference if the FBI traced the call to a nearby cell tower. As long as his name was kept out of this whole fiasco, he'd have no problems returning to his job as a police lieutenant in Suffolk County. This was the main concern of his brother, which was why he was sitting on Sam's deck, instead of running around Cooperstown heavily armed. He'd get there soon enough, after he got some assurances about his involvement.

He dialed the main number for the New York FBI office and was placed on hold several times before someone realized that Agent Reynolds would want to take a call about the whereabouts of Michael Brennan, the country's most wanted man.

After almost five full minutes being routed around the building he was relived to hear the voice he needed to hear.

"Agent Reynolds."

"I've got a message from Michael Brennan that will interest you." Tim read off his script.

"Who am I speaking with?"

"That doesn't matter. I'll give you his location if you'll agree to certain stipulations."

"How do I even know this is real?" Reynolds had dealt with false leads in the past and wasn't about to allow himself to be led on a wild goose chase.

"Mike Brennan and another individual cuffed you to a pole under Rockefeller Center. He took your gun from you and put it back in your holster before he left."

It pained Reynolds to relive that extremely embarrassing moment. He'd never live down the incident as long as he was with his fellow investigator, Pete Battaglia. Brennan had asked for his partner's number and did make the call an hour later. Battaglia mercifully came alone to free him, which spared him the guaranteed ribbing he would have received from the guys in the office. But now Battaglia had this episode to hang over his head for eternity.

The other thing about the incident was that no one else could have possibly known about it other than Mike Brennan and the man he was with.

"Okay, I'm listening. What are the stipulations?" Reynolds asked

"All he asks is that the men who are working with him go free and no names in the papers," Tim said.

"You better have something good."

"Do we have a deal?"

"Yes." He'd catch hell from the Attorney General, but if his own theory panned out, there would be no problems letting these guys go.

"He's currently at Ernest Browning's estate in Cooperstown on Lake Otsego. He wants you to arrive at exactly 9:45pm at the main entrance and you'll have immediate access to the property."

Inside Reynolds' office, Battaglia and the AIC, Jake Holloway, were listening in on the conversation. Reynolds wrote something quickly on a sheet of paper and showed it to Holloway, who looked at Battaglia and said quietly, "Call upstairs and have the chopper ready to go in five minutes."

Battaglia left the room and Reynolds turned his attention back to the caller.

"You can bring as many men as you want but you're the only one who will be allowed in the house. You have his word that no one will be hurt."

"Can I be armed?" Reynolds asked, knowing the answer.

"No. But we recommend you bring as many wagons as you can muster up because you're going to be making the biggest collar of your career tonight."

Tim pressed the red button cutting the call and quickly dialed the next number on his list. It was late but Tim knew someone would pick up the phone because Cynthia Highsmith had a live broadcast scheduled for this evening at 10pm.

"Cynthia Highsmith's office."

"I need to speak with Ms. Highsmith immediately," Tim said.

"Don't we all?" the obnoxious secretary responded.

"I know where Michael Brennan, the subject of her show, is right now and he wants to me to give her a message personally. If you don't put me through to her I'll call the next reporter on my list and I'll be sure to let Cynthia know how uncooperative you were."

There was a pause on the line. Tim knew that the woman wouldn't want to blow an opportunity for her boss. She'd be out on the street in seconds.

"Hold on."

He only waited about a minute before an out of breath Cynthia Highsmith picked up the line. "This is Cynthia."

"Ms. Highsmith, Mike Brennan wanted me to give you a message."

"Why me?"

"Because he knew you wouldn't pass up the opportunity to have the biggest story of the century unfold live on your show tonight."

"What are you talking about?" She didn't sound like she was convinced yet.

"He's being framed for every crime that's been reported. He'll prove to you on your show tonight that he's innocent and he'll have the guilty parties tell you all about it."

"And what did I do to deserve this?"

"Judging by the amount of air time you've given to his alleged crimes, you apparently have the most interest out of all the media."

"What do I have to do?"

"Have a camera crew ready to set up a live feed to your studio and the nation at 9pm tonight in Cooperstown. The situation may get dangerous so you have to remain in the New York studio." He gave her the address and cut the line.

Tim stepped off the deck, walked toward the water and hurled the phone far into the lake. He saw the splash and was satisfied he had officially joined in the fight to help his brother.

CHAPTER SIXTY-SEVEN

Mike looked at his watch and took a deep breath as the last few seconds ticked away. He turned the doorknob and slowly opened the front door. He went in low, sweeping his weapon across the left half of the large entry hall. Haas came in on his heals, standing high, covering the right half.

"All clear," Mike said as he moved immediately to the hallway that led down the left side of the house. At the end were two large double doors that Mike assumed led to the Great Room, as the guard had described to them. The door just before the end was slightly opened and had soft music emanating from within. Mike stepped into the threshold and looked inside. A guard was sitting at a desk with several computer monitors around him. Mike pushed the door open and the man didn't turn around.

"Wilcox and Carey haven't checked in. Should I send one of the others out to check?" He was obviously expecting Hailey, his boss.

"That won't be necessary." Mike said as he and Haas crossed the room and pointed their guns at the man's head. "Back away from the desk."

The man knew he had no chance against these heavily armed intruders and pushed himself back in his chair. Haas removed his weapon and cuffed him.

Mike went back to the door and peered into the hallway. The doors to the Great Room were still closed.

"Grady, are you on your way in?" Mike said into his mouthpiece.

Mike waited a full ten seconds for the reply. "We must have spooked a guard on the way in. He left in a hurry. There's coffee all over the kitchen floor. The only way out was through us, toward the front of the house, or up a back stairway."

"We've secured the guy monitoring the security system. The only one left has to be the boss, Hailey, and he didn't come our way."

"We've got to be careful. He's probably a lot better than the slouches who we just took down," Wessler stated.

"He's got a lot more at stake than the worker bees. Since it looks like the meeting at the end of the hall isn't breaking up any time soon, let's see if we can flush him out. We're coming back."

They walked down the hall to the front door and made a left turn into the kitchen. They found Wessler and Gomez on either side of a stairway leading up to the second floor.

"Let's do this quickly. I don't want him to warn the guys down the hall and give them a chance to slip out." Mike walked to the doorway and looked up the darkened stairs. Since he knew the whole mess was his responsibility, he led the way up the stairs. Each of the men flipped down his night vision goggles and slowly followed Mike.

Mike turned at the top and scanned the empty hall. In the green haze of the goggles, all he could see was a series of closed doors. He continued up to the landing and made the turn. The hallway led in the same direction as the security monitoring room and the meeting room, one floor below. They swept each room, entering two men low and two high, each with their own quadrant to cover. After each room was searched, Mike would lead the way to the next door.

They were just five feet away room the final room when its door exploded into the hall. A shotgun blast turned the heavy wood door into thousands of splinters flying at high velocity. The flash blinded Mike momentarily and he felt the searing pain in the only exposed parts of flesh, his arms and neck. The four men retreated back to the last room they searched and assessed the damage. Mike was the only one close enough to get hit and although there was quite a bit of blood, the injuries were minor.

Before they were ready to approach the door again, another blast came down the hallway, obviously a cover shot because they heard footsteps running down the stairs at the other end of the hall. Mike ran down the hall, counting on the fact that there was only one guard left and approached the room with the mangled door. The shotgun lay on the floor, Hailey must have had only two shells.

Mike dropped all pretenses of keeping their presence a secret from the meeting participants after the booms from the shotgun.

He yelled to his men, "He's headed into the meeting room." Mike took the steps down three at a time and pushed open the door at the bottom of the stairs.

They were very wrong about expecting the men in the room to have heard the shotgun, the room must have been sound proofed. There were twenty men sitting around a large conference table looking at Browning's very distressed head of security. He had his 9mm Glock up in firing position pointed at Mike and his men who just entered the room. It all happened so quickly that no one had time to react.

Mike yelled, "Drop your weapon!"

Wessler, Gomez, and Haas had fanned out behind him, all with their MP3s trained on Hailey.

Browning stood up. "What the hell is going on here?"

"Sit down, Browning." Mike waited for the old man to slowly return to his seat and then repeated his command to Hailey, this time using his name, "Hailey, I said drop your weapon."

Browning didn't miss a chance to belittle a subordinate. "Mark you idiot, drop the gun. They can tear us to shreds in a matter of seconds with those things."

Hailey slowly lowered his gun and dropped it to the floor as Haas and Gomez approached him. They turned him around, pushed him against the wall and quickly searched him for weapons. As a precaution, they cuffed him and sat him in an empty seat at the table.

The men at the table were getting restless and looked to Browning for some sign of leadership. Mike removed his helmet and a flash of recognition crossed Browning's face. The stunned men around the table watched speechless as Browning, in his usual pompous manner, addressed the gunman. "It's pleasure to meet you, Mr. Brennan."

Mike wasn't surprised that the old man recognized him. "You son of a bitch. I'm tempted to put a bullet between your eyes right now." Although Mike had no intention of actually following through with his threat, he wanted to set the tone of this encounter immediately.

"Are you after money, son?" He looked around the table smiling, trying to keep his composure as he attempted to ridicule his captor. "We've got plenty of it."

Mike looked at his watch and then to Gomez and Haas. "It's much too late for any kind of compensation. I suggest at this point that you just keep your mouth shut. Guys, let's proceed as planned."

He removed a small radio from his pocket and spoke into it. "Ross are you ready?"

"We'll touch down in sixty seconds," the pilot replied.

Mike ignored the confused looks on the faces of the men around the table. It only added to the general feeling of fear that he was trying to generate.

Gomez stuck his hand out. "Good luck, man."

Mike shook his hand and said, "Thanks. You take it from here. I'll be in touch." He turned and left the room followed by Wessler, without a word to Browning or the others.

They arrived outside on the lawn, just in time to see Ross Bricker swoop in over the trees and set his Eurocopter down gently in the clearing. The door slid open from the inside and a man jumped down, dressed in fatigues, carrying an MP3.

"You finally get to play soldier, huh big brother?"

Tim Brennan smiled at Mike and replied, "It's been a lifelong dream of mine. Where's the crowd?"

"The sheep are herded in a conference room inside. You've got about fifteen minutes before the camera crew arrives and about forty five until the FBI gets here."

Tim nodded and said, "I'll take it from here." He looked at the blood on his brother's arms and neck. "Are you okay?"

"Just some splinters. I'll be fine."

"Get out of here." He slapped him on the back as he walked by.

Mike and Wessler jumped up into the passenger cabin of the helicopter and the bird took off immediately, banking away from the lake, heading due south.

Ross turned and raised his voice above the noise of the rotors. "We've got to push it if you're going to make it by ten o'clock."

"I hope your tallying up your bill. I owe you a hell of a lot for what you're doing for me."

"Are you kidding? I haven't had this much fun since I was pulling those dumb jarheads out of the jungles in Nam." He winked at Wessler who shot him a smile.

CHAPTER SIXTY-EIGHT

Reynolds and Battaglia landed in the FBI helicopter in downtown Cooperstown, about a quarter mile from the Baseball Hall of Fame. The agents from the Albany office were waiting for them as they landed. They hopped into the back seat of the government issued Chevy and after quick introductions, set off for the quick drive to the Browning estate.

Special Agent Rick McKern was a thirty year guy who had worked in some of the largest cities in the country. After a harrowing experience hunting down a kidnapper, he decided to settle with his family in an area where he would be happy to eventually retire and actually make it there in one piece.

He turned in the front passenger seat to face the two recent arrivals in the back. "I've never seen such a large mobilization of agents in this area. Can you give me some more details?"

"Have you been following the news about a guy named Mike Brennan and his company, BNL?" Reynolds asked.

"You'd have to be deaf, dumb, and blind to miss it." McKern replied.

"I got a message from him to go to the Cooperstown estate of Ernest Browning. He's wrapped up in this mess as well."

"What could Browning have to do with a guy like Brennan?"

Battaglia answered this one, even though Reynolds had come up with the idea to focus on venture capital. "Apparently, Browning is connected to a couple of shell companies that provided start up capital to a company that eventually became BNL."

"Doesn't venture capital get pulled out pretty soon after they start making money?"

Reynolds answered, "That's what you'd expect but it seems once Browning had his claws dug in, he didn't let go."

They arrived at the access road to the Browning estate within minutes. They past a long line of cars similar to the one they were driving and parked near the gate where five FBI wagons were waiting. Just why they were needed, Reynolds had yet to find out.

They got out of the car and approached the gate. Reynolds pressed the button on the intercom and waited only a few moments for a voice to come crackling out of the box.

"Reynolds?"

"Yeah."

"Head up the access road and come to the front of the house. I'll meet you at the door."

"Did I speak with you earlier today?"

"Yes sir. You did," said the voice.

"Can you still guarantee my safety?"

"You have nothing to worry about."

"I'm coming in." Reynolds said. The wrought iron fence buzzed and started to open slowly, creaking as the gap widened. "I'll keep you guys posted."

McKern looked at the younger agent and said, "Are you sure you know what your doing?"

"I trust this guy. I'll be fine."

He removed his gun and handed it to McKern who put it in his waistband. They watched as Reynolds walked up the slight incline until he reached a curve in the road and disappeared behind the foliage.

CHAPTER SIXTY-NINE

Just before 10pm the area around Rockefeller was still bustling with tourists. Mike and Grady got out of the cab on Forty-Ninth Street near Rockefeller Plaza. The entrance to 30 Rockefeller Plaza, where the Browning Aerospace headquarters was located, was just twenty yards away. They walked south on the plaza toward Forty-Eighth Street and past through the crowd on the street waiting to watch Cynthia Highsmith's live broadcast. Mike never understood how these people were present at all these live shows from the studio, homemade posters in hand. Maybe they were gathered by the network to make it look like there were fans willing to brave the elements to get a glimpse of the on air talent.

They had changed into street clothes in the chopper on the way down to be able to blend in a little easier with people on the street. Mike cleaned off the blood on his neck and arms to discover close to fifty tiny cuts. Some anti-bacterial cream from the first aid kit had to hold him over until he could get the wounds properly taken care of at a hospital.

At the side entrance to the studio, the guard let them through without asking for ID. He was expecting them.

Inside the studio, a producer with a headset on approached Mike. "We've got ten minutes till air and Cynthia wants to talk to you before you go on."

They followed her to a dressing room behind the set where Cynthia was having her makeup and hair done. She stood up when they entered the room and ushered the assistants out.

"Mr. Brennan, it's a pleasure to meet you." She stuck her hand out for Mike to shake. He shook her hand and she immediately turned to Grady. "And you are?"

He almost answered her before stopping himself. His name would come out soon enough and it was a better idea to wait for the excitement to die down before that happened.

"A friend." Grady answered

"Hello, friend."

She turned her attention back to Mike. "Are you going to explain all this to me or are we going to break it all out on the air?"

"Let me give you the summary version. The rest will have to come out on air."

Ten minutes later Mike was sitting on the set he must have seen a hundred times over the years. Cynthia Highsmith sat across from him watching the producer count down to the live broadcast.

She looked directly into the camera. "Good evening, I'm Cynthia Highsmith and welcome to the Cutting Edge. Tonight we continue with the incredible story involving BNL and fugitive Michael Brennan. We have a guest here in studio that will blow your mind. Come back after these messages and we'll cut live to the upstate town of Cooperstown, New York where we have a live feed from the estate of Ernest Browning III, chairman of Browning Aerospace."

The stage manager dragged his finger across his neck, telling them they were off the air.

"Are they ready Brian?" Cynthia asked another producer.

"Take a look for yourself." He pointed to a monitor.

Cynthia looked at the screen hanging on the wall behind their small set. The image was shocking. Twenty men in suits, ranging in age from forty to seventy were sitting at a long conference table with their hands cuffed behind them. Three armed men, their faces hidden by ski masks were standing in front of them.

"What are you planning to do with these men Mr. Brennan? I'm taking a huge risk here trusting that you're not planning to commit mass murder on national television."

"Don't worry, Ms. Highsmith. I'm going to have Mr. Browning and his friends tell you all about the organization their fathers and grandfathers started in 1930."

"Why would they decide to come clean now?"

"The fear of death will almost always take precedent over any other fear. These men now know that their organization has collapsed. Someone from the outside has penetrated the walls and is about to splash the news across the country."

"Are you going to hurt them in any way?"

"Not physically."

CHAPTER SEVENTY

It was eerily quiet as Reynolds approached the Browning mansion. The walk up the gently rising slope of the drive in the evening heat made him slightly out of breath and he was now sweating profusely. He made a mental note to get back into the gym when this crazy investigation was finally over. He wiped his face with a handkerchief and loosened his tie slightly. His badge was hooked on the pocket of his suit jacket to make sure everyone on the inside new he was an agent and not part of Brennan's team.

As the massive house came into view through the trees, he could see two vans parked directly in front. His first thought was that they belonged to Brennan but as he got closer and the trees thinned he could see the telescoping arm of a satellite transmitter sticking out the roof of one of the vehicles. They were news vans.

Any fears he had been harboring about entering a trap were immediately dismissed. He actually laughed out loud thinking that this Brennan guy was not messing around. The former BNL executive told him in the darkened space under Rockefeller Center that he was innocent and now he was going to broadcast it to the world. The guy had balls and he had to admire him for it.

Reynolds walked up the steps and knocked on the large wooden door. Within seconds, the door opened and a man in fatigues and a ski mask was standing in the opening.

"Special Agent Reynolds?" Tim Brennan asked from behind his mask.

"Yes." The combination of the military gear, MP3 machine gun, side arm, and ski mask didn't exactly make Reynolds feel comfortable.

"Thanks for coming. Come on back, we're going to broadcast live in about ten minutes."

"You're not expecting me to go on camera are you?"

"No. We just wanted you here to witness first hand the admission of guilt by these sons of bitches."

Reynolds followed Tim back to the conference room but stopped before entering. He stepped into the small security monitoring room and the FBI man followed.

"I thought you'd want to watch this on closed circuit T.V. It may be easier for you to have some deniability of the situation. Our methods are going to seem cruel to some people and probably illegal."

"Where's Brennan?" Reynolds asked.

"You'll see soon enough," Tim said as he turned on the screens, one of which showed the image of the men in the conference room next door.

"Are you planning on killing anybody?"

"Absolutely not."

"Torture?"

"No one will be physically hurt." Tim replied honestly.

"Let's get on with the show then." Reynolds sat down in front of the monitor and the television and noted to himself that he wasn't searched for a weapon. These guys were not here to commit a crime. They just wanted some justice. Judging from the snippets of data his agents uncovered at 26 Federal Plaza about the capital Browning poured into BNL and the sheer vastness of the family's holdings, Brennan probably thought the case would be tied up in the courts for years. The young man's methods were certainly proving unconventional but hopefully effective. The last thing Reynolds wanted was for the case to drag on and the principle players ending up doing easy time.

Reynolds turned his attention to the television and watched as Cynthia Highsmith's show returned from commercials.

"The footage you'll be seeing in a few moments is live and will not be for the faint of heart. Please know that we have been assured that no one will be hurt. I now want to introduce the viewing public to the reason behind this special presentation."

The camera pulled back to reveal Mike sitting calmly in the other chair on the set.

"Michael Brennan, former Executive Vice President of BNL Securities has been accused of the murder of Melvin Barry, a founding partner of the company, Jack Darvish, a coworker, and Albert Claire of Claire Cosmetics, a former client. To add to the list, the FBI has uncovered millions of dollars in numbered accounts in the Caribbean that have been traced back to his name. Mr. Brennan, that's a serious list of charges. How does your life go from being a war hero to winning The Man of the Year award from the Lower East Side Youth Center to being America's most wanted?"

The camera closed in on Mike's face and he looked directly into it before speaking. This was his one chance to prove his innocence and he was going to make the most of it. "Ms. Highsmith, you've had a number of experts on your show over the past few days that have pretty much wrapped up the case against me. Vice President Browning even made an appearance to throw his two cents in. I'm going to prove to you and to the country that I've been framed for each and every crime that has been made public." Mike paused and took a sip of water. He reached down to the coffee table and picked up a manila folder.

"I have proof that in 1930, a number of wealthy and powerful families entered into a major conspiracy to alter the path of this country's economy. It was a year to the day after the stock market crashed. Their organization's power and influence has grown over three quarters of a century and has permeated all facets of our society, including politics."

"Those are considerable charges," Cynthia cut in. "Why not bring your proof to the authorities and see this through in court?"

"Because I believe there's a real possibility that law enforcement and the court system have also been compromised." He wasn't afraid that the police or the FBI would come to the studio and pull him out while he was on the air because of a call Sam placed to Mayor Maddux a few minutes before Mike arrived at the studio. He agreed to hold them back until he had the chance to complete his plan.

"Please give the viewers some background before we cut over to Cooperstown."

Mike went on to describe the documents he uncovered in the offices of Browning Aerospace and the famous names that were included on the lists. Luckily, Cynthia Highsmith was a bit of a maverick and convinced the network executives to air her segment.

"Now I believe we're ready to talk to Mr. Browning," Mike said.

The screen cut to the image of the conference room in the Browning's Cooperstown estate and showed the businessmen sitting with their hands cuffed behind them. They were uncomfortable and becoming increasingly nervous. A microphone was set up on the table in front of Ernest Browning. Gomez, Haas, and Tim were now behind the camera. Mike thought that the scene would go over much easier with the public if they didn't show heavily armed men holding a group of prominent Americans hostage.

Cynthia provided the voiceover. "We're live at the estate of Ernest Browning III, in Cooperstown, New York. Go ahead, Mr. Brennan."

"Mr. Browning, this is Michael Brennan. Do you know who I am?" Mike's voice was coming from a speaker under the camera.

Browning leaned forward and spoke into the microphone. "Of course I know who you are." He was seething mad. "You and your men just took us hostage a couple of hours ago."

"Are you familiar with BNL Securities?"

"Are you going to continue to ask me questions with obvious answers?"

"Mr. Browning, as I just told the national audience that's watching right now, I have proof that your father founded an organization in 1930 that included many well known families from across the country. I also told them that you are now in charge of that organization."

"That's just ludicrous." Browning stated emphatically. The rest of the men at the table were fidgeting a little more now but kept their eyes on their leader.

Mike continued. "We have wire transfer records from subsidiaries connected to Browning Aerospace going to the accounts of the men sitting at your table. In fact, the FBI has tracked an individual by the name of Philip Layden, the lone surviving partner of BNL securities, and my former boss, who was intending to initiate wire transfers today from the Banque Internationale de Zurich located on the island of Aruba."

Paul Schmidt had called Tim Brennan with an update of what happened in Aruba a few hours earlier. When Schmidt and his team entered the BIZ building in Oranjestad, Layden had slipped away but the wires he was going to send were still set up on the bank's computers. François Barrau was taken into custody and was in the process of being extradited.

Browning remained defiant. "I think you'll have a tough time proving that connection in front of a judge and jury, Mr. Brennan."

Mike smiled and said, "Unfortunately for you, I am your judge and jury."

Agent Reynolds remained glued to the television screen in the security room. He knew he was going to take heat for allowing this to go on but there was no way he was going to interrupt. He had a fair idea of what was coming next and very much looked forward to the outcome.

Mike continued. "Are any of you men in the room willing to testify right now to the fact that there is a criminal conspiracy as I've previously described?" The room remained silent.

Mike waited a few seconds before going ahead. The camera panned the faces of the men at the table. Each one remained silent.

"Take the first one out and shoot him." As expected, there was an uproar in the room. For the first time, the armed figures would appear on camera and shock the nation. Gomez and Haas grabbed the man closest to the camera and dragged him from the room.

Reynolds was as shocked as the viewers must have been when Brennan gave the order to execute one of the hostages. He was about to leave the security room and try to intervene when he saw the television screen split. One camera remained on the conference room and the other followed the hostage being taken outside. Flashing across the bottom of the screen was a message in large letters, "There will be no bodily injury caused to these men." One of the masked men placed tape over the man's mouth and sat him in a chair while the other held a pistol in the air. They were right outside the conference room window. The gunman fired straight up into the air and Reynolds turned his attention back to the men in the conference room.

After hearing the gunshot, they began pleading with Browning.

One man said, "It's not worth it Ernest!"

Browning shot back, "Keep your mouth shut!"

One of the gunmen returned while the other remained outside with the very relieved hostage.

Mike spoke again. "I'll ask again. Is anyone willing to come forward and tell the truth?"

Another man looked at Browning and said, "Ernest, are you going to allow this to continue?"

Browning eyes remained icy as he replied, "Shut up, Alan. If this is really being broadcast live, the police will be here at any minute."

"Do I take that as a *no*?" Mike asked.

Again, no reply.

"Take another one outside, gentlemen."

This time the gunman walked to the center of the table and picked a man at random. The man didn't put up much of a fight and walked bravely out of the room. Again the split view followed them outside. Before they reached the door, the gunman taped the second hostage's mouth. As they approached the first hostage the second man realized it was a trick and the relief in his eyes was evident. He collapsed into a chair. The gunman again raised his gun in the air and fired one shot.

This time the men inside the room erupted. Several of the men looked at the camera and said they were willing to talk.

"You jackasses. You have no idea what you're doing!" Browning was turning red with fury.

"Fellas, take Mr. Browning out now. We have no further use for him."

CHAPTER SEVENTY-ONE

Three blocks away from the Cynthia Highsmith's ground floor studio in Rockefeller Center, in his limousine driving down Fifth Avenue, Philip Layden could not believe what he was watching unfold before his eyes on the small screen hanging from the ceiling. He never really believed it would come to this. Even on his way out of Aruba and the close call he had with the FBI, he thought they could salvage the organization. Now it was all over.

He removed his gun from his shoulder holster and looked at the shiny metal. He rubbed the smooth barrel up and down and then clenched his teeth and said out loud, "There's no way he's taking me down without a fight."

He pressed the button to lower the screen separating him from the driver. "Mick, let me out here."

"Are you sure Mr. Layden?"

"Just stop the fucking car here, then pull it up to Forty-Eighth Street and wait for me to come back. Don't wander away!"

The car stopped directly across the street from St. Patrick's Cathedral. It was the same spot where Mike Brennan made the connection between the statues of Atlas and Prometheus and Browning Aerospace. He followed the same route that Mike walked just a couple of days earlier. Walking quickly south on Fifth Avenue, he turned west on the Promenade toward the skating rink and the statue of Prometheus. Instead of heading into 30 Rockefeller Plaza and the Browning building, he turned south again and crossed Forty-Ninth Street.

The crowd outside Cynthia Highsmith's studio had grown to over a hundred people. Layden pushed his way through and turned the corner to the studio entrance where the same guard was manning the door. He didn't slow his pace as he approached and removed his 9mm from under his arm, pointing it the man's head. The unarmed guard backed up slightly but tried to hold his ground.

Layden was shocked at the man's insolence. "Get the hell out of the way or I'll put a bullet in your fucking brain!"

The guard surprisingly kept his cool. "You can't go in there, sir."

Layden took a second to weigh his options. If he shot the guard, he'd lose the element of surprise he was hoping for. Leaving wasn't an option, so the only other choice was to swing at the man's head and hope to knock him out. He lowered the gun and watched the expression of relief form on the guard's face. Unfortunately for the young man it only lasted a second because before he could react, Layden swung the gun as hard as he could, catching the guard in the temple with the hard metal. He quickly crumpled to the floor. Layden stepped over him and continued through the hallway and walked directly into the studio.

The show had wrapped just a few minutes earlier and Mike was standing in front of the cameras talking to Cynthia Highsmith and a producer. Grady was off to the side pouring himself a cup of coffee.

As Layden stepped up on the raised platform of the set, someone yelled, "He's got a gun!"

Everyone turned to the intruder but it was too late for Mike to react because Layden was already on top of him. He pressed the gun into Mike's back and said, "We've got some talking to do. Come with me."

Mike didn't have the chance to turn around and see the face of the man who started to move him toward the exit but he recognized the voice immediately.

"Philip, it's over. Let me go."

Wessler pulled his weapon from his waistband but there was nothing he could do. It would be too risky to make a move.

Layden saw Wessler with his gun drawn and put this own gun to Mike's head. "If I see you come outside the building, I'll shoot him on the spot."

Layden guided Mike out onto the street and continued walking east on Forty-Eighth Street

"Come on Philip, this is only going to make it worse for you."

Layden pushed the gun harder against Mike's head. "Keep your goddamned mouth shut."

As they approached Fifth Avenue and the waiting limo, the driver jumped out and opened the door for his boss.

"Get the hell back in the car and drive." Layden pushed Mike into the back of the limo and followed him in. Mike finally was able to look his captor in the face.

"You've got nothing left, Philip. Let me go and I'll tell the Feds to go easy on you." Mike could barely see the man's face in the darkened interior. Every time they past a street light, his face would be momentarily visible.

Layden ignored the comment, leaned back and closed his eyes. The gun was still trained directly at Mike. He finally opened his eyes and pressed the button to lower the divider.

"Take us over the Brooklyn Bridge, Mick."

"Where the hell are we going?" Mike demanded.

"I suggest you keep your mouth shut, Mike. I'd kill you right here but I've got something much better in mind for you."

CHAPTER SEVENTY-TWO

The line of dark Chevys with tinted windows followed the FBI wagons through the gate and up the drive to the house. They spread out and parked on the grass on either side of the house. Battaglia and McKern got out of the lead car and approached the front entrance. The door opened before they reached the porch and Reynolds came out followed by the three masked gunmen. They came off the porch and the agents began filing into the house to begin the arrest process.

Battaglia addressed the three gunmen. "You guys were absolutely brilliant." He looked at Reynolds. "They played these jerks like cheap violins."

McKern still wasn't convinced that they should allow these guys to walk away. "Did you leave your weapons inside?"

Reynolds replied for them, "I conducted the pat down myself, Rick." He ushered Tim, Gomez, and Haas through the maze of cars and down the drive to the main gate. On the way, they removed their masks.

Reynolds looked at Tim and said, "Are you sure you want to do that?"

Tim replied, "You had me pegged from the beginning."

The FBI man didn't deny it. "You had that much faith in your brother from the start that you'd risk your job and your freedom?"

"If there's one thing I can say about Mike, he's an honest man."

"I had my doubts for a while there. These guys had some convincing evidence stacked up against him."

"Just do me a favor. Don't let these guys walk on plea bargains. They've got to do time."

Reynolds nodded in agreement. "Nothing would make me happier, but unfortunately my involvement ends once these guys are brought in front of a judge."

"Let's just hope it's not a judge on Browning's payroll."

CHAPTER SEVENTY-THREE

The Brooklyn piers stuck out into the East River directly across from the South Street Seaport. There was no better view of lower Manhattan at night than from the piers or the promenade above the Brooklyn-Queens Expressway. Mike wasn't much in the mood for the view tonight. The fact that Layden's gun had been stuck in his back since they left the limo back at the gate had a lot to do with it.

As they walked slowly toward the river, Mike weighed his options. He could try to turn on the guy and hit him before he got a shot off but the chances of not getting shot were near zero. The only other option was trying to talk to him, which probably would do no good at this point, but it was worth a try.

"Did you know that Browning ordered your father's death?" Mike said without looking back at his captor.

"Shut up, Brennan." Layden pushed the gun harder into Mike's lower back.

Mike continued. "I can show you the documents that prove it."

"You don't know what the hell you're talking about," Layden said, this time pushing Mike forward with both hands.

As he stumbled, an idea came to him and he knew it was his only chance to get out of this alive. He'd only have one chance to get it right and he had to do it without alarming Layden enough to pull the trigger.

Mike fell to the ground holding the back of his leg and Layden stood above him, pointing the gun at his head.

"Get up or I'll shoot you where you lay!"

Mike put one hand up in a seemingly defensive position and blocked Layden's view as he slid his other hand into his pants pocket. He felt for the switch on the back of the small two-way radio he got from Wessler and flipped on the transponder.

Two thousand feet above the upper East River, a small red light flashed on the screen of the laptop being monitored by Grady Wessler.

"He did it. We just picked up the signal."

"Where is he?" Ross asked as he kept the chopper in a hover just north of the Fifty-Ninth Street Bridge.

"He's south. I'll get a better reading when we get closer."

Grady held on tight as Ross banked hard right and turned a hundred and eighty degrees heading downtown along the river.

Mike got to his feet and was once again pushed along toward the water. All he could do now was pray that Grady would have the smarts to be monitoring the satellite tracking system and be close enough to actually do something before he took a bullet in the head.

Layden stopped pushing and let Mike move away from him slightly.

"Look across the river, Brennan."

Mike did as he was told and looked at the brightly lit Pier 17 and the many buildings beyond.

"What do you see?"

Mike looked at him again but wasn't sure what answer he was expected to come back with so he didn't answer.

"Tell me what you see Brennan!" He pointed the gun at him, his hands shaking.

Mike turned his head to the view and swallowed hard before replying, "I see Manhattan. The Seaport. The Fulton Fish Market." He paused and waited for Layden to respond.

"Is that all you see, you small minded bastard?"

Mike looked again and listed some more sights. "I see the Brooklyn Bridge, the river." Mike was struggling. Then another thought came to him. "I see the BNL building."

"You're getting warmer." Layden looked up and down the skyline. "I see a city that would never have become the great city it is today if it weren't for the bravery of Ernest Browning's father and the others in 1930." His voice was starting to shake and he pointed the gun at Mike again. "I see a country and its industries that would be second rate if it weren't for the descendants of those men who stayed the course."

Mike figured if this guy was going to go on with his delusions, he'd try to keep him talking. "You perpetuated a crime against this country that probably put thousands of honest men and women out of business!"

"You don't know anything about us! We're the backbone of this country!"

"How many people had to die for Browning and his organization?" Mike wasn't sure how hard he could push Layden. The man was unstable and becoming more so by the second. He was about to make another comment when he heard a very familiar sound. Layden heard it at the same time.

The lights of the Williamsburg Bridge were coming up quickly underneath them as the laptop began to beep louder. The three bridges connecting Brooklyn to Manhattan were lined up directly below them.

"He's on the east side of the river. Probably the piers." Grady said, pointing to the screen.

Ross slowed the bird and dipped down close to the water after passing over the Manhattan Bridge.

"Three hundred yards beyond the Brooklyn Bridge. He's practically in the water."

Ross continued to fly just feet over the water and didn't stop when he reached the large brick support columns of the Brooklyn Bridge.

Layden heard the rotors of the helicopter at the same time Mike did but wasn't alarmed. Helicopters flew around the city twenty four hours a day. What did take him by surprise was the fact that this helicopter just flew under the Brooklyn Bridge.

Ross flew the helicopter under the bridge, clearing the roadway by just feet. He figured if he came in low, he'd have the element of surprise. Grady removed his headset and moved back to the passenger compartment as Ross searched the piers for Mike.

Ross pulled on the stick and slowed to a hover. "I've got him. Ten o'clock. The guy's got a gun on him." Mike was just a hundred yards away on the darkened pier.

"Turn me around to face them."

Ross turned the helicopter quickly so the door was now facing the pier.

Grady said, "When I say go, turn your spotlight on them."

Layden's reaction time was a few seconds too slow. He watched as the door to the helicopter slid open and the blinding spotlight was turned on. He pulled the trigger of his gun but never heard the shot. He also didn't feel the bullet from Grady Wessler's rifle enter his head.

Ross put the chopper down a few feet from where Mike and his captor lay on the pier. Wessler jumped out and ran to Mike and found him unconscious, his head and neck covered in blood.

"God damn it, Captain!" He tried desperately to find the wound.

Mike opened his eyes to see Grady over him and Ross running from the chopper.

"It's about time you guys got here." Mike sat up.

"You son of a bitch! I thought you were dead."

Mike looked at Layden sprawled next to him with half his head missing. "I'll be fine, but I think I'm covered in blue blood."

CHAPTER SEVENTY-FOUR

The cool October air felt good in Mike Brennan's lungs. He'd just spent the better part of the day helping the New York State Attorney General lay the groundwork for the landmark case that was due to begin in December. After Ernest Browning's secret was revealed on national television, more and more people were being found to have some level of involvement.

A sweep of the airports picked up multiple people on the lists trying to leave the country. Mike's testimony would help put them behind bars for a very long time. Anthony Davenport was unfortunately another story. After Mike left Atlanta on his privately chartered flight, Davenport disappeared and had not turned up. The FBI was currently working with their connections in Europe to begin the process of tracking him down. There had been several leads but he was probably well hidden by now.

Vice President Browning was arrested the same night as Cynthia Highsmith's broadcast at a fundraiser in Albany where he was appearing with the President. Joseph Browning was a front runner in polls for the Democratic nomination and the organization formed by his father would have become even more powerful with him in the Oval Office.

After Mike revealed the conversation he had with Sam's father about JFK, William Brodworth was brought in to tell everything he knew to the grand jury. Since he was one of the few members of the organization willing to talk, there was a lot of legwork that needed to be completed before they could build the case.

Mike didn't have to worry about the metal detectors at the entrance to City Hall because he no longer felt the need to carry a gun. Sam's office was just down the hall from the Mayor's on the second floor. On the way in, the guards waved to him and one went so far as to slap him on the back. He was a hero to them.

He knocked on the doorframe, interrupting Sam's conversation with Mayor Maddux.

"Hey, come on in." Sam smiled as she stood and walked across the office. She put her arms around Mike's neck and kissed him.

"Okay, okay. Enough already," the mayor said as he stood and extended a hand to Mike. "How'd it go today."

"I'm glad I'm not a lawyer. I can tell you that much." Mike said, only half joking.

The mayor looked at Sam. "Do you take that kind of crap from this guy?"

"Yes, sir. I do." Sam grinned.

"Are you guys taking a vacation?" Maddux asked.

"Just heading to the Hamptons for a few days." Sam said looking at Mike. "I think we both need a break."

"Are you taking the helicopter service?"

Mike looked at Sam and they both smiled. "No," Mike answered. "I think we'll drive."

Printed in the United States
56853LVS00004B/10